P9-AFS-354

The Long Hunt

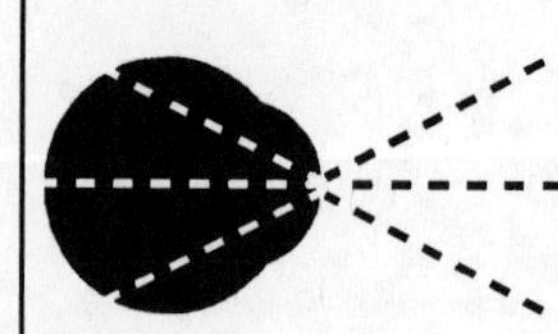

This Large Print Book carries the Seal of Approval of N.A.V.H.

The Long Hunt

Cameron Judd

THORNDIKE PRESS
A part of Gale, Cengage Learning

GALE
CENGAGE Learning

Detroit • New York • San Francisco • New Haven, Conn • Waterville, Maine • London

Thorndike Press® Large Print Western.
The text of this Large Print edition is unabridged.
Other aspects of the book may vary from the original edition.
Set in 16 pt. Plantin.

LIBRARY OF CONGRESS CATALOGING-IN-PUBLICATION DATA

Judd, Cameron.
The long hunt / by Cameron Judd. — Large print ed.
p. cm. — (Thorndike Press large print western)
ISBN 978-1-4104-5157-6 (hardcover) — ISBN 1-4104-5157-7 (hardcover)
1. Large type books. 2. Kidnapping—Fiction. I. Title.
PS3560.U337L66 2012
813'.54—dc23 2012019455

Published in 2012 by arrangement with NAL Signet, a member of Penguin Group (USA) Inc.

Printed in the United States of America
1 2 3 4 5 6 7 16 15 14 13 12

The Long Hunt

Prologue

August, 1786
Wilderness along the Doe River
Future state of Tennessee

She was old now, and hardly able to get out of her bed even on better days. This day was not a better one. She lay in her small, Cherokee-style cabin and stared upward, not even bothering to turn her gaze out the uncovered door to the lush woodlands around her. There was nothing out there for her now. The world had lost its life and luster.

She lifted her hand and looked at what she held. Small as gravel, but much more valuable, these yellowish pebbles had come from *him.* Any inherent worth beyond that was not relevant to her. She held them only because she could no longer hold the one who had given them to her.

Her name was Polly. She had been given another name at birth, but he had always called her Polly, so Polly she was. Names hardly mattered now, anyway.

She closed her eyes and slumbered. It was a hot and muggy day in the mountains, but the breeze was moving and angling itself just right to reach her through the door, so she was content. She moved the little stones in her palm with her fingertips and enjoyed the relative comfort provided by the light wind.

In her girlhood and most of her womanhood, her skin had been coppery and dark, beautiful to see. He had always told her that her skin was her most delightful feature, and she had treasured every moment when he caressed her, his rugged hands gentle on her flesh. She dreamed about it as she slept.

When she awakened the day had progressed and the breeze had changed its course so that it no longer came through the door. It was just as well. When evening came the air would be cooler and she would not want a breeze.

As the afternoon waned, Polly rose and with effort made her way out the door. She visited her privy area in the woods and headed back toward the cabin, but had to stop along the way and sit down on a stone to rest. It was that way now — shortness of breath, frequent dizziness, weakness. She despised what age and infirmity were doing to her.

Her eyes drifted closed, and when she next opened them, it was dusk, she was back in her bed, on her back, and someone was in the room with her. She looked over at the man, who was standing nearby. Like Polly, he bore clear evidence of a Cherokee heritage in his physical appearance, mixed with traits of an *unaka,* or white man. He was grinning at Polly. She said, "Hello, John."

"Polly."

"How long have you been here?"

"Since I carried you in. I found you on the ground, beside the big sitting stone."

"I think I went to sleep."

"Or fainted and went senseless."

"I'm not well, John. I'm old and sick. I'll die soon."

"Don't say such things, Polly."

"I want to die. I'm ready. I want to join McCoy. I am alone here, barely able to feed myself."

"We will keep you fed. I have brought you food today."

"You have been good to me, John. You and all your family. But I am weary of being a burden to other people. I want to go on."

"None of us has ever considered you a

burden," said John. "You have been a friend to us, like McCoy was. We consider you as one of us."

Polly smiled a weary smile. "I have not seen Tom in the longest time," she said. "He used to come and see me sometimes."

"He has hidden himself more than before," John said. "As more people move over the mountain into the backcountry, he hides himself more and more in his shame."

"There is no shame in having been touched by the Creator."

"The *unaka*s do not think in the same way about such things, Polly. To them such things are the mark of badness."

"They are wrong."

"They are. About many things. But there are more and more of them. They keep coming and the Indian people are pushed away."

"I want to go to McCoy's grave now, John. While there is still a bit of sunset light to see it by."

"Can you stand? Can you walk?"

"If you will hold to me, I can."

With her every move deliberate and slow, and the woman growing wearier with each step, John led Polly out of the cabin and around to a small meadow, where they stopped at the side of a mounded grave. It bore a plain wooden grave marker that was already beginning to weather and weaken. On it was inscribed

MCCOY ATLEY
B 1724 D 1786

The old woman, helped by the man, knelt and touched the carved-in name, tracing her fingers over the letters while tears stained her face.

■ ■ ■ ■

Part One: Edohi

■ ■ ■ ■

Chapter One

"We named her Deborah," the old clergyman named Eben Bledsoe said to his visitor. The Reverend Professor Bledsoe puffed lightly on a long clay pipe of the same sort taverns kept atop mantelpieces for the shared use of patrons. "After the Old Testament prophetess and judge. It was our hope she would grow into a strong and God-fearing woman like the one she was named after."

The clergyman's listener nodded. He was a lean, gray-haired frontiersman with a clean-shaven face of leathery countenance, a face long exposed to sun and wind. He, too, puffed a pipe, one made merely of a hollowed half length of corncob stemmed with a hollow reed. The frontiersman's name was Crawford Fain, though he was sometimes called by the Cherokee name of Edohi. He was a man of some fame, known across his own country as a great hunter and tracker, and in parts of Europe because of his mention in a fanciful, idealized, and highly popular epic poem about the American frontier. The poem was the product of a dandified baron who had scarcely set foot off his own English property, much less ever visited America's wilderness.

Wearing a long hunting shirt that was sashed about his lean middle, Fain slumped casually under the flap of a tent pitched in the log station that was home to one James White — hence its name of White's Fort. It was the heart of a settlement that would be known to future generations as Knoxville.

"Yes, you told me her name in the letter you sent me," Fain said, frowning at his pipe, which had gone out. "Fine name, Deborah. I've always favored it. If ever I'd fathered a daughter, I might have so named her."

"You have but the one child, sir? A son, I believe?"

"That's right, Reverend. My boy, Titus. He's a fine young man. Proud of him. A chip off this old chopping block, as they say. Twenty-five years old now. I can't believe that sometimes. I wish his mother was living to see him."

"Same woodcraft talents as his father?"

"The lad could trail a bug's track on

polished granite. Good rifleman and trapper, too."

"Perhaps he can help you with what I'm asking from you." It was Bledsoe's first direct mention of the matter upon which he had summoned Fain to White's Fort. Fain himself lived in a smaller forted station of his own a few miles away on a stream called Edohi Creek.

The frontiersman looked out through the open stockade door. "Truth is, I ain't decided yet as to whether I can do what you're wanting from me."

Bledsoe's countenance fell. "Those were not words I'd hoped to hear from you, sir."

"And I hate to speak them. But I must look at matters as they are, and myself as I am. I'm not the young man who used to drift from fort to fort, station to station, Reverend. I waken each day with ankles and knees aching and a back that don't want to straighten up for a good hour after I've risen. I ain't the spry pup I was back when I hunted with Mansker those years back."

"I do understand, sir. I feel Adam's curse in my own body and bones. But with such an increase in sightings of Deborah of late, it was my hope that the time was right to at last find her."

Fain knocked the dead ashes from his

pipe. “I don’t want to promise what I can’t fulfill. I’ll have to think on this awhile.”

“I would expect nothing else. It’s a daunting challenge I have laid before you. But at the very least there are now signs and trails to follow, something mostly lacking in past years.”

The frontiersman tucked his pipe into the deer-hide pouch that hung across his hunting shirt, slung on a rope strap across one shoulder. “Can I talk to you open and honest, Reverend? Ask you things that need asking without you taking offense to it?”

“Again, I would expect nothing other.”

“All right. You say there are ‘signs and trails’ to follow, but from what you wrote in your letter, I have to consider that these stories you’re hearing could be about any number of people. Your Deborah ain’t the only child who has been took by Indians in this wilderness country of ours.”

Bledsoe nodded. “No, sir, she is not,” he admitted. “But the stories of late talk of a woman with hair yellow as the sun, and describe her as being of the age Deborah would be.”

“Has she any marks or scars or such of the sort that would linger from her earliest days on to her grown-up years?”

“One. A mark in the colored portion of

her left eye. A gray streak in the brown of her eye, spanning from the pupil downward. There since birth, and I'm guessing a mark that would last for life."

"And have you heard anyone say that this yellow-haired woman you're talking about has such a marked eye?"

Bledsoe stared off past Fain, unhappy. "No. No. The honest truth, sir, is that I can't know if the young woman I hear of is my own missing girl. All I know is that she *might* be. I must find the truth, but I am not equipped with the skill, the youth, or the knowledge necessary to engage such a quest myself. And thus I have summoned you here. I wish to hire you to follow the track of these tales, find this yellow-haired maiden, and determine if she is my own Deborah." He paused. "And if she is, I want you to see if she might be persuaded to let her old father see again the child of his loins, after so many years of separation. And of course I would pay you with liberality, and we can strike our agreement in writing, if it would please you."

Fain thought deeply a few moments, silent. He sincerely pitied the old clergyman, but he was a man of the frontier and aware of hard realities Bledsoe might be inclined to overlook or push aside. He had to speak.

"Reverend, sir, you told me I could speak forthrightly, and I shall. The fact is, according to the facts you provided in the letter that brought me here, the woman you believe may be your Deborah appears to be moving about freely, traveling alone, not among the Indians at all. You say she's gone from station to station, settlement to settlement, seemingly unencumbered. So I must point out, sir, that this woman, if she is your daughter, could have sought you out on her own if she had a mind to do so. It is well-known that you are where you are, that you are creating churches across this wilderness and talking much of building an academy to bring schooling to the frontier. The fact that she has not sought you out of her own will might indicate either that she is not Deborah at all or that, if she is, she is content with her state of life and not prone to unsettle it by returning to her long-ago past."

Bledsoe's lips moved slightly as if to reply, but no words came. He appeared to be on the verge of tears.

Fain went on, gently. "It happens, sir. I've seen it more than once. A child, even a child of some age, is taken by the Indians and adopted into their society, and over time becomes accustomed to such a life. Refuses to acknowledge the former life or return to it even if opportunity arises. It is a more common thing than you might guess."

Bledsoe nodded sadly. "I've heard such stories, and acknowledge that such might apply. But keep in mind another possible reason for this state of affairs, sir. If the yellow-haired woman is indeed my Deborah, and if indeed she is now free and moving about the wilderness at her own behest and whim, she might not have come to me simply because she does not know her own parentage, does not know who she is. Deborah was taken as a small child. I doubt any memory remains of her earliest days, or her capture. And those who took her would likely not have either the knowledge or the inclination to tell her of her past."

Fain pondered and nodded. "I won't dispute a word of that, sir."

"There is only one way to settle these mysteries and make peace in my own mind, Mr. Fain. I must locate this enigmatic young woman and learn for myself whether she might be the child wrested from me all those years ago. And there is no one within my reach better suited to undertake such a quest than the famous Crawford Fain, the great long hunter."

"I have to say, sir, that if the woman does not wish to be found, this might be a long hunt indeed."

The conversation went on, the depth of the clergyman's feelings becoming more and more evident. Fain was stirred with compassion for the sad man.

And before he knew it, he heard himself agreeing to Bledsoe's request. Yes, he would go on the trail of the young woman, determine if she was indeed the long-missing Deborah Bledsoe, and if she was, try his best to bring her back to his father.

Bledsoe tried to speak his gratitude but could only weep.

A hundred miles to the northeast, a much younger frontiersman than Crawford Fain rode slowly along the tree-lined bank of the Nolichucky River. The hour was early but the day was already warm, though overcast. His horse plodded lazily along.

A sound came from his left as he passed a sycamore undergrown with scrubby brush. He reflexively reached for the butt of the flintlock pistol tucked into the belt encircling his long, loose hunting shirt. But before he drew it he realized the noise had been no more than a loud belch, its source an obviously drunken man seated heaplike on the ground at the base of the sycamore in a thicket of ivy, clutching a crockery jug.

The frontiersman halted his horse and looked down at the unkempt, slouching man, who grinned up at him, teeth glinting dull yellow through a rough mat of dark and dirty whiskers. It was hard to tell the man's age; the young rider had an impression that he might be younger than he appeared, having been aged, perhaps, by hard living.

"Good day, sir," the mounted young man said. "You startled me."

The other took a pull from his jug and belched again. "Always been explosive on the belch, like my fathers before me, Mr. . . ."

"Potts. Most just call me Potts."

The drunk stuck up his hand, though Potts was far out of handshake range. Still grinning, the man drank again, belched even louder, and shoved the jug toward Potts in a gesture of sharing that Potts was not about to accept. "Got a first name, too, Potts?" the drunk asked.

"Langdon. But just call me plain old Potts."

"I'm John," the man said. "Just plain John."

"Well, just plain John, you often get drunk this early in the day?"

John tried to get up, but his legs seemed lifeless. "Only when I'm celebrating. Man's got a right to celebrate, don't he?" Another pull from the jug followed while John's bleary eyes glittered at the younger man over the grimy, fingerprinted surface of the vessel.

"What are you celebrating?"

"A new son," John said. "Born yesterday. Healthy little fellow. Named him David, after my father."

Potts grinned and congratulated John, commenting that this was a fine spot to be born at, with the quiet river flowing past and Limestone Creek gurgling its way into it just yards from where they were.

"It's a good place, I reckon. But I'm restless. Looking for something better all the time. I figure I'll move on once a better opportunity presents itself." John's voice was quite slurred.

"A man has to follow his opportunities," Potts said agreeably. "Even if they lead him here and there and here again."

"You're wise beyond your years, young man!"

"I don't know about that. Just got my own touch of restlessness, I reckon."

"Sure you don't want a swallow of this corn?" John sloshed the jug.

"Thank you, no."

"You headed to Greeneville?"

"Just a stop for the night. I'm going from there to White's Fort."

"You got some miles before you, then, son. And you ain't going to find much in Greeneville. The town is just now getting laid out. Empty lots and such is what you'll mostly see. A few cabins and houses. Give it a year or two and there'll be plenty more."

"As long as I can find a place to lay my head, that's all I need."

"There's always the good earth to make your bed," John said, drinking again. Potts suspected this man had spent many nights on the "good earth," sleeping the hard sleep of the drunken. "You'd be welcome to stay the night at my cabin yonder, but it's crowded, and with the new baby there, I don't know the missus would want company."

"I appreciate your thoughtfulness. I'll just keep on traveling."

"What takes you to White's?" John asked.

"I'm just passing by there, too, actually," Potts replied. "I'll go on beyond to Fort Edohi."

"Crawford Fain's station?"

"That's right."

"I met Fain once. Two years back."

"I know him, too," said Potts. "Through his son, Titus, who's the very image of his father, and nigh as skilled a woodsman."

John tried again to come to his feet, and to Potts's surprise, succeeded. He wobbled a moment, then stepped clumsily forward, drawing nearer to Potts with the look of a man intent on sharing important information.

"Let me tell you what to do, son," he said in alcohol-tainted gusts that made Potts flinch. "You want to have a good evening tonight, you steer up toward the north side of Greeneville and look for Ott Dixon's place. Kind of a cabin, but it's walled only halfway up, with a tent finishing out the top of the walls and the roof. Old Ott hisself you'll know from his homely face. Uglier than Crale's lump, that man is."

"What's a Crale's lump?"

"Hell, I don't know! It's just something folks say in these parts, 'uglier than Crale's lump.' "

"Does Ott provide lodging?"

"He provides drink. Rum. And whiskey from east of the mountains. I got this very jug from Ott three days back." He sloshed it again, gauging how much was in it. "Surprised I ain't drunk more than I have in that time."

"I ain't much of a drinker, myself," Potts said.

"You're missing one of life's blessings, then," John said.

"I'll be moving on now, John. Need to find me a bite to eat somewhere." Potts looked ahead, around a clump of trees. "That your cabin yonder?" He would never directly ask, but was hoping John might offer food, if he had any to spare. Quite possibly he didn't. . . . John seemed to be a very poor man.

"That's my house, yes," John said. "Not much of a place, is it?" No invitation followed.

"Well, a home is a home. My best to your wife and your new son. David, was it?"

"Yep."

"Take care of yourself and your brood, Mr. . . ."

"Crockett. Name's John Crockett."

"Mr. Crockett. All best to you."

"Right back to you, Potts. And don't forget to stop at Dixon's later on."

As Potts passed the Crockett cabin, he heard from inside the open door the quack-like squall of a newborn, and smiled. But his accompanying thought was sad: that the little Crockett born in that humble cabin had little chance for success — not as the product of such a father as just plain John Crockett.

Chapter Two

John Crockett proved to have been right about Greeneville. Though the town was officially three years old, it was yet early in its transformation from empty land to village.

Despite the rolling terrain on which the town lay, it was lined out in gridlike fashion, with relatively straight streets and squarely shaped lots.

Potts waved and nodded to those working on structures going up in the little town, which was situated where it was because of a rich spring rising near its main avenue. Potts took his horse to the spring, and man and beast enjoyed a refreshing drink. Then they progressed up through the northern side of town, through the dusk and toward the place Crockett had urged Potts to visit.

Potts found Dixon's quickly and easily. A cabin had been started, built none too squarely and with uneven, round-notched logs, and rising only to the height of a man's chest. The upper part of the structure was mere sailcloth, stretched up and across a central ridge pole running from the front to the back, giving the building a decent but flimsy imitation of a peaked roof. Half cabin, half tent.

Potts found a place to sit in the back corner; there he could quietly observe the grubby humanity in the place and ponder his options for passing the night. As darkness thickened, torches were lighted, some burning so close to the tent cloth that Potts worried the place might suddenly flare up. He eyed the front exit and made plans to bolt should it become necessary.

A big, ugly brute of a fellow clad in badly stained, heavy trousers came stumbling across the splintery puncheon floor and looked stupidly down at Potts. "Whatcha drinking?"

"Don't fancy anything to drink, sir," Potts said, wondering if this might be the Dixon whose name was attached to this obviously short-term enterprise. From the look of the place, Potts guessed that the proprietor probably carried a packhorse load of liquor from new town to new town, throwing up temporary log-and-canvas taverns on unclaimed lots and vending liquor to the locals, then moving on when things began to be more settled.

"Gotta drink to stay here," the ogre said.

Potts stood and faced the man, who was a handbreadth shorter than he was, but much thicker. "Then I suppose I'll move on," he said in a cordial tone. "Know any place a man can find a place to sleep for a night?"

The man pointed a finger that wavered in any and all directions. "Go see Katherine Parr up yonder way. Two mile. Only cabin south of the road. She'll bed you down." The man, suddenly friendly, chuckled and winked. "Aye, she'll bed you down, no two ways 'bout it! You know what I'm talking about, young man! You be sure to tell her Dixon steered you there and would favor having some business steered back to him in turn."

"I'm just looking for sleep. That's all," Potts said. "I reckon you might be thinking I'm looking for something that I ain't, Mr. Dixon."

"No drink, no women . . . bah!" The man lost his smile and waved his hand toward the door in a contemptuous gesture of dismissal. Potts wasn't the kind of patron he needed.

Potts had turned to head out when suddenly a figure filled the doorway and made him stop. A voice with the kind of piercing edge that could be heard half a mile away suddenly burst forth: "Sin is a reproach to the God of heaven and earth, and shall be driven forth before him like dried and husky leaves before a divine wind! And *no* drunkard, so says the holy word, shall inherit the kingdom of God!" The declaration was given in a distinctly British accent.

Groans and drunken protests rumbled through the place, and Dixon stepped toward the newcomer, who was shadowed by two stoutly built men of mixed Indian and white blood, seemingly bodyguards. They glared menacingly at Dixon as he neared.

"Bledsoe!" Dixon bellowed. "You think the Lord would want to find you here in this den of sinfulness?"

"Dixon, you rank and randy son of a libertine and his unwashed whore, the Lord calls me to bring the good news even to such as you, and even in such places as this pit of hell you call a tavern!"

Dixon fixed a scornful glare on his face. "Well, you Bible-spouting pox, the Lord calls *me* to deliver good strong drink to his thirsty children! And I heed that call. Why you in here, anyway?"

Potts put the pieces together quickly. The newcomer was obviously a preacher, and

Dixon had called him Bledsoe. That narrowed the field as to who this righteous warrior probably was: one of two Bledsoe brothers, both of them well-known clergymen in this western country, but of decidedly different styles and religious traditions. Both Bledsoes were making names for themselves on the new frontier, one as an educated Presbyterian cleric devoted to the spread of classic Christian institutional learning in an academic environment, the other a much more roughly hewn, self-educated devotee of the kind of fiery revivalism associated with camp and brush arbor meetings. One brother an "old light churchman," the other a "new light man."

There was little doubt in Potts's mind that this was the latter Bledsoe, the new light revivalist, who had just come in. Potts struggled to remember his name. Abner, he thought. Yes, Abner Bledsoe. And his brother, the academic — his name was Eben Bledsoe.

"I want you out of this place," Dixon commanded Abner.

Abner Bledsoe's crimson face twisted into a snarl and for a few seconds he looked very dangerous. His bodyguards stepped up, but he abruptly waved them back, seeming to think better of escalating the confrontation to a physical level.

"Dixon, I'll leave you and your den of perdition happily if I may but tell your patrons here of a great meeting soon to happen that can provide a pathway to a better life for them . . . and for you, too, if you'll have it."

Dixon huffed and snorted, then said, "Well and good, preacher, have your say. No preaching, though! Just announce your meeting and be gone. Ain't going to help you none. My people here ain't your church-going type."

Bledsoe stepped over to a bench that sat against a wall and climbed onto it. "Friends!" he said in a voice meant to pierce the thickest alcoholic murk, "there will be" — he paused, counting on his fingers — "four days hence from this night, a great outpouring of the power of God in the broad meadow nearby Edohi Station. I shall preach the word of truth to all who come, and shall also share the story of Molly Reese, late of the city of London, whose life was given back to her through the power and mercy of God after she fell victim to one who misused her sorely, leaving her with the very tongue cut out of her head! And hear this, friends: Molly Reese herself will be there, in the flesh, so that you may better understand her tale!"

A drunk man hollered, "Going to be mighty hard for her to tell that tale with no tongue in her head!" Several laughed.

Bledsoe pointed at the man. "True enough, sir! You shall hear her story from *my* lips, *my* tongue, reading from the narrative written by Molly herself, recounting her sufferings, her rescue, and ultimate salvation through the power of our Lord! And you shall see her with your own eyes!"

"I done read all that Molly Reese jabber on a broadside over in Charleston," said a man whom few would have identified, by appearance, as a likely literate. "No reason to hear you spew it all over again!"

Indeed, the story of London-born Molly Reese was widely known and had been published frequently on broadsides and in newspapers both British and American. Preachers often recounted paraphrased versions of the Molly Reese saga from pulpits, particularly on the American frontier, where tales of redemption and apparent supernatural intervention were popular. There was even an ongoing stage dramatization of the bloody tale in Boston, a play much discussed for its remarkably believable and graphic depiction of the gore involved in severing a human tongue. "How did they *do* that?" was the question most frequently asked, post-performance, by those who attended the play.

Potts personally had heard Molly Reese's story on three occasions, all proclaimed from pulpits. At mention of her name by the loud preacher, the details of her grim adventure began to spill through his mind.

Those of a religious bent almost invariably saw the experiences of Molly Reese as evidence of the power of divine intervention to save those in distress and danger. Some found in her story specific evidence of protective angelic activity. Less spiritual souls simply believed the woman was just unusually lucky.

There had been little enough evidence of luck in the early life of Molly Reese, beyond the fortunate accident of familial affluence. Raised in a landed family, Molly was brought up without benefit of her mother, who had died during Molly's birth. It was said that her father harbored some related resentment toward Molly, while others believed the man simply to be especially perverse and cruel.

In any case, at around a decade of age, Molly began to fall victim to mistreatment and abuse by her father, who drank heavily. Initially his treatment of her was simple meanness, striking her with his fists at the slightest provocations or hitting her with such objects as fireplace pokers, kitchen implements, and the like. As the girl grew, though, his abuse achieved a darker, depraved aspect, and Molly became the victim of treatment her own narrative euphemistically called "invasions of the most harsh and lewd variety." Yet the more he misused the girl, the more her father seemed to despise her.

At length Molly's father came to realize that his actions put him at great risk of exposure, because Molly was a highly intelligent and articulate girl. A whisper to a sympathetic domestic servant, a neighbor, a constable, or clergyman, and Molly could easily bring destructive public humiliation and punishment upon her sire. When Molly's father realized this, his molestations ceased for a time. Then came an inevitable renewal of his perverse passions, bolstered by the weakening effect of liquor on his moral character. Molly Reese was placed in her most dangerous circumstance yet, though she was too young to fully comprehend the depth of her danger.

There had been a time when John Reese had been a decent man and citizen, and even, in the earliest days of his daughter's life, an occasionally tender father. But alcohol did terrible things to the man, corrupting him body, soul, and mind. His thinking became irrational, his reasoning addled — so much so that he actually became able to believe, one night when he was drunker and more irrational even than usual, that rendering his daughter physically unable to speak would keep his sins hidden forever. He persuaded himself that he could protect his secrets without taking such an extreme step as murdering his own child, an action he had been pondering secretly. Ruined as it was by his drinking, his mind was actually able to fully accept the fallacious notion as not only sensible, but clever.

Thus came the horror that changed the life of Molly Reese forever. Alone one evening in the house with her father, she was caught by him in an upper hallway and dragged into his dark bedchamber, where he clouted her severely with a heavy brass candlestick and knocked her unconscious. He drew out a thin-bladed knife, pried open the senseless girl's mouth . . . and began cruel and bloody work.

It was only afterward, standing over his profusely bleeding daughter with her severed tongue in his hand, that he comprehended the flaw in his plan. He might have rendered it hard for Molly to betray him with spoken words, but the girl was able to read and write. A simple scrawled note passed to a constable or dropped in the charity box at a nearby church, and he would be as fully betrayed as if she'd shouted the truth about him from atop a cathedral. Furthermore, the way he had maimed his daughter could not go unnoticed, and would in itself rouse questions and investigation.

So he had failed. He had mutilated his daughter in a beastly act of cruelty, and still he was in danger.

So she had to die after all. He knew it then, and while he still possessed the will do to it, lowered himself beside her to put the knife to her throat. . . .

Then came the miracle, the divine intervention. Or so it was described in Molly's famous broadside narrative.

From out of the shadows in the room, a figure bolted forth, lean, lithe, and fast, and came upon John Reese with swift violence. Swinging a candlestick that was twin to the one with which Reese had pounded Molly's skull, the intruder, whoever and whatever he was, dropped John Reese like a sack of dirt and pummeled his head repeatedly.

And Molly, regaining partial consciousness, saw and heard it all, albeit in muddled fashion. The flash of the brass candlestick as it caught a reflected gleam from the simmering coals on the nearby grate, up and down, up and down . . . the thud and crush of metal pounding flesh and skull . . . the terrible hiss of John Reese's last breath of life . . .

Then it was done. John Reese was dead. Molly was mutilated but alive, filled with horror and pain as she discovered what had been done to her, having seen her severed tongue lying on the floor near her father's lifeless hand, an ugly thing she could not readily identify in the dim light. The mysterious one who had intervened to save her life knelt beside her, talking softly and gently, telling her he would take her away, and that her father could never follow or hurt her again. He was gone forever, and she was safe.

The young girl did not know the one who had saved her. And as she groped at her painful, bloodied mouth, she did not care. She cared only about what had been done to her. And the fact that her father could do no such terrible things to her again.

According to her famous narrative, Molly Reese's memory failed her at that point. The next thing she was aware of was being away from her home, the body of her father left behind and never seen by her again. Molly came to herself on a rough cot in a dark and dingy room, an unshaven and watery-eyed man leaning over her and wiping blood from her face. His breath smelled of strong rum. He had something like a cloth sack pulled over his head for some reason, but the front was at the moment rolled up so his face was visible from chin to brow.

"Well, there you are, m'lady," he said. "The bleeding is stopped now. You're going to feel a goodly amount of pain for days to come, and much hunger because there'll be no feeding you until you've healed at least a little . . . but you will heal, and you will live. Life will go on and you'll get past this terrible violence that has been done to you."

The impulse was to answer the man, but when she tried to talk she could form no words and the effort brought a shuddering burst of pain. All she could do was groan. The man leaning over her shook his head.

"Don't try to speak, m'lady. 'Twill only frustrate you and bring you fresh hurt and bleeding. Just lie quiet and let yourself begin to heal."

She nodded, but nodding hurt, too. Her vision shimmered and she felt weak and faint, collapsing back onto her dirty pillow.

She closed her eyes and knew nothing more for quite some time.

So declared the famous broadside narrative.

Ott Dixon growled, "You've talked your talk and announced your come-to-Jesus meeting, preacher. Now go."

Abner Bledsoe actually managed a smile at his uncongenial host. Dixon did not smile back.

Bledsoe performed the unexpected friendly gesture of approaching Dixon with his hand extended. Dixon stared down at it as if Bledsoe had just tried to hand him a smelly fish carcass. For a moment, Potts wondered if Dixon might strike the preacher with his fist. No such thing happened.

"I'll not shake your hand, knowing you think of me as less than fit as a man, but I'll offer you a drink of good rum," Dixon said. "That's as Christian an offer as I'm able to make the likes of you, hypocrite."

"I imbibe very seldom of the kill devil," Abner Bledsoe replied pompously. "If a man must wade into Satan's pool, let him dip his toe only into the shallows."

"Bosh and bilge water!" Dixon blustered. "Off with you, babbler! Don't you come around here again, neither!"

"I'll return the day the hound of heaven finally nips your heels and drags you to the Father who calls you," Bledsoe replied in his English-accented voice. "It will be my pleasure indeed to be the one who points the way to you."

Dixon pointed at the door. "There's the way, yonder, that I'm pointing to *you!*" he said. "Be gone, preacher!"

Bledsoe departed, and Potts took advantage of the moment to slip out of the door himself. He still had no place to sleep for the night, and the house of ill fame that Dixon had recommended to him certainly held no appeal. His horse had traveled far and was tired, and Potts was tired himself.

It was time to give up the quest for lodging. As John Crockett had said, a man could always sleep on the good earth. He'd find a grassy meadow where his horse could graze, and he would spread his bedroll and say farewell to what had been a long day.

About five-score miles farther west than Potts, Crawford Fain had harbored no intention of remaining all night at White's Fort, but the conversation with Eben Bledsoe had dragged on far longer than anticipated. The day had passed and evening had fallen, and still Fain and Bledsoe conversed by the light of a nearby cook fire where an aging Cherokee woman tended the contents of a steaming kettle.

"Where were you born, Mr. Fain?" Bledsoe asked. "Virginia, I think?"

"Raised in Virginia, sir, but actually born in London, and raised English through my youthful years. Yes, sir, like you, I am a born Englishman, though now I'm American to the core. My father followed his brother across the sea and brought us to America. My mother took sick after they arrived here — an ague of some kind — and died, leaving me and my father alone."

"Sorrowful story, sir. I'm regretful to hear it."

"I was raised well despite it all. My father remarried, a Virginia woman, and she raised me as if I were her own. Most assumed she *was* my mother. And it was generally not worth the effort to correct that notion."

"What led your family to America?"

"A big part of it was that uncle of mine, who had come over to the Colonies earlier. It was his belief in the future of the new country that inspired my parents to leave London and follow after him. Of course they had no notion of how it was actually going to turn out for them. Neither did my uncle. But when they were gone he rose to the need of the moment and was a great friend to me the rest of his days, though I'm sure I seemed a burden to him."

"Thank God for faithful family relations."

Fain said, "Speaking of families, I've met your brother. I'm sure you must be proud of his work, both of you being men of the cloth."

Eben's eyes rolled toward the night-grayed heavens. "Bah!"

Fain frowned. "Have I misspoken, sir?"

Bledsoe stood on gangly, sharp-kneed legs. He presented an image of ill humor, much at variance with his previous friendly manner. His knees popped audibly as he unfolded himself. "I beg your pardon," he said. "The subject of my brother is distressing to me."

"I fail to understand, Reverend."

Bledsoe drew in a slow breath. "I simply must do a better job of restraining my reactions when the subject of my fraud of a brother comes up."

" 'Fraud'?"

Bledsoe breathed deep again and calmed some. "Mr. Fain, not all who claim the service of the Lord God are truly his servants. Some are pretenders, manipulators of the passions, casting the masses onto a tide of false fervor whose only power is emotional. Such, I regret to say, is my own brother."

"But he's had such success in his preaching! Why, there is a camp meeting soon to happen near my own station that I expect will attract a town's quantity of people to hear him. And some of them will surely join the faithful through his preaching — won't they?"

"I would not pretend an ability to judge the veracity of any individual's conversion."

"Except your own brother's, it sounds like."

Bledsoe frowned. "I have made you see me as judgmental. Perhaps I am, and perhaps I am wrong in being so. It's merely that I know my brother well, not only who he is but what he is. And what he is not."

"Ain't he just spreading the same message as you in a different way?"

"What I seek to 'spread' is the true *knowledge* of the Lord," Eben Bledsoe said. "What my brother spreads has more to do with mere feeling than knowledge, I fear. Have you ever attended one of his camp meetings?"

"I watched part of one from a distance one time. Never took part myself. I hear the voice of God clearer out in the wilderness alone than in the midst of a bunch of worshipers thrashing around like they're dancing on embers."

"Thrashing about. So you witnessed the so-called exercises that are one of the marks of Abner's meetings?"

"I saw folks having the jerks, as they call it. Looked like they was being cracked like whips. Never saw the like before or since."

"Such things, in my view, have little, if anything, to do with a God of dignity who tells us to do things decently and in order, Mr. Fain. I do not believe in a chaotic divinity."

"So it sounds like your objection to your brother boils down to not liking his kind of religion."

"There is more to it than that. There are things I know about him that indict and discredit him. There could never be cooperation between us, and he knows it as well as I."

"I've heard his voice while he was preaching. Why does he sound like a Britisher while you don't?"

Bledsoe chuckled. "Interesting, that little oddity! Both of us are English-born, and spent our young days in London. Once in America, though, I set it as my course and cause to adapt myself fully to my new land, including in my mannerisms and speech.

I'm sure some of my native British tones and ways come through yet, but for the most part I have changed my patterns, I believe."

"So you have. So have I. Living as I have so many years this side of the water, though, and taking the side of the Colonies in the revolt, my British tones have faded away, as yours have. But why not your brother's?"

Bledsoe chuckled and spoke more softly. "Very simply, because he wishes to sound to American ears like the famed English evangelist Whitefield, whom he resembles physically and whose preaching achieved such fame and influence. Whitefield was successful, and my brother worships success." Bledsoe paused, glanced about as if watched, then said in even quieter tones, "I'm ashamed to say it, but I think his fascination with Whitefield began when he learned the man suffered from crossing of the eyes. Abner has the same condition, and even though his condition is slight, I'm told he sometimes deliberately crosses his eyes more extremely while preaching, to make himself look all the more like Whitefield."

"Maybe it's working. Abner Bledsoe has gained fame and influence of his own."

Eben Bledsoe shook his head sadly. "The truth is, Mr. Fain, that success as a preacher can be had without the slightest trace of true religion. The masses are easily stirred by that which touches their passions, their emotions, particularly in new country where education is lacking. Stirring the emotions is the operating method of the camp meeting preacher. And such is why education and wisdom of the sort I seek to bring to this border country is so vital: so that the rational mind will prevail over the irrational heart. It is with the *mind* that truth is apprehended and understood, Mr. Fain — the *mind.* Not the heart, not the passions. Man is called to *know* God, not merely *feel* him."

Bledsoe filled his pipe again and lighted it with a flaming splinter from the nearby cook fire, then continued. "Here, tersely told, is the difference between me and my brother: He values success and adulation; he values religion as a show, a spectacle. I value it as the conduit whereby the elect are connected to God through his sovereign power. Abner values the individual, self-chosen spiritual experience; I value the covenant life as established by God and given to those whom he elects."

Fain wasn't sure he fully grasped the distinctions Bledsoe was making, and besides, his empty stomach was drawing his attention increasingly away from spiritual matters to a physical one: the bubbling kettle of venison stew being stirred by the Cherokee woman. Surely Bledsoe would invite him to eat. He was, after all, his guest.

Ultimately it was not Bledsoe, but James White, who issued the invitation. White, a pleasant-looking man in his late thirties, had been away from his fort through the day, and he was hungry upon returning. Fain, who knew White already as a neighbor, was pleased to accept the invitation. He waited with straining patience while Bledsoe led a long and windy prayer of thanks, then ate eagerly and sumptuously, praised the excellent seasoning of the venison, and its tenderness, to the delight of the Indian woman who had cooked it.

Fain passed the night in one of the fort's several cabins, sleeping comfortably on a mat woven from reeds and cane. The next morning he took pains to avoid engaging in any deep conversations with Eben Bledsoe, eager to get on his way back to his own station, where other duties awaited.

But Bledsoe would not be fully put off. He cajoled Fain about the need for frequent communications via messenger regarding his progress in seeking his daughter. With that pledge made, he brought out a small leather purse bag with a substantial jingle.

Advance pay for the undertaking. Bledsoe would cover all costs related to hiring messengers, finding lodging, and so on. It was an arrangement with which Fain could find little fault.

So Fain made all necessary promises and managed to maintain a pleasant demeanor, but struggled with the question as to whether he had made a sensible decision in agreeing to all this. To find a lone woman who could be almost anywhere in a broad wilderness, a woman who might have no interest at all in being found . . . could he do it? Should he?

There had been a time when such a big task would not have been daunting. He had gained the nickname of "Edohi" from his eternally traveling ways as a younger man, and particularly from his habit of moving from settlement to settlement all along the advancing borders of American civilization. He had visited or lived in so many different settlements that there was hardly a well-established fort or village that didn't claim him as its own. The "Edohi" name came from the Cherokee, among whom he had moved freely and safely when times allowed. Edohi designated a traveler or a walker. So associated did the name become with Crawford Fain that when he established his own frontier station a few score miles away from White's Fort, it quickly came to be called Fort Edohi, or Edohi Station. Several popular bards and storytellers, attracted by the poetry of the Edohi name and the adventurous life of the man to whom it was attached, presented works imaginatively based on his exploits that made him "Edohi" forever, and brought him a significant amount of fame besides.

Once away from White's Fort and Eben Bledsoe, Fain set his horse on the woodland wagon trail toward Fort Edohi. As he rode, he felt a sharp prod of pain in his left ankle, and winced. It was a rheumatic reminder that he was not the young man he'd once been, a result of too many years spent treading miles of cold and damp wilderness ground on feet clad in moccasins that did little to keep out the chill or to support the ankles. Fain knew several aging long hunters like himself, and almost every one of them now walked with a limp and suffered in damp weather.

"Why did you tell him yes, you fool?" Fain asked himself aloud. He answered his own question with more self-reproof: "Sentiment, old mammy kind of sentiment! You felt pity for a poor fellow missing his daughter. So you threw away all common sense and agreed to a job you may not be fit to do."

Maybe Titus would lend a hand. And a pair of strong, young ankles that could still go when his father's aching and aging ones would not.

Fain pulled himself out of his reverie and turned his attention forward, onto the trail ahead, the path to Fort Edohi.

CHAPTER THREE

Standing a few days later on a wood-fringed crag overlooking a broad valley nearly devoid of trees, a husky, thick-bearded man peered at the lone rider moving toward Fort Edohi on the edge of the big meadow. Though the distance was too far to let him be sure, the watcher was persuaded that the rider was none other than the famed Edohi himself, Crawford Fain. Jeremiah Littleton had seen the man often and could easily recognize the particular slump of his shoulders and tilt of his broad-brimmed slouch hat. Fain had traveled in and out of the fort several times over past few days while Littleton had been camped nearby, watching and awaiting an associate he'd summoned to meet him.

"Damn your eyes, Edohi!" he muttered softly toward the distant rider. "Your time will come, old fool!"

Movement on the side of the meadow

where the stockade stood diverted Littleton's attention. A wagon was rolling around the side of the fort, bearing timbers, atop which sat a few men. The wagon jolted along a little faster than it should, hit a bump, and one of the men perched on the cargo was knocked off and hit the ground hard. The others laughed, but were too far away for Littleton to hear them.

The fallen man got up fast to make sure he avoided the rear wheels of the wagon. One of his companions extended his hand down to help him back onto the wagon, but the man shook his head, opting to walk. The wagon hit another bump, the man with the extended hand almost fell off, and this time it was the walking man's turn to laugh.

Littleton looked back toward Crawford Fain and saw that Fain, like him, was watching the moving wagon. Fain lifted his arm and waved at the men, a couple of whom waved back.

"Know what they're doing, don't you?" said a voice behind Littleton. The big man wheeled, startled, moving his hand toward the big butcher knife he carried sheathed in rawhide at his belt.

The man who had spoken was emerging from a stand of scrubby trees, a big grin on his lean face. He was a small fellow, clad like Littleton in woodsman's garb, and carrying a loaded and primed flintlock pistol that he held at his side, pointed downward, but ready to raise in only a moment.

Littleton sucked in a deep breath and made tense sounds deep in his throat, which he then cleared. "Hello, Gilly," he said. "You surprised me."

The other laughed, a strange cackle. "Surprised? Why? By jingo, it was you who told me to meet you here, Jeremiah."

"I know. I mean, you startled me by appearing so fast."

Gilly chuckled. He looked past Littleton and across the valley. "See that rider yonder? That's old Fain himself! The mighty Edohi!"

"I know. I recognized him, too. From the way he sits his saddle."

"You see them others? With the wagon? Know who they are?"

"Can't see faces from this distance and don't know that I'd know them if I could."

"Hell, I mean, you know what they're up to?"

"Getting ready for the glory to fall, I reckon. Building a platform for the preaching going to happen down there. Big camp meeting, famous preacher. Old Bledsoe hisself!"

"That's right. Place will be filled up with

every kind of saint and sinner, and old Bledsoe will collect himself an offering, sure as anything, and leave all the good Christian converts skint out of whatever coin is in their pockets."

"Yep. I know about the camp meeting."

An awkward pause followed, during which Littleton kept his eye on the pistol in Gilly's hand. Gilly noticed but did not put the weapon away.

"What'd you want to meet me up here for?" Gilly asked.

"I believe you know."

"B'jingo, I did what had to be done, Jeremiah. There was reason."

Littleton shook his head. "No. Not for that. Our purpose was robbing, Gilly. Robbing. Not murder. You killed a man who didn't lift a finger against us. We robbed him and his folk, he made no resistance, and you shot him dead. With that very pistol you hold in your hand right now."

"There was reason."

"That kind of thing is what gets men hanged, Gilly. You know when we agreed to band up that we settled on me being the captain, me making the rules. My rule was, and is, no killing except to protect your own life or the lives of your fellow members of the band. You broke that rule. Killed a man for no cause."

"I said it before: There was reason."

"He was on his knees, Gilly! Hands clasped behind his back. Even had his eyes closed. He was no danger to you or me or anybody else. And you shot him through the head, right before the eyes of his family. There was no reason."

"There was. An old one."

"What was it, then?"

"Because he deserved it, for something he'd done years ago."

"What?"

"What business is this of yours, Jeremiah?"

"Because we're partners, Gilly. Or I thought we was! You and me and the other boys, we teamed up together to get what we could off all these folks traveling to the Cumberland Settlements. We partnered up to be thieves and highwaymen, to work together and to keep one another safe . . . and when you start killing folks for no reason anybody else can see, well, you put us all in danger. Of the hanging rope."

Gilly gave a snort of exasperation. "Hell, Jeremiah, they can hang us just as quick for being highwaymen as for murder! I didn't put us in no danger we weren't already in anyway."

Littleton shook his head. "Murder's a

worse crime, Gilly. Murder will get a man hanged faster than anything else. We're thieves, but by God, murderers we can't afford to be."

"It wasn't murder, not really. The man I killed earned that pistol ball, b'jingo."

"How? He was giving no resistance."

Gilly's face reddened. "That man killed my father, Jeremiah. Years ago. Shot him dead."

Littleton frowned. "Your father was a second-story man in Baltimore. If he was shot it was probably in the midst of robbing a house or a shop."

"He was shot. I was just a boy and I saw it happen with my own eyes." Gilly's eyes grew moist. "I vowed I'd find that man and make him settle his debt. And I did."

Littleton pondered his partner a few moments. "Your father was a murderous scoundrel, Gilly. Worse even than you. Any other such debts still lingering out there you're going to demand payment for?"

Gilly glared at him in silence. Littleton shook his head. "Can't continue, Gilly. Not like this."

"You're cutting me out, Jeremiah?"

Littleton was, and the truth was he'd probably have done so even without the provocation of Gilly's indiscreet shooting of their recent robbery victim. Littleton had begun to detect instability in his partner sometime back, and had been expecting to have to take such action even before Gilly's last exhibition of poor judgment.

"I'm cutting you out," Littleton replied.

Gilly's face reddened even more, and his body gave a hard tremble. Then, from somewhere in his throat, a grumbling, strange sound rose, soft but fast-building, until it erupted in a violent screech of pure anger that made Littleton step back involuntarily.

"Gilly, calm yourself. No reason for —"

He never finished the sentence. The lithe Gilly burst forward toward Littleton like a startled hare coming out of trailside brush. Littleton sucked in his breath and stepped back again.

The heels of Gilly's hands caught him in the center of his broad chest and threw him off balance. He stumbled backward and over the brink of the bluff, plunging backward over the fifty-foot drop, his big body doing a full flip in the air as he fell. When he dropped into the yawning mouth of a pitlike cave near the base of the escarpment, where it bulged outward, he went in feet-first, down into blackness.

Only Gilly's light weight and natural athleticism enabled him to heel back his momentum and avoid pitching over the cliff right after Littleton. His feet scuffed up grit and gravel that rained over the edge, but Gilly himself kept his footing and did not fall. Looking over the bluff, he saw the black hole that had swallowed Littleton. But in the shadows of its mouth he could detect no details, no movement. Nor did any sound emerge, any cries of pain or pleas for rescue.

"Done in, I reckon," Gilly Cobble muttered to the wind. "Good-bye, Jeremiah. Shouldn't have behaved like you did to me. It might have saved your life. Ah well."

He thrust the flintlock pistol back under the rope belt that bound his hunting shirt tight around his scrawny middle, and looked back out across the big meadow below. The men were off the wagon now, and removing the puncheon lumber from the wagon bed. A couple were already driving heavy stakes that would provide the bracing for the preaching platform.

Gilly shook his head, pondering the foolishness of the kind of folk who would fill a meadow just to hear a man give them a religious harangue while holding his eyes crossed. Gilly couldn't fathom it. He was not educated or literate or trained in any kind of faith himself, but he was sure he was right to ignore all things religious. Liquor, money, women, and good tobacco — these were his objects of worship and veneration. Good enough for Gilly.

"So long, Jeremiah," he said quietly. "Sorry I had to kill you like that."

He turned and walked away. Out in the big meadow, work continued on the preaching platform. One of the sharper-eyed workmen happened to glance up at the right moment to see Gilly Cobble disappearing into the tree line back behind the cliff. The workman wondered for a moment who that distant man was, then forgot about it and went back to his task.

Jeremiah Littleton's senses returned slowly at first, like the light from a slow-spreading flame, then faster, until the final leap into awareness left the man convinced he was dead and gone to hell.

Pain was everything and everywhere, filling him body and soul. He could see only darkness, though it seemed that above him was a faint vestige of light. He was far too bathed in pain to care, and for a time his consciousness flickered in and out, on and off. Then it set in to stay, and he suffered.

Though his pain was all through him, it

was centered most intensely in his left leg. This was pain like he'd never known, the pain of a leg that had been broken on a wheel or shattered by cudgeling on a St. Andrew's cross. And it would not subside, and in fact merely worsened if he tried to shift his position to gain relief.

Littleton was upright, his arms free to move within the pinching confines of whatever place this was that held him. He could not put together how he had come to be here or even where "here" was. All he knew was that it was as if he was in the base of a funnel, his weight pulling him downward into the tightest part of it, his left leg already hopelessly wedged into the funnel's hole, and pulverized. Miserable throbs of torment came up from that leg in waves, filling him again and again, building upon itself.

He heard himself scream and his voice seemed louder than it should have been. He opened his eyes just as a pale wash of light came down upon him. Looking up, Littleton saw an irregular circle of sky. It was night and the moon had just moved past the black edge surrounding the circle, and it was that light he had just seen.

It came back to him then: the memory of being on the bluff, of his tense words with Gilly Cobble, and Gilly's treachery in pushing him over the bluff. This "funnel" around him was the lower portion of a pit into which he had plunged feetfirst, and the hole of the funnel was simply a crevice in the rock that was too small to accommodate his hips and upper body, but which had received his left foot and leg easily, though destroying both flesh and bone from the knee down. Littleton's right leg, amazingly, had found a resting place in a smooth recess in the stone wall, and seemed uninjured, though the pain radiating from his destroyed left limb was so intense he could hardly tell what was hurting and what was not.

How long had he been down here? It was afternoon when Gilly had pushed him over, but now it was dark. He might have been here for hours, bleeding from that shattered leg. God above, it hurt! How it hurt! He was quite sure that his shinbone was broken clean through with the broken end protruding through his flesh. Torn and bleeding flesh was all that kept his ankle and foot connected to his body.

But his arms were free, and maybe, if he could find purchase to push himself up, he could pull out of the terrible pinch. Then maybe it would hurt less . . . but he would still be trapped in this pit. And Gilly, he was sure, was gone by now, probably hoping and assuming Littleton was dead.

It was that thought that gave Littleton the will to place his hands on the rock and give his body a heave upward. The only result was a horrible intensifying of his pain, a throb of agony pulsing up from the ruined leg. Littleton screamed and fainted, and when he came around again, he knew he could not be freed from this place. He would die here simply because it hurt too terribly to try to pull his leg free.

His right hand flopped limply and touched something . . . the grip of the butcher knife he always carried. Another throb of pain came and he knew this could not go on. If he was to die here, he would rather do it fast, to ease the suffering. And he would rather die by a hand other than that of Gilly. That betraying killer did not merit the achievement of causing his death. Littleton would do the job himself.

With effort he worked the knife from its sheath . . . and dropped it. Reflexively reaching after it, he inflicted another jolt of suffering upon himself, and groaned loudly in his constricting prison of rock.

"So thirsty," he whispered. "Hurting . . . and so *thirsty!*"

Despite the discomfort that groping for the knife had caused, he had managed to get it. He moved it into position against his chest, pressing the tip of it against his flesh until he could feel the pulsing of his heart vibrating the blade — then, hesitation.

Littleton was no praying man, but his eyes drifted skyward and he stared at the moon through tears. "I . . . I don't want to die, God," he said. "But I hurt so bad . . . and if I don't do this, I'll die anyway, just longer and slower and hurting worse, and I can't bear it. Forgive me, Lord. Forgive me for what I've got to do."

His leg throbbed worse than ever now, and he sobbed.

Pressing harder with the knife, he wondered how badly it would hurt when he pushed the metal into his heart; but as the blade broke skin, he discovered something unexpected. The pain of his smashed and torn leg was so intense that he hardly noticed the new pain caused by the knife beginning to enter his chest, a mere pinprick of discomfort by comparison to what already overwhelmed him.

Even so, he hesitated. The impulse to live was strong — but so also was the need to be free of his pain.

"Forgive me, God," he said again, and pushed a little harder.

Chapter Four

People began gathering early in the morning, arriving in wagons and on horseback. Those on foot began to show up a while later. By noon the great valley meadow near Edohi Station was well populated, several tents pitched and even a few arborlike shelters in place, the materials for them mostly carried in by the families who made them.

Crawford Fain stood on the rifle platform inside the stockade wall of his fort and watched the crowd grow. The platform from which Abner Bledsoe would preach had been completed two days earlier, and during that time Bledsoe had hauled in, by wagon, a stout oaken pulpit lectern that would not have been out of place in an ornate chapel in England or one of the older New England cities, but which was incongruous indeed on this rustic frontier setting. Abner Bledsoe, it was said, insisted upon always having that lectern with him when he preached. There was a story behind it; something to do with Whitefield, the famed preacher, once having preached from behind it.

"Fain!"

The call came from somewhere among the scattered crowd of people below, and it took a moment for Fain to locate who had called to him. A waving hand finally caught his eye and he saw an old acquaintance, Zeb Cable, who was busy stoking a cook fire over which his wife, Mae, had hung a black kettle. With a keener sense of smell than most men — another legacy of his long hunter days — Fain could smell the simmering stew even across the distance.

"How fare you, Zeb?" Fain called.

"Quite fine, Edohi! You?"

"Well indeed! Come to the gate!"

He saw Cable speak to his wife and gesture toward the fort, then begin to advance in Fain's direction, a broad grin on his face. At the same time, Fain heard a bumping on the nearby ladder that led up to the rifle ledge. He looked around and saw that Langdon Potts, who had arrived at Fort Edohi the day before, was climbing up to join him. Potts stepped lithely to Fain's side, looked out, and saw the approaching man.

"Fellow looks familiar," Potts said. "Somebody I should know?"

Fain shrugged. "Don't know if you've ever met him. His name's Cable, and last I knowed of him, he was living over on the Nolichucky. The fact that he's come farther west might indicate he's moved off from there, or maybe that he's such a follower of Abner Bledsoe's preaching that he just didn't want to miss the camp meeting."

Potts noticed that Fain was watching Cable's approach with a look in his eye that didn't seem entirely a happy one, and commented upon it. Fain sighed. "Truth is, Potts, Cable is one of them singers that only knows one song. By which I mean he talks about the same thing all the time. Franklin and Carolina and the government and all such as that. Blast my soul! Why did I call him into the fort? I should have left him out there with his family around their stewpot."

"He a Franklin man or does he favor Carolina government?"

"He's Franklin, unless he's changed since last I spoke with him."

"I reckon that's good."

"Do you?"

"Reckon so," replied Potts, shrugging. "I don't pay a lot of heed to such things. I'm taking it that maybe you think t'other way?"

"I don't think on it at all, son, if I can avoid it. Let the folks over round Jonesborough and Greeneville fight that one out. They can just leave me be on the matter."

Cable reached the gate and came through. With effort, Fain slapped a smile on his face and descended the ladder to greet him. Potts followed, and was introduced to the newcomer. They found a shady spot in a corner of the stockade, under a post oak, and sat on the ground.

It did not take long for the conversation to be led by Cable into a discussion of the governmental issues of the day. Potts listened without saying much. Fain pretended to be interested and Cable droned on like an undying mountain wind, never tiring of his subject.

Uninteresting as it might have been to Fain, the governance situation Cable loved to talk about was unusual indeed, and left many of the settlers in the so-called backcountry wilderness honestly unsure as to what government they owed allegiance.

At the close of the Revolutionary War, the region of North Carolina was vast, extending all the way from the Atlantic coast to the waterway the Algonquin called the "Great River," or in their language, the

"Misi-ziibi."

Just west of the Unaka Mountains, along rivers with names such as Holston, Nolichucky, Watauga, and Clinch, were settlements populated by thousands. Beyond was a long stretch of wilderness, reaching to the Cumberland River and its Nashborough settlement, and other neighboring settlements. The Cumberland River settlements were particularly vulnerable to attacks from Indians who did not welcome the intrusion into what had been before rich hunting ground for the Cherokee and other natives, and for long hunters such as Casper Mansker, Alphus Colter, John Rains, Joseph Drake, and Crawford Fain.

As part of North Carolina, the backcountry people believed themselves due protection from their mother state — but therein lay a problem. Distance and the mountain barrier made it impractical for North Carolina to respond to troubles in the outlying settlements or offer them significant protection, so the settlers were for the most part left on their own.

The situation was diplomatically clumsy for North Carolina. At the close of the Revolutionary War a solution, or an attempt at a solution, was finally contrived. North Carolina opened its western lands to purchase and settlement, then made a gift of those lands to the government of the United States, effectively washing its hands of the responsibility to protect the far-flung settlements. But before it made the move, it first went through some legislative maneuvers that allowed Carolina leaders the chance to claim ownership for themselves of great tracts of backcountry lands. The move came to be known as the "Land Grab Act." And in ceding the land to the federal government, the land grabbers set as one term of the cession that their North Carolina land grants would continue to be honored.

Cut off by their mother state and with little ground to believe the federals would do any better protecting them than had the Carolinian government, the resentful backcountry leaders came up with their own idea: an independent, separate state, one that they hoped would be approved and taken in by the Continental Congress. They named their proposed new state Frankland, meaning "land of the free," though they eventually got around to changing the name to Franklin, in honor of America's most popular statesman.

The affair took another twist when North Carolina changed its mind and rescinded its cession of lands to federal control. The settlers who had begun the process of state-making now were under a strange double banner, their allegiance being asked by both North Carolina and the fledgling entity of Franklin. There were, at some times and places, two simultaneously acting sets of government leaders, one with Franklinian authority, the other acting for North Carolina.

Efforts to have Franklin recognized by the Continental Congress failed, the vote falling short of what was required by the Articles of Confederation. Those strongly in favor of the Franklin effort huffily proposed becoming an independent republic, while others favored the old North Carolinian association. Crawford Fain, for one, was persuaded that the heated feelings the issue stirred in some quarters would inevitably lead to flying rifle balls at some point, and prayed fervently for a resolution before matters took such a bad turn.

Fain wondered if he would ever be able to stop grinning. He'd forced a muted but agreeable smile onto his face in order to politely make it through the conversation with the boring, monotone Cable, and now he'd held it so long he wasn't sure he could relax his jaws. But he did, and found his will to be polite fading fast. He had to escape Cable and his unending Franklinite talk, even if it meant leaving poor Potts to sit there and endure it alone.

How was it possible for a man to live his life thinking of nothing but politics? Fain, unlike Cable, just didn't have it in him to do that. Fain loved to let his mind drift free, to think upon whatever it happened to find, like a man stumbling down an unexplored path. Fain knew from long experience that the unexplored paths often proved to be the ones that opened on the finest vistas.

Fain had not had much interest in observing the camp meeting commencing outside the walls of his stockade. He'd planned to watch a few minutes of it from the vantage point of the blockhouse on the southeast corner of the fort, then quietly drift back to his own cabin to turn in early for a long night's sleep.

If the choice ended up being between listening to old cross-eyed Bledsoe and political blabber Cable, Fain was inclined to choose the former. Cable was showing no sign of reaching the end of his Franklinian discourse.

Conveniently, singing voices arose from outside the stockade, distracting Cable from his talk and rendering him silent a few moments.

Come, ye sinners, poor and needy,
weak and wounded, sick and sore;
Jesus ready stands to save you,
full of pity, love and power.

"Sounds like they're getting started," Fain said, grabbing the opportunity. "Mr. Cable, I'm supposing your family awaits you out there."

"Why . . . yes. They do. Perhaps I should go. Though there was more I wanted to say about —"

"Yes, perhaps it is time to rejoin them. We'll continue our conversation some other time. Now, I believe I'll retire to the blockhouse and listen to the preaching from there."

For a moment Cable looked intrigued by that idea, and Fain wished he'd kept his last words to himself. If Cable climbed up into that blockhouse with him, Fain would remain his captive.

"You are a fortunate man to have so fine a family to enjoy such an evening with," Fain said. "Though I do thank you for taking a few minutes away from them to visit me."

Cable nodded and shook hands with Fain

and Potts, and at last made his way out of the fort. Fain grinned at Potts. "Got your politics all figured out now, son?"

"If I don't I reckon I've got no excuse for it, having heard all that."

Fain chuckled, and the pair headed toward the ladder leading up into the blockhouse, which was a square log structure, built on poles, rising above the top of the stockade palisades, with a wide rifle slot in the blockhouse wall at shoulder level. From inside the blockhouse a few riflemen could lay down a wide field of fire in almost total safety, protected by thick log walls.

Fain and Potts positioned themselves at the rifle slot, from where they had a panoramic view of the meadow and what was now a large crowd indeed, hundreds in number. Arbors, tents, parked wagons, and makeshift horse pens were scattered throughout the throng. Here and there a small clump of people were gathered around would-be preachers who stood on stumps or wagon beds, preaching their own unwanted sermons in a vain hope of winning over the crowd before Bledsoe could get rolling with his crafted British accent and crossed George Whitefield eyes. Bledsoe, at the moment seated on a bench at the back of the preaching platform, didn't worry about such usurpers. They showed up at every camp meeting, and never drew more than a handful of listeners. The crowd belonged to Bledsoe, and he knew how to play it.

At Bledsoe's side sat a gray-haired woman, locks wrapped up in a kerchief, a placid expression on her face. This, Fain knew, was the woman who would become the focus of attention when the Molly Reese narrative portion of the presentation began. Fain opened his mouth to make a comment to Potts, but just then a figure clambered up the ladder through the entrance hole in the blockhouse floor.

Fain frowned and started to say something to encourage Cable to go back where he'd come from; then he saw it was not Cable.

"Hello, Doctor," Fain said to the new arrival. "Fine-looking rifle you got there."

Peter Houser moved away from the entrance hole and approached Fain with arms outstretched, the rifle held horizontal in his upturned hands like a gift. For a moment Fain wondered if perhaps a gift was just what it was. He hoped so, for Houser was known as the finest gunsmith west of the mountains.

"Is that the one you've been working on?" Fain asked.

"It is," Houser replied through his auburn whiskers. "Finished just yesterday. I spent the morning making bullets for it and polishing it so you would see it to greatest advantage."

Fain took the rifle and admired it with a knowing eye from butt plate to sight. "It's a beauty, sir," he said. "If you're as fine a physician as you are a gun maker, those of us privileged to be your neighbors will surely live forever."

Houser smiled. "Even without Holy Bledsoe's help?" He nodded in the direction of the camp meeting.

"Even so," Fain said.

Houser chuckled. Houser, a man of multiple fields of expertise and a seemingly endless range of skills, was known to be no devotee of camp meetings, emotional displays, or other traits of new light religion. Even so, he sometimes described his choice to leave the settled East and move to the frontier West to be the result of responding to a "calling." His goals were to be an agent of better life on the frontier, using not only his medical skills (gained through years of apprenticeship with one of Philadelphia's best physicians) but also as an innkeeper, real estate broker, gunsmith, and supporter of education. Rumor had it he had made a sizable monetary gift to Eben Bledsoe's fledgling college, whose loftier and less emotive style of religion was more in keeping with Houser's preferences.

"I'm pleased you like the rifle," Houser said. "It's yours."

Fain gaped. "I beg your . . . Did you say . . . ?"

The physician/gunsmith/innkeeper beamed. "I *did* say. I consider it an honor to be able to present a rifle to so fine a hunter and woodsman as Crawford 'Edohi' Fain."

"But I . . . I've done nothing to merit . . ."

"You have done more for me than I can ever repay. You opened your station to me as soon as I and my family arrived. You provided us shelter, a cabin of our own within these very walls. You treated us as if we were your own kin. You provided land upon which we could build our permanent home, establish my medical office, and build our inn. This rifle is but a small and inadequate effort to show my appreciation."

"I'm — I'm grateful. More than grateful."

"That's a beautiful piece of craft, sir," said Potts.

Fain said, "Doctor, I don't know that you've met my friend Langdon Potts before. He came here to see Titus, only to find he's away."

Another song had begun outside, and swelled up loudly, interrupting the conversation. Preaching had not yet begun on the main platform, though a few of the uninvited small-time competitors were still holding forth out among the throng.

When the music lulled, a wild, screaming yell arose from the camp meeting. A man's voice, harsh and high, as if someone had just hit him with a hot iron.

"What the deuce?" Fain said.

Potts was already looking out. "It's Bledsoe," he said. "I think the preaching is about to commence."

"That wasn't preaching; that was a howl," Fain said.

"Little difference between the two in Bledsoe's approach to religion," said Houser. "Vent the emotions! Stir the passions! Disconnect yourself from the rational mind." He shook his head. "How can a man suppose he can find truth when he disdains the very organ of reason? It's more than Abner Bledsoe's eyes that are crossed, in my opinion."

"Bledsoe's brother, Eben, thinks the same, Doctor."

"I know. I know. And had he not disavowed his brother's nonsense, his new academy would have received no support from me."

"What the devil?" said Potts, looking out the rifle port.

"What is it, Potts?"

"There — see? Coming through the crowd?"

Dr. Houser, whose eyes were as keen as his mind, was already at Potts's side. "Lord in heaven!" he said. "Come with me, young man. I think I may be needed out there, and I may benefit from your strong, young back."

Chapter Five

Reuben McCart was only fourteen years old, but tall and big for his age, as muscled as his father and uncles. Partly because he looked so much like a man, he particularly resented the fact that his family still treated him as a child, sending him on trivial errands, leaving him to oversee his younger siblings when his parents were away, and speaking to him in a condescending manner.

His latest resentment was that his mother had sent him to fetch his youngest sister's lost dog, which had chased a rabbit away from the camp meeting grounds and back into the brush and trees around the base of the bluff overlooking the meadow. As far as Reuben was concerned, the dog could be left to its own devices and fate. The fact that his sister consistently failed to keep control of the animal was not *his* fault! And how was he expected to find a free-roaming dog at night, especially considering that this particular dog had never taken to him much and would probably hide if he got near? Despite making that point to his mother, she was unrelenting and sent him on his surely vain errand while his tearful sister smugly looked on. He might have appealed to his father, but his father was off somewhere else on the meeting ground, talking to other men. So Reuben simply went on, back toward the cliff looming behind them all.

"Here, boy! Here, Tater! Show yourself, dog!"

Nothing. He went on, past the back edge of assembled camp meeting worshipers. The meeting was beginning to really come to life, a few people showing the first signs of the "exercises" that often marked these events: spasmodic, violent jerking back and forth, so hard that men's hats were flung fifteen feet away and women's long hair flailed like cracking whips.

It all seemed odd and unpleasant to Reuben, who decided that maybe looking for a lost dog was at least better than being stuck in the midst of such seeming madness.

Half an hour later, as he trudged back to the meeting ground, he did not have the dog with him, but was unconcerned. He'd fetched back something much more important than a dog.

He'd heard the sound shortly after penetrating the brush at the bottom of the escarpment: a low, mournful moaning that he thought might have been wind moving through the small cavern passages that penetrated the bluff. He'd seen the dog then, standing at the rim of a pit below the cliff, growling and barking down into the hole. As Reuben sneaked nearer, intent on grabbing the dog before it knew he was there, he realized two things: the moaning was coming up from the pit itself, and it was not caused by wind. It was a human voice, the voice of a man who was seemingly in great pain.

At that moment Reuben hadn't felt much like a grown man at all, but a scared boy. Someone was down in that hole, hurt, and he wasn't sure he wanted to see the situation. But duty and curiosity drove him to the pit's edge, and just as he looked over, the moan rose to a full scream.

It was dark in the pit, and Reuben had no light except for the feeble illumination of the moon. He lay on his belly and looked down into the hole, hands resting on the rim of the pit, and listened as the screaming faded down until it was merely moaning again.

"Who's down there?" he finally dared ask. His voice trembled more than he liked.

"I . . . need help. . . ."

"Are you trapped down there?"

"Need . . . help to get out . . ."

As Reuben strained to see, his eyes adjusted somewhat and he thought he saw something white moving below in the murk. A moment of closer study revealed it to be a hand. Drawing in a deep breath, he braced himself as best he could and reached down.

The man's hand was thick and rough-skinned. It closed around Reuben's hand with great force. "Pull now," the man below said.

Reuben pulled hard. The man's hand held firm and Reuben could tell the fellow was pushing up from below with his legs, but as he did he moaned pitifully, like a victim of torture. The effort for both Reuben and the man in the pit became more difficult, but both persisted, and slowly the man rose until Reuben could just make out the dim image of a bearded face.

Reuben was sure he was going to lose his grip, but it didn't much matter because the man now found purchase with his other hand, gripping an out-thrusting rock on the side of the pit. Still groaning, he pulled up, then let go of Reuben's hand and at the same moment took hold of the edge of the pit. Reuben could hear the scuff of the man's feet on stone as he struggled to climb.

The fellow was burly and strong, but something in his manner and look, as he became more clearly visible in the moonlight, did not seem right. Reuben had the impression that he was pallid, but it was too dark to really know. When the fellow suddenly slipped backward a little, as if stricken with weakness, Reuben grabbed his hands and pulled him forward. The man managed to writhe over the edge of the hole, where he collapsed onto his belly with great heaving breaths. He moaned again.

Reuben stood erect and stepped back to look the fellow over, and saw at once that he'd been wrong when he'd thought that the man was pushing himself up with his feet. He had used only one foot, for one was all he had. Where the other leg should be was only emptiness, with ragged dark meat visible about knee level.

"Your leg, mister . . ."

"Gone," the man said, his voice raspy. "Left it in the pit, wedged tight in a hole." Then he groaned again and said no more.

"Mister?"

No answer. Not even a moan now. Reuben thought for a moment the man had died, but then he saw movement between his shoulder blades, his lungs weakly inflating and deflating.

"Can you hear me, mister? We got to get you out to the camp meeting. There's people there and we can get you help. You're hurt bad, sir. Hurt bad."

No reply. Reuben knelt beside the man and tried to see the fellow's face, but the moon vanished behind a cloud and he could not.

"I'm going to have to try to get you up," Reuben said. "But you're a big man, and I don't know how well I can hoist you."

His hope was that the man would come around again, and have enough strength and balance to lean against him and stay upright. Together they could work their way out through the trees and brush and enter the campground, where surely others would come to their aid. Reuben was unsure whether he should position himself on the man's right side, where he still had a leg and foot, or on the left, where there was nothing.

He chose the right side because the ragged bloodiness of the other side made him queasy. He'd be no use to this man if he passed out in a faint and let him fall.

Kneeling, he slid the man's limp right arm over his shoulder and tried to stand him up. He got only part of the way before the fellow's weight pulled him down again. Another try, another failure. And again, the same.

Reuben changed positions and tried a fourth time, still to no avail. He'd managed to help the man out of the pit, but that might be as much success as he'd see. He decided he'd have to abandon the man and go bring back rescuers from the camp meeting. But just as he stood to do so, the man groaned loudly and rolled a little onto his right side.

"One more . . . try, friend," he said hoarsely.

"Have you got the strength for it? You're missing a leg, sir. Part of one, anyway. Gone from the knee on down."

"Yes . . . had to cut it off . . . to get free . . ."

"You cut it off your own self?"

"Yes . . . Help me up. . . . Let me lean on you."

The man seemed to be gaining a little strength and clarity. But with it came renewed pain. Even so he put forth great effort to rise, and with Reuben joining his strength to the man's, he managed to get upright after several more attempts, his weight resting on his one remaining foot and on Reuben.

"Come on, let's figure out how to walk together," Reuben said. And they moved forward, an odd kind of shuffle that relied on instinct and mutual coordination — and on the injured man managing to hold on to his consciousness.

The trees, darkness, brush, and the physical clumsiness of their mode of locomotion served as impediments, yet step by step they advanced, until at last they cleared the stand of woods at the base of the bluff and entered the back edge of the meadow. As they entered the back perimeter of the camp meeting, no one noticed them initially, their attention turned toward the speaking platform where Abner Bledsoe was talking in his piping voice and gesticulating freely, pacing from one end to the other. They went forward, and then the injured man drew in his breath sharply and passed out, his weight dragging him off Reuben's supporting shoulder. Littleton hit the ground with a sound like that of a dropped sack of grain.

Reuben looked around. They were still unnoticed. Then one man, who was jerking slightly with the religious spasms that marked Bledsoe's meetings, noticed Reuben struggling to rouse his companion again. The man didn't move to help, but turned his eyes forward toward the preacher again. Reuben felt a burst of resentment.

Littleton groaned and moved a little.

He was never quite sure thereafter how he did it, but Reuben pulled his companion up to his single foot, managed to balance him for a moment while he positioned himself, then heaved the mostly unconscious man up onto his shoulder, completely off the ground. He tottered under the weight, but somehow didn't fall. Astonished at his own strength, he took a step, and again didn't fall. Then another, and another, and another, and slowly he advanced through the crowded camp of worshipers, tents, and arbors, going mostly unnoticed, but in a few cases drawing the attention of people who gasped in horror when they noticed the state of Littleton's severed leg. So distressing was the sight that people withdrew as Reuben advanced, mothers covering the eyes of their children and men taking on tense stances of wariness, as if anticipating a fight.

Reuben had no thought of carrying the injured man back to the place where his own family was emplaced. They were unequipped to deal with such as this. He would take him to the stockade, where, he had heard, an actual trained physician was usually present, some fellow who was settling in the area and building a fine new hostelry.

Reuben was most of the way through the crowd when he saw men coming out of the open stockade door and trotting his way. Help at last! He'd been seen from inside the fort, obviously.

Exhausted, he fell, the bulky form of the man he carried crushing down upon him.

The camp meeting continued unabated, the worshipers fully distracted by the theatrical preacher, who himself seemed to have not even noticed the odd sight of a boy carrying a large one-legged man on his shoulder through the middle of a camp meeting, then falling beneath the burden.

With the air crushed out of him by the weight of the limp figure lying upon him, the exhausted Reuben passed out for a few moments, and next was aware of walking along beside an older man through the interior court of the stockade. He no longer bore his human burden. He looked toward the man and recognized a face that was famous through the region: Crawford "Edohi" Fain, the very man who had built

Fort Edohi. Reuben had seen him twice before, once when the family had first come to the region, and a second time when consideration was being given to a possible farther move to the Cumberland Settlements, and Reuben had joined his father in a visit to Fort Edohi to talk to Fain about the safety of such a move. Fain had spoken honestly about the dangers posed by Indians and white bandits along the way, and Reuben's father had been dissuaded from his notions of moving farther west.

"Are you all right, son?" Fain asked Reuben as they walked toward Fain's cabin. Others now carried the injured man Reuben had hauled, a few steps ahead. The man seemed to have passed out again and his one remaining foot merely dragged the ground beneath him as he was borne along.

"I'm fine, Mr. Fain."

"You're that McCart boy, I believe."

"I am." Reuben was surprised to be remembered.

"When we get inside and the doctor does what tending to this fellow he can, we'll want to hear everything you can tell us about how you came by him."

"Yes, sir."

"You know his name?"

"He never said, sir."

"Looks familiar to me, but I can't place him."

Houser got directly to his task, which was illuminated mostly by the fireplace, plus a few candles grouped nearby. Reuben was at first intrigued, but when he got his first clear look at the raggedly severed leg stump, he felt his gorge rise as a wave of faintness lightened his head. Fain noticed and moved him toward a bench against the cabin wall.

"He cut it off himself," Reuben said. "He told me that. He said the bottom part of his leg was left stuck in a hole down in the pit he was in."

"A devil of a task, cutting on yourself that way," Fain said. "Don't look at it and don't think on it. I believe it's bothering you a mite."

"More than a mite, sir."

"Dr. Houser will see him put as right as he can be. I've known others who lost extremities, and every one of them came through and did pretty well after. He's got enough leg left that he'll probably peg-leg it pretty well, if a peg can be made that fits him right." In his mind, Fain was already going through the process of whittling out a peg leg for this man. A proficient whittler, Fain had made three such prosthetics in his life: one for a neighbor whose leg had been crushed in a tree-cutting accident, and removed after, and two more for survivors of a fierce siege by a band of Chickamauga, or "Lower Cherokee," so called because of the location of their towns farther south than the ancient and revered Overhill Cherokee villages.

Conversation dwindled. Houser bent to his work, and the injured man remained mercifully unconscious, making Houser's labors easier. Reuben kept his eyes on the leaping flames in the fireplace and tried not to hear the meaty, ugly cutting sounds made by Houser's blade. He began to feel a bit better and decided at last he could even sustain a glance at what the doctor was doing.

"Why is he cutting on his leg stump, when it's already cut?" Reuben asked Fain.

"I'm no physician, son, but I think what he's doing is getting that leg in shape to heal better. He'll pull what skin he can down over the wounded flesh and stitch it all up right neatly. I've seen something like that done before. Makes a world of difference in the healing if it's done right."

Reuben was pale. "Lord, how did that fellow do it? Cut through his own leg? Wouldn't the pain have made him stop? I'd never be able to do that."

"Men do what they have to do in such moments. And generally they can do more than anybody would think they could. I'm guessing that this gent probably was in such pain already that he might not have much felt his own cutting. All the hurting kind of mixing in together, you know."

Reuben shuddered. "God, I hope I never have to do such a . . ." He trailed off.

"Likely you'll never face such a situation, son, but if you did, you know what you'd do?"

"No, sir. But I think I'd just throw down the knife and hope for the best."

"No. You'd do what you had to do, whatever it was. It's the way the good Lord made us . . . and maybe part of the reason he lets us face such dreadful things at times. So we can learn just what we're capable of doing."

"I don't know that I want to know what I'm capable of doing, sir," the youth said.

"I understand what you mean, son. I do. I think most of us hope to pass the tests we're put to, but that's no reason to hope we get put to them in the first place."

"I need to go back and get with my kin," Reuben said. "Thank you for helping me get that fellow some aid."

"Nothing but what I'd have done for

anybody, and hope anybody would do for me."

"Evening, Mr. Fain."

"Evening, son."

Chapter Six

The Molly Reese presentation had been given so many times that the preacher could have recited most of it without the aid of the papers on the lectern before him, just as the woman did her part without prompting or direction. She had it easier than he, of course, possessing no tongue and being able to produce only the most rudimentary approximations of understandable speech. She was not required to say anything to the congregants.

Repetition of the performance had helped her overcome any sense of shyness or hesitancy she had once possessed. In earlier days she had felt a normal human resistance to letting others see her abnormality, and had gone through life with her mouth clamped tightly shut most of the time. Those who sought to see for themselves what was, or was not, inside the oral orifice were turned away consistently. She would not be treated like some living horror or mutilation.

All that had changed when she met Abner Bledsoe. Something about the man had drawn her, pulled her out of herself, and filled her with fascination for him. Just what it was she could not say. It was certainly not physical — he was a plain enough fellow, to be sure — nor was it a serious interest in his religious teachings. God had done little for her, in her estimation, and she had decided years ago she could and would do without him. And if that meant she would also do without him when she entered the next life, whatever it was . . . well, so be it. Fine with her.

She had met Bledsoe on a street in a town in Virginia. A purely random meeting, made memorable by the injury she had suffered when Bledsoe rode too close to her on his horse and a hoof crushed her foot into the dirt street, breaking two of her toes. She had gone down with a cry and Bledsoe had dismounted to see what he had unwittingly done. It was a fated meeting for them both.

It didn't take long for Bledsoe to realize that the woman he'd injured had a distinctive handicap. Her first effort at speaking revealed it: muddied, murky approximations of word sounds, only a few of which he understood.

As coincidence or fate would have it, Bledsoe had, only the day before, read the already-famous account of Molly Reese and her bloody girlhood adventure — and a fascinating possibility suddenly presented itself.

"Are you by chance named Molly Reese?" he asked. The woman's answer was impossible to understand, but it didn't matter. Bledsoe had continued: "Because if you are, ma'am, we stand to benefit nicely from this encounter, you and I." From the look of her he could tell she was impoverished, and would surely respond to any prospect of "benefit."

She did respond. She accepted an invitation from him to dine at a nearby tavern — having not eaten a real meal in days — and her usual defensiveness quickly faded. He told her about himself and his preaching life, working his way delicately around the nature of his motives and interests, allowing her to realize slowly that his "calling" was not really a spiritual one. Rather than be put off by his blatant and unrepentant hypocrisy, she was drawn to it, finding in his willingness to exploit others a ground of hope that perhaps her life could become something better than she had known.

She had not left the preacher's presence that night, and was still with him when the next morning came. He sent her away from the inn where they had stayed long before he left, so they would not be seen departing overnight lodgings together. They rejoined outside the town. They had not parted since, forming a partnership both personal and professional: He told the sordid Molly Reese tale and she allowed the gaping devotees of the false preacher to stare into her empty mouth while she sat beneath torchlight with her jaw dropped for their viewing convenience. She hated them all but pretended otherwise for the sake of the gifts some of them gave her in pity. In all her lonely life she'd never fared so well as she had since she took up with the preacher Bledsoe.

She'd done better than usual here beside Fort Edohi. Her little wooden collection bowl was filled with coins and other items, even a ring and a locket, a generosity quite surprising and unexpected from a population of people one would expect to be quite poor. She could not account for her good fortune, but gladly accepted it, and without guilt. She'd been deprived of much in her life, and it was surely only fitting that she receive something in recompense.

She'd grown bored, though, sitting there as she had so many times, maw lolled open like an idiot's, men, women, and children filing by and ogling so they could see for themselves that, yes, indeed, this woman had no tongue in her head! She despised their morbid curiosity, their looks of pity and revulsion. Fools! They could use her as an entertaining display if they chose, because she was in turn using them. The jingle in her wooden bowl more than made up for the shame of being stared at like an object of pathos.

At last the line of gawkers melted away and she stood, giving a quick smile to Abner Bledsoe, who remained on the platform, waving his dignified farewells to the scattering worshipers. She had turned to step away from her post when Bledsoe suddenly made a subtle gesture indicating she should remain, and tossed his head slightly to make her look to her left.

A man was approaching her, a gray-haired, slender fellow in excellent clothes, a man who would have looked more in place in a Boston parlor than in an open meadow beside a frontier fort. She smiled at him and sat down again as he reached her, and thought he looked affluent, maybe able to give her more than the usual pittance.

"Ma'am?" he said pleasantly. "I'm late, I know, but I've been occupied within the stockade, tending to an injury. I am a physician, and my name is Peter Houser."

She smiled again and nodded, putting out her hand for him to shake. He did so delicately, holding her by the fingertips.

"As a man of medicine who is often called upon to tend to injuries involving injury and mayhem, I am intrigued by you. I've never had occasion to see the type of injury you have suffered. I would like to make a quick inspection for the sake of my own education. May I?"

She seldom encountered such politeness. Almost no one ever asked permission to inspect her mutilated mouth. They simply walked past, giving no greeting, acknowledgment, or thanks, and gawked at her like a pathetic object rather than a person.

She nodded and dropped open her mouth, turning her face up to the light of the nearby torch. Dr. Houser leaned over and stared in. She studied his eyes as he examined what he saw. He was no idle, ignorant gawker; he looked at her with a knowing and understanding eye. As she realized this, she suddenly clamped her mouth closed.

"Is something wrong, sir?" Bledsoe asked

him, having watched all this from the platform.

Houser hesitated, his eyes flicking between the preacher and the seated woman, who now rose to her feet again. "I would like to speak with you privately, Reverend."

Bledsoe repeated his question. "Is something wrong?"

Houser climbed the little flight of steps leading up to the platform and went to Bledsoe. He put his hand on Bledsoe's upper arm and gently prodded him to the rear corner of the platform, away from where the woman was.

"Sir, what is wrong?" Bledsoe asked, concerned now.

Houser paused a moment, glanced over his shoulder to make sure the woman would not hear him, then said quietly, "I am afraid you might have been misled by your associate."

"Miss Reese?"

"The woman who professes to be Miss Reese, you should say."

"Explain, sir."

"Sir, if Molly Reese lost her tongue in an act of violence during her girlhood, then the woman standing over there is not Molly Reese."

Bledsoe jerked as if he'd been stung, his

slightly crossed eyes narrowing as he stared at Houser. "Why would you say such a thing, sir?"

"Because the woman there is indeed missing her tongue, but I can assure you, as a physician, that it was never cut out of her mouth. The deformity is one of birth. Her tongue was never cut out because she never possessed one. She was born in her current condition, and if she has presented herself to you as Molly Reese, she has deceived you."

Bledsoe glared at Houser and for a moment struggled for words. "I — I don't believe that, sir. I'm sorry. I'm sure you speak what you think is truth, but I tell you, before God, that she is Molly Reese! I have spent too much time with her, shared her story so frequently. . . . I cannot, will not, believe she is anything or anyone other than the Molly Reese I have known for years."

"Well, then, if she is in fact Miss Reese, then it is her account of her misadventure that is false. For I must tell you with the firmest of conviction, that woman's tongue was never removed from her head! She lives today in the condition in which she was born."

"No." A firm shake of the head. "No, sir. She is who she says she is. She was attacked by her own father, mutilated, then rescued by a being who well might have been an angel sent for her protection."

"Reverend, with all respect due to you, may I ask you why, then, did the angel not present itself sooner and stop the assault aborning? If protection had been the divine intention, why was it not given before the severing of her tongue?"

"Aha!" Bledsoe said, aiming a stubby, pointing finger at the physician's face. "You admit, then, that her tongue was severed! You just said as much!"

"I am presenting a hypothetical, not a statement of fact. And that is beside the point in any case. What I say, I say on the basis of trained observation. I know scarring when I see it, and the marks left by cutting and severing. Those are absent from this woman's mouth. I must stand by what I have declared."

"You do not know what you speak of!" Bledsoe's piping voice was getting louder and more shrill.

Houser took pains to keep his own voice calm. "I know that woman never suffered the violence described in the famed Reese narrative. That I know. What I do not know is whether or not the fraud derives from her alone, or from the both of you together."

"You insult me, sir."

"My intent is not to insult. I am simply making a physician's observation of the facts, sir, and —"

He had not finished his sentence before a furious Bledsoe lunged at him shoulder-first and shoved him back toward the rear of the high platform. Houser groped reflexively at the preacher's shoulder and grasped his shirt, so that when Houser fell he pulled Bledsoe down after him. They hit the ground hard, Houser landing on his back and Bledsoe on Houser's chest, driving the air from the doctor's lungs so thoroughly that it seemed it would be forever before he could draw it in again.

Simultaneously an unexplainable sharp pain exploded just to the inside of Houser's right shoulder blade. It surged through him, worsening when he tried to move. It was the last thing Houser was aware of before he closed his eyes and passed out cold.

Fain was looking down into Houser's face when the physician came around again. Houser looked up in puzzlement, trying to remember just what had happened, at the same time moving a little. The movement caused a new stab of pain beneath his right shoulder.

"You ought to hold still, Doc," Fain said, touching Houser's left shoulder and hold him down. "You took a sharp root stab under your wing, and it's going to hurt you if you do much moving."

"Root stab?"

"There was a sharp root poking up from the ground right where you and the preacher fell, and it jammed up right into your back. Long as my finger, it was. If it had struck into you on t'other side, I might wonder if it would have probed into the backside of your heart."

"Hurts," Houser said, closing his eyes. "Damn that preacher! He pushed me off that platform — I know he did — because he didn't like having his fraud revealed." Houser, growing a bit impassioned, stirred involuntarily and groaned loudly at the pain.

"Easy, Doctor. Don't stir. What fraud are you talking about?"

"The woman he passes off as Molly Reese. Either she is not Molly Reese, or if she is, Molly Reese never lost her tongue to violence. That woman out there tonight was born with no tongue. As a man of medicine and science, I can say that with certainty."

Fain did not look surprised. "I knew she was not who and what he claimed."

"You knew? How?"

Fain smiled. "I knew."

Houser's injury, though painful, was not serious. Within an hour of his fall from the platform, he was up and moving about, admitting that in doing so, he was in violation of the advice he would have given had the injury been suffered by someone else. Twice Fain had to replace the bandaging of the doctor's wound because his movement caused renewed bleeding.

"Doctor, it's no surprise your wife left you," Fain said. "You are a stubborn man intent on doing himself harm."

Houser frowned. "Fain, you know as well as I do that my Beth's return to Carolina is only temporary, and done for the sake of her ailing father."

"I know, I know. I only wish she was here so she could be your nursemaid, not me."

They were in the spacious front room of Fain's large cabin within the walls of Fort Edohi. The door opened and Langdon Potts entered.

"He's gone," Potts said.

"Who?"

"Preacher Bledsoe. I saw his wagon pulling away, him driving. There was a loose wheel, or so it looked to be, so I hailed him to a stop. He didn't look glad for it. He was in a hurry to leave. I checked the wheel and thought it needed fixing, but he declined it and said it would be fine to travel on. He pulled on out and as he went on, I caught a look inside the back, 'neath the wagon cover. I'll leave it to you to guess what I saw."

"The woman," Fain said. "The one they foist off as Molly Reese. Probably naked as the day she was born."

Houser laughed, then yelped in pain. "Don't make me laugh, Fain. It hurts to laugh."

"I did see the woman," Potts said. "But she had her garments on. Still, you could tell, just kind of get the feeling. . . ."

"That the two of them ain't spending their free time studying the scriptures?" Fain suggested. "Maybe doing a little something else?"

Potts nodded.

"They are frauds, you know," Houser said. "That woman did not lose her tongue. She never had one. I saw it for myself when I examined her."

"So the preacher's a fraud, too?"

"Almost certainly. I suppose the woman might be fooling him, but he seems the kind to do a bit of fooling himself. She's probably some malformed whore that Bledsoe ran across somewhere, and then came up with the notion of presenting her as Molly Reese to spark up his camp meetings a bit."

"A preacher would do that?"

"If he's a fraud and hypocrite, indeed he would," Houser said.

Fain rose in the middle of the night and paced through his cabin, his rheumatic pain causing him to limp. Houser slept on a thick bearskin pallet made on the puncheon floor near the cold fireplace. Houser's own house stood not far away from the stockade, on the side opposite the great meadow where Bledsoe had held forth, but Fain had insisted that Houser remain close by in case Houser's injury proved worse than it appeared. He also wanted the physician handy should trouble arise with the bearded man who had lost his leg; that man snored on another pallet on the opposite side of the room.

Potts had a pallet of his own up in the loft overlooking the cabin's main room. He quietly slipped down the ladder and joined Fain.

"Having trouble sleeping, are you?" he asked his host.

"Tell you the truth, son, I'm thinking of

Titus. Wondering where he is and why he ain't come home in such a spell of time."

"I wish he was here, too. I came a long way to see him and to tell him about the express plans. I think he'll be interested in that."

"I think he will. That's the kind of thing that would suit him just right."

The express plans to which Potts referred involved a scheme by some of the backcountry leaders in the Watauga country to create a system of mounted messengers who would serve as a private postal service in the frontier country, carrying mail and messages and the like between the Watauga, Holston, and Nolichucky settlements to the area of James White's fort and Fort Edohi, and probably on beyond all the way to the Cumberland Settlements. With success, the effort could be expanded later to provide service into the Kentucky country to the north.

It would be dangerous work, requiring bold and skilled young riders to carry it out. Indian dangers would be nearly constant along the wilderness routes. But such a service would be useful beyond measure and provide an avenue of greatly enhanced communication between far-flung settlements. Potts had been drawn to the idea from the first time he'd heard it, and had known that Fain's son, Titus, would be equally intrigued and as ready to become one of the express riders.

Crawford Fain stared out into the night between the shutters of a side window and sighed. Potts drifted over to his side.

"You worried about Titus?"

Fain said, "Not so much worried as just wondering. Titus is a capable young man, and he can see to his safety as well as anyone I know. But the fact is that these are dangerous times even for capable men. I just hope the boy hasn't gotten himself into some problem he can't find a way out of."

"He's fine, wherever he is," Potts said. "He might come riding through the stockade gate come morning. You never know."

"I wish I did know. He's the only son I've got. And besides that I've got a task I need his help with. A job I took on that I don't know I can do alone. With Titus, though, I think I could get it done."

"He'll be back," Potts assured again.

"Littleton," Fain said abruptly. He turned and looked Potts square in the face. "Littleton! I just remembered it."

"Who?"

"Littleton. Jeremiah Littleton. You heard of him?"

"I don't know. Who is he?"

"A bad man. Outlaw. Been known to rob travelers and emigrants. Runs with a band of outlaws as bad as he is. They killed a man recently while he was kneeling down and giving no trouble. That's the story, anyway."

"Why do you mention his name now?"

"I think that's who old stub-leg over there might be. I'd heard him described before, and his looks fit what I heard."

"He looks like any number of men you see every day, to me," Potts said, looking over to where Littleton continued his snoring, lying flat on his back.

"He's got the scar. Little one up near his eye, right side. Runs back toward his ear a thumb-width or so. Littleton's got that, they say. That's what was tugging at my mind but I couldn't get a full grip upon."

"Is he the one who killed the man?"

"He leads the gang. Has made bargains with the Indians, and has a few who rob with him sometimes. He's as guilty as any of them, in my book, whether he directly did the killing or not."

"Guess we have to keep him from getting away, then."

"That leg will help with that. Hard to run on a stump."

"But what if it ain't Littleton?"

"Let's go see."

They walked over to the sleeping bear of a man, whose lips vibrated with each snore. One eyelid flickered but he did not waken.

"Littleton!" Fain said in a sharp, loud whisper.

The man flinched some but slept on. "Littleton!" Fain said a little more loudly. Still he slept. A third call of the name, louder yet.

Littleton started and opened his eyes. For a moment he looked past the two faces staring down at him, then focused in blearily on Fain.

"Littleton, right?" Fain asked.

"What do you want from me?"

"Your name's Littleton. Jeremiah Littleton. Ain't that right?"

Littleton shook his head. "No . . . no. Name's Kirk. Lyle Kirk." He tried to sit up, then winced sharply. "God!" he swore. "Why's my leg hurt so?" Then he managed to lift himself enough to see, and the memory came back. "God . . . I'd forgot. Damned Gilly . . ."

Fain looked over at Potts. "Gilly's the name of one of Littleton's robbers. I think this is our man."

"Name's Kirk," Littleton repeated.

"Hell you say," muttered Fain.

"Don't know no Littleton."

"Very well, Mr. Kirk. Whatever you say." And he and Potts withdrew, leaving Littleton alone. A minute later the bearded man was snoring again.

"That's him, I'm right sure," Fain said. "I thought maybe he'd spill the truth if we caught him just waking up, but he's smart. Came up with a false name without so much as a hitch."

"I suppose he'll be staying put awhile, whoever he is," Potts said. "With that leg and all."

Fain was silent. He went to the bench against the wall and sat down. Potts joined him.

"That task you mentioned . . ."

Fain said, "Man has hired me to make a hunt for him. Not a hunt for bear or deer or any such as that. He wants me to find his daughter who went missing years ago, thought to have been taken by Indians. He thinks she may still be living. He's heard tales of somebody matching her, of a blond-haired woman."

"That's all? Blond hair? Not much to go on, just that."

"She's got a marked eye, gray streak in the brown. If I can find a yellow-haired woman with a gray streak in the brown of her eye, she might be his gal. Name's Deborah, if she's still using the name she was given at birth."

Potts was thoughtful a few moments. Littleton snored and Houser rolled over a bit and groaned. Fain pondered the oddity of being in a roomful of injured men when there had been no Indian attack or bandit raid, just a revivalist camp meeting.

"Tell you what," Potts said. "If Titus don't get back in time, and you're still of a mind to make that long hunt for the yellow-haired woman, I'd be glad to go with you and help you just like Titus would."

"You'd do that?"

"I would."

"You're a good boy, Potts. Just like Titus."

"Thank you, sir. Though I ain't really a boy, no more than Titus is. We're both men now. Been men for some years."

Fain grinned. "You're right. I just lose my bearings sometimes and forget. He's a man, and a good one."

He slumped back against the log wall. "I surely do wish that boy would come home." Then he began repeatedly casting his eyes toward a nearby shelf. Potts noticed.

"Want your pipe?"

"You're a good boy — good *man* — indeed, Potts. Sot weed pouch ought to be right there with it. And if you can bring the flint box, too, I can make a little fire for it."

Potts got up from the bench and fetched the items. Fain used his flint box to get a small piece of punk burning in a little recess made into the side of the box, and from that lit a splinter he had fingernailed out of the log wall. With that he lit his pipe.

Potts left the frontiersman contentedly puffing and made his way back up to the loft and his sleeping pallet. When Potts awakened the next morning, Fain was slumped to one side on the bench, sound asleep, the now-cold pipe having been dropped to the floor long before.

Littleton was gone, pallet empty. And when Potts checked, he found his own horse missing. He hurried back inside and told Fain.

"I'm smote," he said. "Plumb smote. I thought he might try to get away like that, but I didn't figure him to do it right off like that, with his leg fresh gone."

"He took my horse," Potts said, trying to make himself believe it. He'd raised that horse since it was a colt.

"He did?" Fain replied. "He's stout to do such a thing. Hard flint and oak tree stout. Got to give him credit for that — hop out of a stranger's house in the middle of the night on one foot, fresh-cut leg stump swinging and hurting, then steal another stranger's horse and get himself up on it to get away, and nobody catch him at it. Yep. That's stout as they come. And bold."

"He stole my horse!"

"He did, son. He did."

It was Houser who spotted the note.

Littleton had written it on a page torn from a Bible, using ink Fain had manufactured the year before from the juice of pokeberries and kept stored in a little crockery bottle on a nearby shelf. The letters were dim but well formed despite having been written without benefit of light sometime after Fain and Potts had gone back to sleep.

Heard you speak, Littleton had written across the Bible page, which he had left in the middle of his sleeping pallet. *Saw yellow-hair woman marked eye Crockett Spring three month past.*

"I'm smote yet again," Fain said. "Who would have thought he could have got away like that, the shape he was in? And I never even thought about him hearing what we said, him snoring away like he was."

"Will you go to Crockett Spring to look for this woman? Is this fellow somebody whose word you can take?"

"Likely not. It's not much of a clue, coming from such a source as our one-footed friend. But it's the only real clue I got, and following it holds more promise than just launching out without any hints at all. Will you come with me, Potts? I need the help of younger muscles and bones, and I can't know when Titus will return."

"I'll go, sir. Be glad to. But do you think it's real, what he says? Maybe he's just trying to get us chasing off to find this yellow-haired woman so we won't follow him. If we're off after her, we ain't off after him."

"That could be. But the fact is I've made a bargain with Eben Bledsoe, and I must fulfill it. You and me, Potts, we're going to Crockett Spring."

■ ■ ■ ■

Part Two: Journey

■ ■ ■ ■

Chapter Seven

The cabin door stood open and movement was visible in the shadows inside. Even so, the watching frontiersman on the ridge facing the cabin was unable to discern exactly what he was seeing.

A man approached quietly from behind and dropped to his belly beside the first man. "How many killed, Titus?" he asked softly.

"Don't know for certain. There's one man visible there by the woodpile — he's been scalped. Around the back there's a woman and a boy, both dead, both scalped. But somebody is inside the door, moving around. Can't see enough to know who or how many, though."

The other man reached beneath his hunting shirt and drew out a small spyglass, which he slowly expanded after examining the angle of the sun to make sure no reflective glint from the lens would reach into the cabin.

"What can you see, Micah?" Titus Fain asked. He was a youthful-looking man, in his midtwenties, his hair a sandy brown and tied behind his head in a queue. His lean face mirrored his late mother's visage, except for the eyes. His eyes were those of his father, and just as keen of vision.

Micah Tate squinted through his spyglass and said, "There's a body in there. A man, I think, though I can't see anything but the feet. But there's somebody else, too. Can't tell much, but I think it may be a child, still living."

"A child — Lord! What a fearsome and sad thing for a child to see!"

Micah handed the spyglass to Fain, who adjusted it to his eye and peered into the shadowed doorway. Fain lowered the glass slowly. "It's a little girl, Micah. I'd say ten years old, maybe eleven."

"Any other sign of movement?"

"None. I'm going down there."

"Hold a moment. That may be just a little girl, but she's seen her people slaughtered, and if she has a gun within reach, she could shoot you dead as you approach."

"So she might. Life is risky, Micah. I'm going down there. It's likely the poor little gal needs help."

"Then we'll go together."

"Fine. Now's the time." He came to his feet and stepped down the slope, Micah joining him.

"Hello the house!" Titus called. "Little miss, don't be afraid. We are friends coming down to help you! We are not Indians, but white men!"

They were halfway there when the girl appeared at the door, and true to the warning, she had in her hand a flintlock pistol, already cocked. The two men froze and then Titus made a slow display of laying his rifle on the ground, nodding to Micah to do the same. The two frontiersmen raised their hands and looked at the little girl, thinking how incongruous it was that a mere child had them at bay.

They were near the corpse lying beside the woodpile, and Titus said, "Is this your father's body lying here on the ground, miss?"

"No," said the girl in a voice more clear and strong than they would have expected. "That's my uncle. His name was Tom Deveraux."

"And what is your name?"

"I'm Mary. Mary Deveraux."

"Mary, my name is Titus Fain, and this is Micah Tate. Like I said before, we're friends.

You can count on that. Friends. We've come to find out what happened here and to help you and anybody else who may yet be living."

This time her voice wasn't as strong, and quivered some as she spoke. "There ain't no others living. They're dead, all of them but me. Indians done it. Did . . . did they take Tom's hair off him?"

Titus said, "Yes, Mary, they did."

She nodded sadly as if she'd expected nothing else. "Poor Uncle Tom. He was always so proud of his hair. My papa's pate was clean bald, but Tom's had a lot of hair, and he used to laugh at my papa for not having any."

"Mary, could you lay down that pistol so we can feel safe as we approach you?"

The little girl gently placed the pistol on the doorstep of the cabin. Then she stepped back inside a single step.

"We're going to pick up our rifles now, and come on in," Titus said, keeping his voice gentle.

The little girl nodded back in the interior shadows, shoulders slumping as the strength and courage seemed to drain from her. By the time they reached her, she was crying, her thin body shaking.

Titus had little experience with children

and felt frozen with helplessness. But Micah, himself an uncle to several little ones, knelt and put his hand out to touch Mary on the shoulder. He spoke softly. "We're so sorry for what has happened here, Mary. I wish we could have been here to stop it."

The girl, who had rather stringy brown hair, quite dirty and limp-hanging, looked into his face and sobbed loudly. She threw her arms around Micah's neck and hugged him strongly, seeking a protection that was now too late to make a difference. When Micah looked up at Titus with the girl's frail arms encircling his neck, there were tears in his eyes, too.

"You're safe now, Mary," Micah said, patting her shoulder. "Titus and me, we've been traveling all around here today, and there's no Indians hereabouts now. We'd have seen them if they were still about."

She sobbed again and hugged him even tighter.

The story was simple, sad, and typical of such tragedies. The Indians had simply appeared, almost ghostlike, at the front edge of the Deveraux cabin clearing. No words had been spoken. Mary's uncle had been the first to die, tomahawked by a warrior who had rushed down upon him so swiftly he hadn't even had time to cry out or reach for his nearby rifle. Mary had been at the door and saw her uncle fall, head ruptured. But apparently he hadn't died at once, because the same Indian who had felled him picked up Deveraux's rifle and crushed his head a second time with the butt of the stock. Then he knelt and took the scalp, which he waved tauntingly for the little girl to see.

Mary had withdrawn into the cabin and hidden in the little loft, and all else that followed she had more heard than seen from her elevated hiding place. The sounds alone had been terrible: her father being shot and cursed at with English-American vulgarities the Indians had picked up from white men — cursed because he had no hair and therefore no scalp to take — and then the sounds of her mother and older brother falling victim to belt ax and scalping knife, her older brother fighting hard and screaming at his attackers before he died, her mother dying quietly with a prayer on her lips.

Mary did not know why the raiders had not climbed to the loft to seek her, because they had seen her in the doorway and surely knew she was hidden somewhere. "I wish they had killed me, too," she said to Titus and Micah. "My family is dead. I should be dead, too."

"That's no way for you to speak, Mary. God has spared you," said Titus. "He's got something ahead for you, so he has saved you. Something good and happy, not bad and sorrowful like today."

She cried again, and went to the corpse of her father, which was clad only in trousers and moccasins. "They took his shirt," she said. "Why did they take his shirt? I had decorated it for him. I stitched a red flower into it for his birthday. It was here." She touched her chest. "He said it was the finest flower he'd ever seen. Why did they take his shirt?"

"I suppose they thought it was a pretty flower, too," said Micah. "But they shouldn't have took it. And they shouldn't have done this to your kin."

She was crying again now, and Titus wondered whether the child would ever grow past this and be free of the ghosts of this terrible day.

"Mary, where is your mother's body?" Titus asked. "And your brother's?"

"They dragged her out when they killed her," Mary said weakly. "My brother they killed outside, in the back. I saw them cut off his scalp through a crack in the wall up in the loft."

"Put those visions out of your mind as best you can, Mary," Titus said. "You are alive and now you must do your family's living for them, since they can no longer do it themselves. Do you understand me?"

She nodded, staring at her father's dead face.

"Mary, Micah and I are good men, friends, men who will help you and get you to a safe place. We can't bring your family back, nor make you able to forget all that happened here, but we can be good to you and give you protection and friendship. But you must be willing to come with us, to go away from here."

Titus wasn't at all sure the child would be willing to do that. He knew of many cases in which individuals inexplicably clung to the site of calamities and loss. But Mary was differently inclined. She seemed pleased to hear that she could leave this scene of horror.

"I'll go. I'll go now."

"Titus," Micah said, "what about the dead ones?"

Titus pondered the matter, then felt Mary's gaze upon him. He asked, "Mary, I'm going to leave this up to you. Me and Micah can bury your family here, and leave here later on, or we can leave now and send somebody else back to do the burying. But if it would make you sad to think of them left lying here for a time, we can bury them now."

Her chin shook and eyes welled. She shook her head. "I want to go now," she said. "They aren't really here. This ain't them. . . . This is what used to be them, but ain't anymore."

Titus hugged the little girl. "You are a wise young woman, Mary. Wiser than many who are a lot older than you. Have you got kin anywhere else, Mary?"

"No, sir. No family at all now."

Titus said, "Don't worry, Mary. We'll take you with us, back to a safer place, and we'll find you a home and a family. I promise you that."

She nodded and wept.

The sound of approaching horses drew their attention. Riders came over the rise and down toward the house, armed frontiersmen, each with a bit of white cloth tied to his hat. The hats were of many varieties: animal skins, French-styled woven caps, battered tricorns, and common slouch hats, those being the most numerous among the group of nineteen.

Titus came out of the cabin as they drew

near, eyes shifting between him and the corpse by the woodpile. The apparent leader of the group rode down near Titus and dismounted. Micah remained inside with the girl.

"Andrew DeVault," the man said in a deep, gruff voice. "These here men make up the Cumberland Scouts and we've come because we hear there's been an Indian attack here." DeVault glanced down at the dead man. "I can see we were told aright."

Titus nodded. "I've heard of the Cumberland Scouts, gentlemen. My name is Fain. Titus Fain."

DeVault froze a moment as a murmur swept through the rank of mounted riflemen. "Fain," he repeated. "Titus Fain . . . son of Edohi hisself?"

"I am."

DeVault handed his rifle to another man and dismounted. He approached Titus with an outstretched hand, and as they shook, examined Titus's face. He nodded. "I can see it. I can see my friend Edohi in your looks, sir. It's an honor to meet you. How's your father?"

"His ankle bones hurt him a lot these days. All the miles, all the years, you know."

"When you see him next, tell him Andy DeVault sent him greeting."

"I'll see him soon, and do that. There's a little girl in there who survived this, and my partner and me will take her with us to Fort Edohi and find a new situation for her."

Titus found himself the object of much attention from the scouts, who were quite familiar with the fame and reputation of his father. It was vaguely uncomfortable for Titus, who shunned attention when possible, but he realized that he provided distraction from the grim job that now fell to the Cumberland Scouts: burying the dead of what would thereafter be known as the Deveraux massacre.

The best trackers from the group set out to follow the Indians responsible. Titus was inclined to join them, but Mary had attached herself to him and Micah, her emotions boiling at any hint her two saviors might leave her.

Later, when Titus and Micah rode away from the Deveraux cabin in the late afternoon, a third horse accompanied them, Mary perched on its broad back and looking very small indeed.

Chapter Eight

The first night was spent in the home of a family named Colyer, seven miles from the site of the Deveraux slayings, a home surrounded by a small stockade. Little Mary was almost smothered with pity and gentleness by the mother of the family, a brood of five, all of the children older than Mary except for one boy of two, who toddled about the cabin providing some diversion from the general overcast of gloom and sorrow within the place.

Oddly, Mary was the least depressed of the group. She seemed to crave the distraction of being among friendly strangers, and found the toddler to be quite entertaining. Titus took pleasure in seeing Mary laugh at the child's babble and tendency to fall down. He himself could not so easily put behind him the horror of what he had seen at the Deveraux cabin. Nor could Micah, who excused himself regularly to go outside and pace about the cabin clearing, determined to make his body as active as his racing mind, which dwelled on thoughts of the massacre. Only when the hour grew late did he finally begin to settle, eager for sleep and the chance to put a difficult day behind him.

Titus noticed that Ben Colyer, father of the hosting family, was intensely withdrawn, sitting most of the evening in the corner of the room, leaning forward, staring at the floor with his chin in his hands.

When the others had headed off to their beds, Mary having been offered a place on the single large straw tick that was the sleeping place of the three girls in the family, Micah reentered the cabin and sat down near Colyer. Noting his host's obvious depression, he reached over and gently slapped his shoulder.

"Terrible thing to happen to a neighbor," Micah said as an intended prelude to words of comfort that he hoped would come to him of their own accord. None did, and the thought hung alone in the room like a ghost.

Colyer, to the surprise of the other two men, began to weep softly. "My fault," he said in a cracking, nearly silent voice. "My fault."

"It was Indians who done it, Mr. Colyer. Not you. You can't take blame for something done by others, especially red men."

"No, sir . . . but fault I can take for having seen early sign of those savages, yet saying nothing of it. I should have spoke up. Should have given warning."

"Why didn't you?" asked Micah.

"I was unsure of what I was seeing," Colyer said, looking earnestly at the other two. "I am a man of the city by birth. I'm no woodsman as you two are. But now that I reflect on it, I know that what I saw was Indian sign. A full day before the poor Deverauxs were slaughtered. If I had spoke up we could have stopped it from happening."

"All lives have their regrets," Titus said. "My father says that often."

"But you're right," Micah added. "You should have spoke up."

"And next time you will," Titus added.

Colyer stood and paced in a small circle for a few moments. "There will be no 'next time,' " he said. "I am taking my family back to Fredericksburg. I came west only in hope of becoming a merchant when the country was settled and safe. I came too soon. This is a bloody land and I am not a man fit to stay here."

"There are dangers everywhere, Mr. Colyer. Even in the cities."

The man sighed deeply, slumped, and

stared at his visitors. "It is hard for me to put in words the guilt I feel. If only I had been more quick and clever and sure of myself, I could have saved their lives. It all would have been different."

Titus shook his head. "My father has also said to me, many times, 'There is no place named "Would Have Been" where a man's foot can find ground to stand.' There is only what is. And all you can do is look square at it, find your trail through it, and trudge on, whether it is good land or bad."

Colyer nodded. "Your father is a wise man as well as a famous one, then," he said. "But there is no comfort in words for me now."

Titus said, "Just let your sorrow flow through you until it's gone. Then move on."

"If only I could have saved them . . ."

"The past is past. Leave it there."

Micah, seeking to shift the conversation onto less somber ground, pointed toward the base of the door, where sat a yellow-hued stone about the size of a large man's foot. "Something about that stone there draws my eye," he said. "Is it just a door-stop?"

Colyer lost a little of his gloom, clearly glad to have something mundane to which he could shift his focus. "It is a doorstop, but it isn't just a stone I happened to pick up for that purpose. It was given to me three years back by an uncle, who in turn had gotten it from a long hunter who'd come out of Carolina. He told me I should guard that stone because it is 'something important.' What that meant, he never said."

"But you've kept it anyway."

"There is something about it that draws the eye, as you just said," Colyer said. "And if it is viewed in certain lights . . ."

"May I take a better look at it?"

"Certainly."

Micah rose and fetched the rock. Returning to his seat, he examined it by the flicker of candlelight, squinting hard. "I suppose this might be an ore of some kind," he said. "A metal-bearing stone."

"There is a certain shine to parts of the stone when the light hits it," Colyer said. "You'll see it when the sun comes back round again."

"Have you had anyone look at it to see what it is?"

"I don't know anyone who has knowledge about such things."

"I think I'd want to carry it to a town somewhere and let a silversmith have a look," Micah said. "A silversmith would know right off what it is — if it is anything."

"You've roused my curiosity about it all

over again, Mr. Tate."

"If you're thinking of asking me to take a piece of it with me and have a silversmith look at it, I'll do it. We're heading east, and there will be opportunity."

Colyer said, "If that stone proves to have any value to it, I know what I'll do with it. It'll go to help poor little Mary, since I failed to help her before."

"You'll have to let that go, Mr. Colyer. You can't carry around worry over something you can no longer change."

Colyer closed his mouth and said no more.

Micah and Titus spent the night on blankets spread in Colyer's log barn, and did not stir until morning.

Mary slept inside the house on a pallet. Her sleep was restless. In the morning Ben Colyer's wife, Gundred, reported quietly and out of Mary's hearing that she heard the girl whimpering and softly calling out in her sleep, reliving the terror and loss she had just experienced, and had once found her roaming silently through the cabin, staring fearfully at the dark windows. Gundred had spoken to her and quickly ascertained that the girl was not awake. When morning came, there was nothing to indicate Mary had any awareness of having been sleepwalking.

"What will become of her?" Gundred asked the men. "She has no kin to see her through such a hard time."

"I have promised her that I will find her a home," Titus said. "I shall." He paused, gathered his boldness, then asked, "Might you take her in here?"

The Colyers looked at each other, wordless. Gundred spoke.

"We cannot do it," she said. "We simply cannot." No reasons were given and none were demanded by Titus and Micah. Micah, in fact, seemed relieved at the woman's words. Titus asked him about it later, in private.

"Why did you look so pleased that they turned away from that idea?" Titus queried. "It would have solved the problem straightaway."

Micah shook his head. "It might have provided an answer, but it would not have been the right one. There's a better place for that child, and we'll take her to it."

"Where? What place?"

"We don't know yet," Micah said with cheerfulness. "Our duty is to find it."

Titus chuckled. "I never heard you talk about duty before, Micah. You've always shunned such a grim subject in the past."

"Don't mock this, Titus. We saw a child's

world destroyed all around her, like the ground had dropped away under her feet and left her with nothing, not even a place to stand. And it was into our hands she was placed, so it's our duty to provide for her welfare. I figure the good Lord has put this girl into our care, and he's going to whisper in our ears to let us know the right things to do for her. I got one of those whispers while we were talking to the Colyers. It told me they are not the ones who little Mary needs to stay with. Besides, they turned her down and took the matter out of our hands. Maybe they got the same whisper I did."

Titus marveled at his friend. This was not the Micah he had known since boyhood. "Well, brother, far be it from me to speak against the very whisper of God in your ear. But be aware that it won't be easy, traveling with a child, particularly a maiden child. Two men and a half-grown girl . . ."

"Ah, folks travel together all the time," said Micah. "They bundle together at night, stand guard for each other when they go for a squat in the woods — ain't nothing. It's just life in the backcountry."

"I wish she could just stay here."

"They said no."

"I heard them, Micah. I was there, too."

■ ■ ■ ■

If Mary Deveraux herself had any qualms about traveling with the two men whom she barely knew, she did not reveal them. After the trio departed the Colyer cabin and began their eastward journey, the girl presented a much brighter demeanor and was clearly glad to be leaving the area of her family's slaughter. As the hours and miles fell away behind them, there was virtually none of the awkwardness Titus had feared.

Titus found himself beginning to admire his partner Micah in ways he never would have anticipated. The man possessed a natural ability to relate to the orphaned girl, speaking to her in ways both frankly honest about her tragedy but also gentle. Though Mary possessed some residual shakiness and startled easily at any unexpected sound or shadow-shift in the forest, she was calmed by Micah's presence and voice, and Titus pondered that it was too bad that Micah's young wife, Rachel, had died before they had produced any children. Micah would have been an excellent father.

Long travel was not required before the settlements of the Cumberland country gave way to a wilderness virtually untouched by white hands. Settlement of the over-mountain Carolina/Franklin west was following a broken rather than steady progression. The first settlements had occurred just west of the mountains, along the Holston, the Nolichucky, the Watauga, and then leapfrogged farther west to the Cumberland region with a riverborne settlement voyage from the Holston to the so-called French Lick of the Cumberland, and a parallel immigration overland to the same end point. Between the areas of settlement was a broad wilderness of woodlands, mountains, and valleys. Traveling that wilderness was a dangerous venture. Titus did not undertake it lightly, particularly with a child to be guarded.

Two hundred miles of untamed country to be crossed before they reached Fort Edohi. Not until they were there would Titus begin seriously to look for a solution to the question of where, and with whom, the orphaned girl could begin a new life. Such considerations were too distracting during wilderness travel, when a man needed his wits and full attention working for him. Solve one problem at a time, Crawford Fain had always advised his son. One at a time.

"I need to stop," Mary said after having

ridden for two hours in silence.

Titus twisted in the saddle and looked at her. She was riding to his side and slightly behind him, with Micah in the rear.

"Are you well?" Titus asked.

"I need to . . . I need to visit the woods for a minute or two."

Titus nodded. Just as he'd predicted: clumsy. But not very. Frontier folk grew accustomed to doing without much privacy for even the basest functions of life. Plenty of cabins had no more than an elevated horizontal rail somewhere nearby to serve as a privy. One simply sat on the railing, hindquarters extended, and did what had to be done.

"Very well," Titus said. Looking around, he noted, "Plenty of brush here. You can hide easy enough, but if you hear or see anything at all to give you a fright or make you think anybody besides us is around, you come back up here, straight off. Now go ahead."

The girl got down from her horse and vanished into the lush August green to the left of the trail, if trail this could really be called. It took a woodsman to discern it, mostly by following occasional blazes on the sides of trees or faint phantoms of tracks left by earlier travelers. With such poorly delineated trails, there were those who had set out through this country who had simply vanished, reaching no destination and returning to no point of earlier embarkation.

The two men dismounted to let their legs stretch a bit while Mary was out of sight. Titus considered walking beside his horse for the next several miles. He changed his mind as he remembered how his father had suffered for years from rheumatism exacerbated by his years of on-foot wilderness traversing. Don't walk if you can ride, his father had often advised. Such will preserve your joints longer.

The girl safely returned and travel resumed. Mary hurried her horse forward so she could ride directly beside Titus to speak easily. "Mr. Titus," she said, "who will I live with?"

He smiled rather sadly at her. "We don't know yet, Mary. But I promised you we'd find you a new situation you can be happy in, and we will."

"Where do you live?"

"In a way I kind of live all over. I travel, answer the call if there's a need for men to protect a fort or settlement against Indian attack, and I hunt. I explore for good lands that I might someday want to live on, if ever

I get settled down and have a family. But if I do have a home, it's at the place we're heading, Fort Edohi. My father's station, over near White's Fort. You heard of those places?"

"Yes. You got no wife?"

"I don't, Mary."

"Ain't you lonely?"

He smiled. "Sometimes I suppose I am."

"Well, you ought to find you a wife, then."

"You tell him, Mary!" said Micah from behind. "I been telling him that for nigh forever now."

"He has, Mary. Can't deny it. And one of these days I will marry. Hope to, anyway."

"I wish I was older so I could get married," Mary said.

Titus smiled. "If you was older I might just ask you to marry me."

Mary laughed, and Titus thought it was good to hear this little bereaved girl sounding happy, even if only for a moment. "I couldn't marry you even if I was older," she said.

"Why not?"

" 'Cause I'll be married to somebody else. To him." She tossed her head back in the direction of Micah.

Micah roared in laughter. "You hear that, Titus? Looks like you've been passed over in favor of a better man."

"Uglier man is more like it. Mary, you telling me you'd marry an ugly gent like Micah there?"

"He ain't ugly," the girl said. "I think he's right fine-looking. Handsome."

"You're mighty young to have eyes going bad like that, girl."

"She sees just fine, thankee," Micah said. "But, Mary, you're a bit young for me."

"I'm getting older. Every day."

"So am I. You'll never catch up with me."

Titus said, "Consider yourself lucky that you dodged that bit of trouble, Mary. You don't want this one."

Mary, growing ever more comfortable in the company of the two men, turned and smiled back at Micah. "You never been married?" she asked.

A slight pause. "I was, once. She died, Mary. I lost her."

Mary's smile went away. "I'm mighty sorry."

"I 'preciate that."

" 'Cause I know how it feels, losing family."

"You do. That's a fact. A sad fact for both of us."

The conversation died away, Mary withdrawing into herself and her grief again. But the brief round of levity had been good for them all.

They rode farther, then paused to rest the horses and eat a meal of jerked beef and hardened biscuit while the horses ate from the supply of grain Titus carried in a pack behind the saddle of his mount.

Then back on the trail, moving steadily east.

Mary found the old hunter's shed the next day, while away from the others for a few moments of privacy to see to personal needs. It blended so naturally into the leafy environment that she looked at for several moments before she began to discern it.

It did not startle her to see such a man-made structure here in the forest. She knew that this country had been extensively explored years before by long hunters and trappers such as Titus Fain's father, and such men had built many shelters in the wilderness, particularly to see them through the winter months. Most hunter shelters were mere "half-faced" structures made of leaning pole frames topped by branches and sheets of bark. Others, like this one, were squatty, very rough cabins notched just well enough to hold them together and support whatever crude roofing their builders could provide them.

Mary stood where she was when she saw the little hut, looking closely at it to make sure there was no one in or around it. She doubted the place had seen human occupancy for years, but her father had taught her to be cautious. She finally began edging toward the structure, eyes fixed on its uncovered doorway and tiny window, the latter being no more than a gap cut through two adjacent logs in the front wall.

When she reached the shelter, she was confident it was empty. She paused at the door and quietly called, "Hello the house. Is anyone there?"

No sound. She put her head inside the door. "Hello?"

A moment later she withdrew, gasping hard. Turning on her heels, she ran away from the little cabin and back toward the trail. "Mr. Micah! Mr. Titus! Come here! Come now!"

"Is he dead?" Mary asked, barely able to speak. She was standing again at the door of the little hunter's cabin, which was now occupied by Titus and Micah and the man Mary had found unconscious inside the structure.

Titus, kneeling beside the supine man,

shook his head. "Not dead. But in a bad way."

"Apoplexy, almost sure," Micah said. "I've seen it before. You can tell it from the way his mouth pulls down on the side like that. His eye, too, on the same side. See it?"

Mary nodded. She was struggling visibly to maintain her composure.

"You got to kill him," she managed to say.

"Kill him? Mary, why would we do such as that?" Micah asked.

"He's an Indian," she said. "He's an Indian and I know what they do. You got to kill him!"

"He's old, Mary. Very old. And he's dying; I'm sure of it. We're decent men, good men. And you're a good young lady. We wouldn't want to do such a thing as murder."

"He's just an Indian!" Mary said sharply, tears coming now. "He's an Indian, just like the ones who . . . who . . ."

Titus rose and came out of the shelter, taking Mary by the arm and leading her aside. "Mary, this poor old man ain't nothing like the Indians who killed your family. I'm sure those were much younger and stronger men. This fellow is probably eighty years old, maybe older. I don't even believe he knows anybody's with him. He can't move, can't speak. He would have had nothing to do with what happened at your cabin."

Mary gazed at him through tears. "He's an Indian. Indians killed my family. So now I'm going to kill Indians, whenever I can."

"Even them who had nothing to do with hurting you? Even them who are too old to walk?"

"He's an Indian. Just like they were."

"Mary, what you're saying is the very thinking that has cost so many people their lives. Maybe even what cost your family theirs. You see, what happens is that somebody somewhere kills another person — an Indian kills a white man, say — and other white men decide to even the balance by killing that Indian in turn. But maybe they can't find that same Indian, so they kill another one, or another one or two or three. And you know what? The Cherokee have a whole system they follow of vengeance that calls for them to pay back them who kill one of their own, even if it ain't the same ones who did the original murder. One white man kills a Cherokee, and other Cherokees pick out a white man in turn and kill him. Usually not the guilty one. And so it goes, killing going back and forth, never ending, just growing. It's not the way things ought to be. It just ain't."

"I saw them do it. I see my family dying when I close my eyes."

"But you didn't see that poor old man in there do it, did you? He couldn't have. He's no more guilty of it than you or me. He's old and dying and can't even walk."

"If he can't walk, how'd he get in there?"

"Somebody might have put him in there and left him to die, by his choice or theirs. Or he might have been out here, walking, and got struck with apoplexy and dragged himself inside for the sake of shelter. I think he went into that little cabin expecting to die, however he got here."

"I'll make him die, if he wants to die."

"Mary, that's no kind of talk to be coming from the lips of a girl so young as you."

"But I . . . I . . ." She burst into a loud wail and Titus embraced her gently. Her small frame shook violently with her sobs.

"Mary, I'm not an old man, but I've lived long enough to learn that sometimes, you just have to scribe a line across everything and make a clean start on the far side of it. You have to draw in a deep breath, and as much as you can make yourself, try to forgive."

"I don't think I can."

"Nobody can do it perfect. You just got to try."

"I hate 'em. I hate Indians." A tear glistened.

"Put that out of you, Mary. Hate is a poison that only hurts the one carrying it around."

Micah called for Titus to return to the shelter, and Titus told Mary to stay where she was. He went back inside.

Mary stayed still only a few moments, then went around the stand of trees between her and where the horses remained tethered beside the trail. She went to Micah's horse and from a saddlebag drew out a small flintlock pistol she'd seen him place there earlier after loading it. Her hand trembled as she held it, and she bit her lip.

"I got to," she said to herself. "I got to do it." She hid the pistol in her clothing and went back around the trees to the hunter's shelter.

Chapter Nine

Crawford Fain knew he had to make a stop at White's Fort on his way toward Crockett Spring, where Littleton's note had indicated the women with the marked eye had been seen. He didn't want to do it, because he didn't doubt that the Reverend Professor Eben Bledsoe probably believed he was hundreds of miles away by now, tracking down his long-missing daughter. He dreaded seeing how Bledsoe would react when he learned that Fain was only just now getting started on the task he'd agreed to do.

As he and Potts rode into view of the White's Fort stockade, Fain halted his horse and leaned forward wearily, sighing aloud.

"What are you thinking about?" Potts asked.

"Ah, I just don't look forward much to talking with old Bledsoe," he said.

"Is he like his brother?"

"Hardly at all." Fain grinned. "Eyes don't

even cross. But it's a lot more than that. They're both preachers, but they don't agree on much, it seems. And Eben hints that his brother is a downright bad man. I don't know all he's talking about with that, but maybe it's about him and that woman he travels with. The false Molly Reese."

"I heard you tell Houser that you knew she wasn't the real Molly Reese even before he figured it out. How did you know?"

Fain sighed again. "I might tell you that story sometime, Potts. Not now."

Potts did not argue. He'd spent just enough time with Fain to realize he was not a man to be persuaded away from something he'd already settled upon.

"Well, let's head on down," Fain said.

Fain was not unhappy to learn that Eben Bledsoe was absent. He'd gone to Virginia in pursuit of financial donations for his fledgling college as well as to lay claim on a library's worth of books he'd been promised by a wealthy benefactor who was believed to be wheezing through his final days.

"I confess I'm relieved," Fain said to Potts. "I wasn't looking forward to talking to him just now."

"On to Crockett Spring, then?"

"On to Crockett Spring. But not until

tomorrow morning. It's late enough that there's little gain to be had from leaving earlier."

Potts wasn't inclined to argue. It was always best to sleep in a real bed, under a real roof, if such was an option. Better to undertake a journey in fresh daylight than fading dusk.

The man with no hair wiped sweat from his broad and fleshy brow and reset his position on the puncheon bench in his log-walled workshop. Around him, in various degrees of completion, lay or stood assorted chairs, stools, tables, benches, and other items of furniture, surrounded by mountains of wood chips.

Adding to those mountains moment by moment were abundant shavings and chips flying off a log clamped in place on a shaving horse, a simple but effective device that held worked wood items in place by pressure of a foot on a plank pedal. The log was being shaved down rapidly by the hairless man's expert and experienced efforts with a two-handled draw knife. The bearded man for whose benefit the work was being done sat watching from the side of the workshop.

"How long do you think it will be?" asked Jeremiah Littleton, still going by his alias of

Lyle Kirk.

The man with no hair stopped his work and caught his breath. "It'll be just the right length. I measured you, you remember."

Littleton didn't want to laugh, but had to. "I meant, how long until you're finished?"

The other chuckled. "Oh. I see. Well, I've still got to do some smoothing inside the cup, and make sure those straps are fixed good and firm. Otherwise you might find it not as comfortable a fit, may bruise you some."

"Don't want that. But I don't want to wait forevermore, either. I need to get away from these parts."

"Why's that?"

"Don't ask questions. Just work on that peg leg."

"Very well." He redoubled his efforts, perspiration flying with the wood shavings.

"Is it all right to ask you, mister, how you lost the leg?" asked the carpenter.

"None of your affair, but I don't mind saying. I had to cut it off to get out of a rock pit I'd fell into over by Fort Edohi."

"Lord! You cut it off yourself?"

"With my own knife. Hardly felt it. . . . Well, hardly felt it mixed in with all the hurting I was already doing. The bones were broke clean in two and poking through the meat. Nothing holding the bottom part of that leg on except for a few strips of bloody flesh. That's all I had to cut through to get the leg off so I could get out. Foot and anklebone and all were wedged too tight in the hole to pull out, you see."

Simultaneously revolted and fascinated, the carpenter had slowed his work to listen. Littleton pointed out that fact gruffly, and the man went at it hard again.

"How long has it been?" the man asked.

"Well, a good deal longer than it is now, considering the bottom part of it is cut off."

The carpenter puzzled over that a moment, then laughed. "I admire a man who can be jocular in such circumstances, sir," he said. " 'Good deal longer than it is now.' *Ha!*"

"I'm supposing what you're really asking is how long since the leg was lost."

"Yes."

"Days. That's all. Just days."

The carpenter stopped all motion for a moment, frowning. "Mister, you won't be able to wear this leg for a time, then. It would be like torture to put weight down on that stump with the wound not healed yet."

"I know. But I want to get it now anyway

to take it with me to wear when I *am* able to."

"I see. I'll . . . I'll fix you up a crutch, too, so you can use that until you're able to wear the peg."

"I 'preciate that. But I ain't willing to pay for a crutch. I got me a stout stick with a fork on the end where I rest my armpit, and that's serving me fine."

"You don't need to pay, nor wait for me to make one. I had a crushed ankle two years ago and made a crutch for myself then, and I still got it, but have no use for it now. It's yours. You and me are about the same height, so it should fit you."

"Kind of you, sir. I thank you."

"My pleasure, Mr. Kirk. I try to do good by folks."

Though they had cooked for him a very thin, bready gruel and passed a little of it through his lips, the old Indian looked as if death would come at any moment. Yet the thin chest kept rising and falling and the lips of the twisted mouth moved slightly from time to time. He managed to lick away the watery gruel and seemingly get it down, and with care Titus found he could successfully administer the old man a bit of water.

Occasionally the Indian would make

whispering sounds, something between words and mere noise, but no meaning could be discerned. As best the men could tell, the old man probably did not understand much English, though he did react very slightly to words of kindness.

"He's mighty pallid for a Cherokee, don't you think?" Micah asked Titus.

"I'd had the same thought myself," said Titus. "I'm wondering if he might have some white blood, or maybe even be a white man . . . maybe a trader who lived in the Upper Towns."

"Well, if he was, he ought to understand English."

Titus went to the old man, who was at the moment coming awake. The bleary eyes moved about and finally settled on Titus's face. Titus smiled at the fellow, and to his surprise the half-paralyzed face managed to make a smile of its own.

"Old Gentleman," Titus said, using a name he'd contrived for the fellow because he couldn't know his real one, "are you Cherokee? *Tsalagi?* Or are you white . . . *unaka?*"

The old man seemed to want to answer, but made only vague sounds. Frustration filled his eyes.

"Your skin is light," Titus said. "That's

why I ask. I'm wondering if you might be a white man who lived among the Indians."

Somehow the weak old fellow managed to give a small nod. Or so it appeared to Titus. "You understand what we say here, then."

Another nod, this one even weaker and obviously requiring excruciating effort. The old man's eyes fluttered closed and it took nearly a minute for them to open again.

"You were a trader, maybe. Or maybe you just married a *Tsalagi* woman."

Another tiny nod, and this time, to Titus's astonishment, a breathed-out sigh that could understand as an attempt to say the word yes.

Titus nodded and began to explore possibilities. "I'm going to make some guesses here, some suppositions. I don't know if I'll be right, but maybe you can let me know."

No response from Old Gentleman.

Titus began. "I think your wife died not long ago. Left you alone in your old age. And you lost your interest in living. It just didn't matter anymore with her gone."

The old man's eyes fixed on Titus more firmly than anytime before, and Titus knew his surmises, which were half deduction, half pure imagination, were close to the truth.

"You decided finally that life couldn't go

on for you, and you picked a place to come and die. This place. But when you came, something happened to you. You were stricken — you could hardly move, and you couldn't really speak. You became *udalina*. Weak and feeble. You couldn't walk, of course, so you used the one side of your body that you still had power over and dragged yourself into this little cabin that some old hunter had built and left My father is a hunter, and in his younger days he built many shelters and huts on his hunting grounds."

Then the most surprising thing yet. Old Gentleman looked squarely into Titus's face and said in words with little form to them, "Your father?"

"His name is Fain. He is called Edohi."

Now the old face smiled clearly, and a more firm nod came. Titus was pleased to see that the old man's apoplexy apparently was not as severe as it first had appeared.

"Do you know Edohi?"

"Yes," said the old man. "When young, he and I."

"Friend or enemy?"

"Friend." The old man raised a hand and indicated the structure around them. "Edohi," he said softly.

"You mean . . . Are you saying that Edohi

built this shelter?"

"Yes. *Uh.*" The affirmative spoken in both English and Cherokee.

"It ain't that unusual, you know," said Micah's voice from behind. Titus glanced back at him. Micah came up and knelt beside the old man's resting place alongside Titus. "The talking, I mean. My grandfather was rendered apoplectic and couldn't speak a word, hardly even make a sound, for three days. Then, all at once, it was back, his ability to talk. Hardly any trace of the apoplexy left in his speaking. He never was able to walk normal again, but his speech was same as before."

"What is your name?" Titus asked the old man.

"Sisalee."

"Indian way of saying 'Cecil,' " Titus said to Micah.

"I know, I know," Micah said. He was frequently annoyed by Titus's obvious assumptions that he was more knowledgeable about most things than he was.

"Cecil — I will call you by your English name because it is more natural for me — I am glad to see you starting to do better," Titus said.

"Thank . . . you." The words required effort, and were poorly formed. One side of

Cecil's face drooped and his tongue moved visibly and sluggishly when he spoke.

"Do you think of yourself as white or *Tsalagi?*" Titus asked.

"I am . . . *Tsalagi.*"

"You are my honored friend, as you were to my father."

Cecil smiled again, crookedly and excruciatingly, and closed his eyes a moment. He said a word Titus could not understand.

"What was that? Say again?"

He did, and Titus remained unable to decipher it. But Micah said, "I think he said 'granddaughter.' "

The old man nodded weakly, eyes still closed.

"You have a granddaughter?" Titus asked him.

"Tla. Tla," he said in Cherokee, then in English: "No." He waved toward the door. "Granddaughter."

"He's asking for Mary," Micah said. "I can fetch her. . . ."

"No," Titus said quickly, remembering Mary's hateful words about the old man. With Sisalee taking a clear turn for the better, now was not the time to confront him with hostility from a child toward whom he perhaps held some tenderness.

"Is it Mary you ask for?" Titus said, smiling.

"Mary. Yes."

"Titus, I'm going to go get her and bring —"

Titus again waved off Micah's plan. "Cecil, there's something you must know. Mary just lost her family to an attack by Cherokee. Probably a band of Dragging Canoe's followers come up from the Lower Towns. But it has put in her a hatred of Indians, and even though you are white by blood, you claim yourself as Indian and live as Indian, and I don't know how she'll act with you."

Cecil pondered this, and seemed to sink farther into his resting place. After a minute or two it was obvious he was sleeping. Titus took Micah by the arm and they left the shelter.

"Who would have figured him for a white man?" Micah said. "I know the skin is light, but I've known other Indians who weren't dark. I had wondered if the paleness just came from him being ill."

"Now that he's starting to show a little more strength, we've got to figure out what to do with him," Titus said. "We can't just leave him here alone. And I got a feeling none of his people know he's here, since he came out here alone."

"We'll make a drag-pole bed and take him with us," Micah said. "That physician at Fort Edohi can take a look at him."

"That's a mighty long way to go, bumping along on drag poles," Titus said.

"You got a better idea? He can't sit a horse in the shape he's in. And we don't have an extra horse, anyway. One of us would be put afoot if he was riding."

"Drag poles it is, I reckon."

"I'll go now and find us some saplings with a good spring to them," Micah said.

They said nothing of what they had learned to Mary. Though she had seemed to be growing brighter and less brooding, she now reverted abruptly and fell into a cold silence, not even willing to look her companions in the eye. Titus's intuition told him that asking her to at some level accept the old man in the hunter's shelter might be more than she could handle. And letting her know that the "Indian" was by birth a white man would be unlikely to make a difference. If anything, she might even find it more upsetting to realize that a white man could willingly embrace the people who had slaughtered her loved ones, and redefine himself as one of them.

So Titus kept quiet and told Micah to do the same. Mary continued her brooding, stayed away from the hunter's shelter, and had nothing to say about the apoplectic old man inside.

The effects of the apoplexy continued to diminish. Cecil's words remained muddied and hard to understand, but he spoke them more easily. He was able to eat more of the thin gruel, and seemed stronger for it. When Titus told him they planned to take him with them to find help from a physician at Fort Edohi, Cecil was pleased and agreeable, despite the prospect of uncomfortable travel slung between two drag poles.

In the middle of the night, Mary Deveraux rose in her sleep, retrieved Micah Tate's small flintlock pistol from where she'd hidden it, and entered the hunter's shelter. Still as asleep as if she had never risen at all, she moved silently to the place where the old man slumbered.

The sound and jolt of the firing pistol was what woke her up. The old man never awakened at all, the ball having entered his forehead and passed into his apoplexy-damaged brain.

Mary dropped the pistol at her feet and stared down at what she had done, though it was so dark she could barely make out the unmoving shape of the old man who was no more.

Chapter Ten

The town growing up around the stream called Crockett Spring lay up the Holston River from Fort Edohi and White's Fort, in a new county organized by the state of Franklin and called Spencer County. Fain had visited the locale many times in past years and knew many of the settlers, including Colonel Thomas Amis, who lived in a fine stone house surrounded by protective palisades, and who had also been instrumental in building a separate fort on Big Spring.

On the morning Fain and Potts rode slowly into the little settlement that a few years hence would be called Rogersville, Potts said, "Crockett Spring. Who's that named for?"

"That would be David Crockett. I knew him, just a bit. He's gone now."

"Moved off?"

"Dead. Killed in the Year of the Three

Sevens by Indian raiders. Him and his wife and some of their children, slaughtered. Had a deaf-and-dumb boy named Jimmy who got carried off prisoner, and another boy captured, too. Three of their sons were away from home when the raid happened. That saved their lives, probably."

"There's another David Crockett now," Potts said.

"There is? Where?"

"Limestone Creek over where it enters the 'Chucky River. Just a little baby, born the day I passed by their house. I met the father. . . . He was drunk at the time."

"His name was John, I'll wager."

"That was him. 'Just plain John' Crockett, as he put it to me. Said he'd named his new baby boy David, after his own pap."

"John was one of the sons who was away from home when the Indians killed the Crocketts. John, he loves his spirits."

"I could tell."

"Come with me and I'll show you something."

The "something" was a pair of graves, one crudely marked with the name of David Crockett, the other marked Elizabeth Crockett. "This is them?" Potts asked.

"It is. This land around here used to all be theirs. Colonel Amis has it now."

Potts looked around. "Now that we're here, how do we find out if Bledsoe's daughter is around?"

"Well, I don't think we can just start going up to every woman we run across and looking to see if she's got a gray streak in her eye. All I know to do is start asking people who might have seen such a gal if she ever really was in these parts."

"Innkeepers and such?"

"That's right." Fain shrugged. "It's clumsy, but all I can come up with."

Potts frowned silently a few moments. "Why the deuce did you agree to do this? And why did Eben Bledsoe believe a man skilled in tracking wild game and such would have any particular advantage in tracking people? It's a whole different situation."

Fain shook his head. "I don't know. I think the man is just desperate to know what became of his little girl. I understand that. That's why I agreed."

Potts exhaled slowly and said, "I can understand that."

"Well, I figure we'll be around here for two, three days at the least. Let's go find us an inn where we can get some lodging. The older I get, Potts, the less inclined I am to sleep out if I can have a real bed."

"I ain't old, but I'm the same way." They went back to their horses. "Mr. Fain, sir, I've found myself wondering —"

"Call me Crawford. I've told you that before. Or Edohi if it suits you."

"All right . . . Edohi."

"You been wondering what?"

"How many folks have streaks in their eyes like Deborah Bledsoe does."

"Potts, that's a question I got a feeling we're about to become experts in answering."

Micah found a sinkhole in the nearby forest, and there they interred the corpse of the "white Indian" named Sisalee in his chosen world, Cecil in the one he was born into. It was important that the old man's body not be found by any Cherokee who might come through, because a visible bullet wound in the forehead would be clear evidence of murder and likely further inflame Indian passions and violence. So they hid him and vowed to put the matter out of their minds. What Mary had done could not now be changed.

The girl was nearly destroyed by realization of what she had done. All her earlier talk of hating Indians and vowing to kill them had been only chatter, a mere verbal venting of emotion. She hadn't meant it.

Obviously, though, some portion of her had meant it. Something inside her had caused her to rise in her sleep and carry out an act she could never have done had her full wits been about her.

"I'm going to hell," she said to Micah, through tears. "I'm a murderer, and I'll go to hell. Won't I? Murderers go to hell."

"Mary, there's only one great judge of mankind and sin and guilt, and it ain't me. Don't look to me for answers to that question. And another thing — it ain't you, either, so don't judge yourself just yet. Right now all you can do is face what happened, ask the Lord to forgive you, and move on. There's not many who would condemn you for what you done, considering what you've been through yourself. You shouldn't have killed the old Indian, true enough . . . but that band of raiders shouldn't have killed your kinfolk, either."

Micah and Titus had agreed not to tell Mary that the old man had not been Indian by blood. In her mind she had killed a member of the race who had brought harm to her family. For her to learn that she actually had killed one of her own people would only redouble her sense of guilt.

Micah asked in private: "Titus, you reckon

it's possible for somebody to do something big, something bad, while he's not himself, and not really be guilty of it? Responsible, maybe, in the sense that it was him who done it . . . but not guilty?"

Titus weighed it in his mind. "That kind of question makes me glad I don't sit a magistrate's bench in a court of law," he said. "I don't know how to answer."

"Well, I'm thinking that the Mary who went in there and killed old Cecil wasn't the same Mary as we know during the waking daylight. She was asleep. On her feet, but asleep. And you know how things can be in your dreams and such. . . . It's all different. You can do and say things in your dreams that you'd never think of doing or saying in the light of day."

Titus shrugged. "All I know is that what's done is done, and the best all of us can do is to never talk of this again, to anyone. She's just a little girl. She'd never have done what she did if not for the things she'd gone through. Old Cecil's corpse will likely never be found, so no Indian vengeance is likely to come from him being killed. Best to leave things where they are and move on down the trail. You agree?"

"I agree." Micah looked over to where Mary sat stiffly on the ground, rocking back and forth mechanically, staring into the woods around her like a scared animal. "The question is whether Mary herself will agree. In the state she's in, she might just go and confess what she done to somebody, trying to lay the guilt burden off her shoulders."

"We've still got some travel time with her ahead of us. Maybe we can explain the situation to her and persuade her not to do that."

Micah nodded. "I sure wish I hadn't let her see that I had that pistol in my saddlebag. If she hadn't had that pistol, none of this would have happened."

"Let it go, Micah. It wasn't your fault that a little girl's mind got so overburdened with sorrow that she couldn't stop herself from doing a bad act."

Micah nodded. "I'm ready to travel, Titus. Shall we?"

"Let's go."

Minutes later they were on the trail again, heading east toward Fort Edohi, still many miles distant.

The three travelers found Fort Edohi in a jovial state when they arrived. The family of Dr. Peter Houser had returned unannounced from family business in the East, and Houser was so glad to see them that he hosted a celebration for one and all: food, drink, even a couple of Irish fiddlers who played reels. The site was the courtyard of the stockade, where Houser had made a pit to be dug and a hog now roasted aromatically in the ground.

"I fear your father isn't here at present," Houser said to Titus. "He's taken on a job, a hunting quest, and has gone up toward Crockett Springs in hopes of finding who he's seeking."

"Did you say 'who'?"

"I did. He's engaged to find the long-missing daughter of the Reverend Eben Bledsoe. She was taken as a child by Indians, but her father has reason to believe she is still living. He hired your father to find her. A different kind of long hunt for an old long hunter."

"Bledsoe . . . the camp meeting preacher?"

"No, no. That one is this one's brother. Very different kind of preachers, Eben being more an academic type. He's the one founding a college over near White's Fort."

"I've heard about that."

Houser looked across the stockade yard to where Mary was sitting on a bench beside Houser's wife, Beth. The two were talking intently and cheerfully, Mary actually smiling, so Titus had no fear the child was revealing what had happened in the hunter's shelter. There would be no smile if she were.

Sitting at a roughly made table outdoors, in the shade of a big maple standing inside the stockade, Titus and Micah looked across the tabletop at Houser. The physician was wiping his mouth rather daintily on a linsey-woolsey rag after having finished a trencher full of steaming roast pork. Torchlight played across the scene, adding an unwelcome heat to the already sticky atmosphere of late August.

Houser yawned and stretched, feeling the effects of a filling, fatty meal combined with the evening heat. "Ah, nothing better than good food and good company," he said.

"I'm glad you consider us so," said Titus.

"Oh, I do. Your surname alone is enough to recommend you to me, Titus. I have come to admire the name of Fain through my associations with your father."

"Tates are a good bunch, too," Micah muttered, swatting at an insect buzzing his ear.

"I'm sure of that," Houser said. "I simply haven't had the pleasure of knowing your people."

"I'll vouch for them," Titus said. "Good

family. Only one disappointment among the whole bunch." He lightly kicked Micah's ankle under the table.

Micah ignored it. He was looking past the doctor to the next table over, where Beth Houser was still keeping company with Mary Deveraux. Mary was looking quite cheerful, very different than she had on the long trail. Clearly Beth Houser was the kind of company the girl needed. Titus supposed that he and Micah had probably not been the most comfortable or natural companions for a ten-year-old girl freshly bereaved of her family and guilty of a murder she had done literally in her sleep. But they had done for her what they could.

Peter Houser followed Titus's gaze and looked over his shoulder. Turning back, he said, "Beth seems to have taken quite a liking to your little friend. And I think the sentiment might be mutual."

"That little girl bears a huge burden," Titus said.

"Yes . . . losing her family in a massacre . . . God, what a tragic thing for one so young to have to deal with!"

"There's more burden than that," Micah muttered. Titus flashed him a look as if to shut him up, but Micah was not in a humor to follow direction. "It needs to be said,

Titus," Micah stated. "It's a burden on me, too, just knowing it and having to keep my mouth shut."

Houser looked puzzled. "I seem to have failed to pick up on what we are talking of," he said.

Titus sighed. "I'd not figured we'd say anything of it," he said. "But I think it is grinding on Micah to hold silence." He looked the doctor squarely in the face. "And perhaps he is right. Can I trust you, Houser, to hold what we tell you in confidentiality?"

"Well . . . certainly. But I'm still mystified by what we are even talking of here."

"There was a sad event along the way here, involving Mary. She stumbled across an old long hunter shelter, and inside was an old Indian who had been stricken with apoplexy and seemed likely to die. It didn't seem Christian to just leave him, so we tended to his care. But Mary was still full of all the misery of what had happened to her, and she sleepwalks, and she got her hands on a small pistol, and in the night . . ."

"I think I understand," said Houser. "She killed the Indian."

Titus nodded.

"She didn't even know she'd done it until the sound of her own gunshot woke her up," Micah said.

"Good God!"

"She was a misery to herself after that," Titus said. "Not saying much, never looking us in the face, riding along like there was hell-smoke surrounding her — all the way here. Not a trace of joy in her until your wife took her under wing."

"Beth has a way with children." The physician paused, deeply thinking. "She has no kin, you said?"

"None. She's alone in the world, and I promised her I'd find her a home to take her in."

Houser said, "You've found one."

"You mean . . ."

"I mean exactly what it sounds like. I'll agree here and now to take her in. And Beth will agree. I know my wife well enough to tell you that without any hesitation. The question is whether Mary will want it."

At that moment Mary laughed loudly at something Beth had said, and Beth laughed as well, putting her arm around the child with obvious affection.

"I think we have our answer," said Titus.

Chapter Eleven

"Edohi!"

The voice came from somewhere behind them. Fain and Potts reined to a halt and twisted their heads. A ruddy-faced man with a shock of white hair was walking up behind them rapidly, face alight with health and a broad grin, hand waving widely.

"Edohi, I knew it was you as soon as I saw you ride by my window!" the man said. "How are you, you addle-headed old wanderer?"

"Still wandering, Dill. How are you?"

"Quite fine. Thank you. Not doing much wandering myself these days."

"Glad to hear it. You were the sorriest excuse for a hunter I ever knew."

"Ain't it the truth!" the man said. He glanced over toward Potts. "Who's your young friend here?"

"Dill Talbott, meet Langdon Potts, a friend of my son's. You knew I had a son, didn't you?"

"I didn't. It's been that many years now since you and I have stood on the same piece of ground, Fain."

"Several more than twenty. Yeah, my son, Titus, was born about a year and a half past the time I saw you last, Dill. He's about the age of Potts here. And like Potts, he's a fine, strong young man who is as good a woodsman as I've ever been, or any I've rode and hunted with."

"Good to meet you, Mr. Talbott," Potts said, leaning down to shake hands.

"Call me Dill," said the ruddy man. "And both of you, get down from those mounts and put them up in my stable over there. You can just see the side of it over there beyond the trees. The inn itself you can't see at all from here."

"Did you say 'inn'?" asked Fain. "You an innkeeper now, Dill?"

"I am indeed. And you'll be among my first guests. What think you of that, Fain?"

Fain grinned. "Well, I think innkeeping is surely more what you're cut out for than hunting. Potts, Dill here couldn't hit the side of a mountain from twenty paces, much less a deer from thirty. He ran off a lot more deerskin than he ever collected. I'd be a rich man today if I had collected the hide of every deer this man here run off with the noise of a wild shot."

Dill Talbott was laughing. "I can't deny it, Potts. I had no business trying my hand at that business, if you can make sense of that."

"I can." Potts grinned. Dill was one of those men it was impossible not to like.

"Yes, sir, the town life is the life for me," Talbott said. "I'd rather have my fire blazing on the hearth of my own inn than in the middle of some freezing hollow like Edohi here always favored. Still that way, Edohi? Shunning the life of civilized men so you can live in the woods?"

"Not so much these days, Dill. Rheumatiz has 'bout done in my ankles. All that walking in rain and snow."

"There's a price to be paid for any life we choose, I reckon," said Talbott, patting his rather round belly. "Here's the price of the innkeeping life," he said. "What Nelly cooks for the guests gets eat up by the host."

"Nelly. Your wife?"

"She is. And she's a real wife, too, married up all legal, papers and everything. Not like that pretty little Cherokee gal you wintered up with that year in that cabin up near Cumberland Gap."

Potts raised his brows. "I'm going to have to hear more about that."

"Well, Potts, she was a pretty little red gal, sweet one, too, and even though she and old Edohi here weren't married in any white man's sense of the word, they acted just as married as can be. You following me?"

"I believe I am."

Fain dismounted and Potts did the same, glad for it, because it indicated they were going to take up Talbott on his invitation. The joviality and friendliness of Dill Talbott roused an expectation that he would be a fine host and innkeeper. And clearly, judging from Dill's somewhat expansive girth, the food would be fine.

"Dill, I can do without you rehashing all my past sins and failures to my young friend here. I want to influence him toward the good, not the bad."

"What you did, Edohi, was no different than what many others did. How many men did we know who had a white family east of the mountains, and an Indian family in the west? You recall Charles Floren? A wife and children back home, but also, on the sneak, a Negro 'wife' who bore him two sons, and in the west, a Creek girl who bore him three daughters?"

"Charles was the worst I ever knew for that," Fain said, nodding slowly.

"When his white wife in Carolina finally

figured out what he was doing, she left him."

"Can't blame her."

"Then he up and married another woman to replace her, and took a mistress on the side as well. Charles is dead now, you know."

"Not surprised. It would take a young rabbit to keep up such a level of carnal activity," Fain said. "The heart would fail most men."

"What killed him was some kind of an ailment he caught from a harlot in Virginia. One of them French pox afflictions, if you know what I'm talking of."

"Live by the sword, die by the sword," Fain said with a shrug.

Talbott's inn was a significantly better building than Potts had expected. It was one of those frontier rarities of the time: a frame building. At least, the front portion was frame, though that part adjoined a large, square log building that held the guest rooms.

At the dark oaken bar that Dill Talbott said he had built himself, the group imbibed in some rum and Talbott and Fain continued their reminiscences.

"Just so young Potts here will have a full picture of the actions of my youth, I want it said that I had only that one time of taking up, husband-style, with an Indian woman.

And them were odd circumstances. Her father was a war chief and for some reason thought highly of me. He said that if I would take his daughter to wife, he would keep peace with the white men. I had to agree."

"Of course, the fact that she was pretty as a sunrise made it a little easier to say yes," Talbott threw in.

"I can't deny that . . . but I did what I had to do," Fain said. "Same thing Indian agents have to do sometimes — join in with the people they're dealing with in order to keep peace and order with them."

"Like Joe Martin," said Talbott.

"Exactly. And his white wife knew all about the Cherokee one. And didn't mind it, they say," Fain declared.

"Like you already said, a man does what he has to do," said Talbott.

"What became of your Indian wife?" Potts asked Fain.

"She never really was my wife. And the times and our situations forced us apart, eventually. She wound up marrying another man. Whether red or white, I don't know."

"I can tell you," said Talbott. "It was a white man who threw in with the Cherokee, got himself adopted into the tribe. His name, I think, is Cecil. Cecil Watson."

Fain's eyes lighted with revived memory.

"Oh yes! I remember him. Met him the same year I built that stout little hunting shelter that became such a favorite of mine." Fain paused. "He was the first man ever to call me Edohi." Fain's look suddenly darkened a little. "I didn't know he wound up with my woman, though."

"It was the times, Edohi. They was what they was, and we was what we was, too."

"I wonder what became of Cecil," Fain said.

"Last I knew, he was still living among the Cherokee," Talbott replied.

Fain looked at Potts. "I got a favor I must seek of you, Potts."

"Just ask it."

"Titus don't know about that Indian gal I was with. I never talked of it to any of my kin. I'd as soon he never know about it. I'm not sure he'd understand his father doing such a thing, for it goes against the raising I gave him. Can you keep what you've heard today under your hat? Forever?"

"I can, and I will." Potts paused and made a show of poking a finger into his ear and twisting it. "Hearing's getting bad these days, anyway. I don't know that I've actually heard a single word today that I could be sure I heard aright. And you should know that I make a practice of never repeating nothing I'm not sure I heard aright."

Fain chuckled. "Thank you, lad."

"My pleasure, Crawford Fain."

Fain had brought with him the rifle he had been presented by Houser back at the fort. As the day drew toward a close, he brought Talbott outside to let him take a look at the fine weapon. Talbott was suitably impressed. He held it to his shoulder and sighted down its long barrel.

"Fine balance of weight, Fain," Talbott said. "Not so front-heavy as some rifles tend to be."

"You're right," said Fain. "It's something Houser has figured out how to do, balancing a rifle so well. I'm not sure what it is and he don't tell. Calls it a 'crafter's secret.' Makes it easy to shoot more accurate, that's for certain. Hell's bells, even *you* might be able to hit something besides the sky with *that* rifle, Dill!"

Talbott laughed. "Hang it all, Edohi, you know as well as I do that I can already shoot a squirrel out of a tree as clean as any man!"

Fain laughed, too, then said to Potts: "I'll explain that to you, son. I told you how Dill here has run off more deer than he ever shot, firing off wild shots like he tends to do. Well, one time we were hunting out near the Fish Creek in the Cumberland country, and old dead-eye Dill here took aim at a buck that had more points on him than a Baltimore beggar man has lice. Well, he leveled in, pulled that butt plate up tight against his shoulder, squinched up that eye, and squeezed off a good clean shot. Only problem was he shot higher than a high-standing chimney top and sent them deer running, as usual. Except that over way beyond them, a squirrel come tumbling down out of a tree, shot cleaner than if Dill had been aiming at him from ten feet away. Which is how close he would have had to be to have made that shot on purpose. And in his case, even then he probably couldn't have hit it."

Potts made a wry comment, but it went unheard, covered by the laughter of the two older men.

That evening, smoking pipes outside Talbott's inn, Fain brought up the matter that had drawn him to this settlement. "Dill, have you happened to see a yellow-haired woman around here who has a brown eye with a gray streak in it?"

Talbott screwed up his brow in thought. "I don't think I have, but I couldn't say for sure. People pass through here a good deal these days."

Nelly Talbott, Dill's plump wife, walked up to the group, having overheard the question and answer. "Dill," she said sternly, "even if you had talked with that woman, you'd not recollect it." She looked at Fain. "He's worse than I've ever seen for hearing but not hearing and seeing but not seeing. Know what I mean?"

Fain didn't speak but subtly nodded at the woman while flashing a quick grin.

Nelly surprised him then. "There was such a woman here," she said. "I noticed her because her hair was so lovely. When I was a little girl I always wanted to have golden hair, and I suppose a part of that is still inside me, because I still notice such hair when I see it."

"But her eye . . ."

"I didn't notice that right away. But when I spoke to her and brought her a trencher of food, I saw it. Her left eye. Her eyes were brown, which is something you don't see much in a yellow-haired person, but that left eye had a lighter streak in the brown that was as gray as it could be. I fear I may have stared at it more than I should have. I worried later that I might have caused her offense. Then I considered that she was probably accustomed to people staring."

"Do you know her name?"

Nelly frowned, hesitated. "Now it's my turn to appear as the one who can't remember much. I did hear her name, but I don't recall it now. I'm sorry."

Dill grinned. "She's worse than I've ever seen for hearing but not hearing, and seeing but not seeing. Know what I mean?"

"Leave her be, Dill. Nelly, was her name Deborah?"

"I — I just can't remember. I can't . . . Wait a moment. Wait! Her last name was Corey. The first name I can't recall, but the last name was Corey."

"You're looking for a Bledsoe, though, ain't you?" Potts said.

"I don't know. If she married, her name might have changed. Or even if she didn't marry, she might have been raised by a family whose name she took for her own."

"Who is this woman, and why are you looking for her, if I might ask?" Nelly said.

Fain saw no reason to be secretive. "You've heard of the preaching Bledsoe brothers, maybe? One of them a fire-breathing camp meeting preacher, the other a book-learning kind of fellow starting up a college near White's Fort? Well, the latter one, Eben Bledsoe, had a daughter who was took from their home years ago, when she was little, seemingly by Indians. The girl had yellow hair and a gray-streaked brown eye. Seems that Eben has heard of such a female, grown up, being seen in the backcountry. He hired me to try to find her. Her name used to be Deborah Bledsoe, but what it is now, we can't know. If the woman he's heard of is even his daughter. It could be somebody else entirely, though the rarity of yellow hair and brown eyes, combined with the extra rarity of one of those brown eyes having a gray streak, well, it does seem likely the missing little Deborah and the woman might be one and the same."

"What a quest!" Nelly said, struck by the romance of it all. "A father seeking his long-lost daughter. . . . Why, a good poet could make quite the epic out of such a tale!"

"Nelly tries her hand at poetry sometimes," Dill said without enthusiasm.

"Well, if this all goes well, I'll give you the details and you can just poetize the very devil out of it," Fain said. "But let me ask something, Miz Nelly. Did this Corey woman happen to say where she might be living, or if she was traveling, where she was going to? And was she with others, or alone?"

"I didn't talk to her much, and nothing was said about where she was going. And she was alone. . . . But a day after she left, a man came asking after her, looking for her. I didn't like the look of him, or his manner. He seemed to me to be a man with something wrong about him. It was very hard to put my finger on, and I didn't dwell on him much. He told me his name was Taylor. I could tell he was just making it up. False name. He seemed a small and unimportant mouse of a man. I'd forgotten about him until just now." Nelly paused. "I'm sorry I haven't been much help to you. If I had known it would matter, I would have talked to her more."

"You've been a great help, Nelly. I have a name, or possible name, to attach to her now. That will make it easier as I ask others about her."

"So you're going to be looking further for her."

"I have to. It's a hired job, and I agreed to take it on."

"Where will you go from here?"

"On to the next town or station, I suppose. And ask the same questions. If she has been roaming about, and if there's somebody following her and asking after her, somebody will be able to tell me something."

"Seems a daunting task, sir," Nelly said.

"It is. Could be a long hunt. But I must do it."

Chapter Twelve

Along the way over the next month, Fain presented to Potts, several times, the option of leaving. The quest for the yellow-haired woman was Fain's, not Potts's. The only reason Potts was involved at all was his own unselfish spirit and loyalty to his friend Titus and, by extension, to Titus's father. So Potts stayed on, having no better way to spend his time at the moment.

Besides, the advance payment Fain had received from Eben Bledsoe was providing Potts food he did not have to purchase or kill himself, and, on many nights, lodging in good inns, all in exchange for nothing more than his willingness to travel with, and stick with, Crawford Fain.

"Why were you looking for Titus, anyway?" Fain asked. "Last I'd heard of you, you were up at Sapling Grove at your grandfather's."

"I'd gotten a letter from Titus," Potts

replied. "He'd sent it by messenger in care of my grandfather, before he left for the Cumberland with that friend of his. . . ."

"Micah Tate."

"That's him. Anyhow, Titus had an idea he thought I might be interested in, and I was, so I came to talk to him about it. Truth is, I'd been looking for a reason to get away from Sapling Grove, anyway. I was growing a touch restless there."

"What was Titus's idea?"

"He had come up with the thought of setting up an express rider service between the Watauga settlements and them in the vicinity of White's and Edohi's forts. Something that would operate regular, rider stations all along the way, a whole little troop of riders who would move parcels and letters and such pretty much all the time. He talked to some of the leaders of the settlements about it, and they thought it a good idea."

Fain was nodding briskly. "It's a good idea indeed. But it ain't Titus's. It's mine."

"He took credit for one of your ideas?"

Fain shrugged. "It don't really matter. He's my boy, and there's no jealousy. I'm glad he thought it was a good enough idea that he'd try to put some feet under it and make it run."

"I'm ready to sign on, if it turns to something real."

"It's going to happen sooner or later," Fain said. "One of the things that makes life in the backcountry hard is just getting things from one place to another and back again. And the more people come in, the more an express will be needed."

They traveled on, passing through Cumberland Gap and entering the Kentucky country. At the first settlement they reached, they found no news of Deborah Bledsoe Corey. They lodged one night and moved on.

At the next station the results were just as unpromising, but at Bryan's they discovered that the yellow-haired woman had been there, her marked eye had been noted, and someone at the settlement had heard her say she was going on to Harrodsburg. So on to Harrodsburg Fain and Potts went. There they picked up the surprising information that the woman had indicated she was heading back down again, intent on reaching Jonesborough in Franklin.

"Why is she following such a twisting pattern, turning back on herself like that?" Potts asked Fain.

"I think she may be trying to make her trail hard to follow. . . . Trying to shake somebody off."

"Us, you mean?"

"Maybe, though I doubt she knows we're after her. More likely she's trying to shun the other follower, the one Talbott talked about."

"Who do you reckon he is?"

"No way to know. A husband, maybe. Or somebody who wants to be a husband."

"Maybe we'll encounter him since we're both on the same track. But let me ask you something. If she's trying to shake him or us or whoever off her trail, why is she telling folks at every stop where she's going next?"

"Again, Potts, I have no answer for you. Maybe she's just not thinking things through very clearly. Scared of something, or somebody, maybe."

"We need to find this fellow who's tracking her."

"I'd rather just find her," Fain replied. "That's what I'm hired to do — and I would as soon avoid butting heads with some stranger if I don't have to."

Titus Fain and Micah Tate reached Crockett Spring in late afternoon and almost inevitably made their way to Dill Talbott's inn. Once Titus's identity was realized, the Talbotts rushed to welcome them and tell them of the earlier visit of Potts and Fain.

"Glad to hear of it," Titus said. "It was in hope of finding them that we came here."

"You've come too late," Dill said. "They moved on north into Kentucky to try to find the woman they're looking for."

"Eben Bledsoe's missing daughter."

"Yes. So you know about that?"

"We learned of it when we got back from the Cumberland River country to Fort Edohi. So we left there and followed Pap's path."

"Who is this Potts fellow?" Micah asked. "I don't know him."

"He's a friend of mine, about our age. Good woodsman, smart, pleasant fellow to be around."

"Just like me, then." Micah grinned.

"Uh . . . yep. Just what I was about to say."

Dill laughed. "Young gentlemen, what fare can we serve you? We have an excellent stew available."

That served the purpose nicely, and the two tired young frontiersman dined well. Dill refused any payment.

The next morning Titus and Micah departed, heading again along the route taken by Fain and Potts, hoping that, with any luck, they might find them.

■ ■ ■ ■

The encounter came by pure chance, on the famed Wilderness Road. Fain's mind was drifting back to a hunt he'd made with Casper Mansker years before on a day when the breeze was cool and blustery as it was this day. Fain turned to speak to Potts, who was riding along at his side, when at the same moment Potts beamed and called out, "Titus!" his hand shooting up and waving broadly.

Fain followed Potts's gaze and saw, riding over a hump on the trail and coming back toward them, his son and Micah Tate. Both stopped and gaped, Fain gaping right back, Potts still gleefully waving.

After halting for a few moments to comprehend the situation, the two parties quickly closed the gap on the trail to give greeting. Hands were clasped, broad grins exchanged, and in the case of Potts and Micah, introductions made.

"Where are you heading?" Titus asked his father. "We'd heard from Dill Talbott that you'd headed into Kentucky on the trail of Eben Bledsoe's daughter."

"You know about that, do you?"

"Houser told us about it at the fort. I was

a mite surprised to hear you were hunting people instead of deer, for once. Not exactly what an old long hunter is known for."

"No, and this hunt may turn out to be the longest kind of them all," Fain said. "We managed to pick up track of this woman, who it seems is going now by the name of Deborah Corey. But she is following an odd route. We trailed her as far as Harrodsburg and discovered she'd turned back the way she'd come and was heading for Jonesborough."

"Lord, have mercy. We could have made Jonesborough easy from Crockett Spring if we'd known all of this at the right time," Micah said.

"Yes, but then we'd not have met up here," Fain said. "Now, at least, we get the pleasure of traveling together."

No inn that night. They made camp along the trail and stayed up far later than any of them had intended, talking and catching up on what had gone on over recent weeks.

The story of the massacre at the Deveraux cabin, the taking in of young Mary, and the tragic end of the "white Indian" Sisalee shook Fain, and it showed. Titus and Micah presumed Fain was impacted by the story simply because he had known and hunted with Sisalee, but Potts, having heard the conversation regarding Cecil Watson between Fain and the Talbotts, recognized who Sisalee was and understood the true delicacy of the subject to Fain.

"Pap, you look to be upset," Titus said. "The old man said you and him had hunted together. You were good friends, were you?"

"I'd . . . I'd as soon not talk of it," Fain replied.

He had little to say thereafter, and was the first to take to his bedroll that night.

In his bed at White's Fort, Eben Bledsoe stirred and mumbled as something sought to intrude itself into his sleep. Rolling over, he began to sink deeper into slumber again, but then came a repeat of the intrusion, which he was able this time to recognize as a persistent knocking on the door of his log-walled room. He sat up, leaning back on one hand and rubbing his face with the other, and stared at the dimly visible image of the door.

Another knock. "Eben?"

Now he was almost fully awake. He had recognized the voice, but having done so, was not at all sure he wanted to answer the door.

"Open up, Eben! We've got to talk."

Eben rose from his bed, the straw of the

tick making a loud rustle, dust stirring from the fabric, unseen in the dark room but detected by his nose. He let out a magnificent sneeze, then stood, rubbing his nose on the sleeve of his well-worn and dirty nightshirt. He went to the door and opened it.

"Hello, Abner," he said to his brother, who waited outside with an eager look on his tropia-distorted visage. "Come in."

Abner was halfway inside before the short invitation was complete.

Eben, so at a loss from this unlikely visit that he seriously wondered whether he was dreaming, waved his brother toward a nearby stool. Abner sat down, but without relaxation. He perched in a stiff posture, hands cupping his knees, fingers drumming audibly on kneecaps. It made Eben nervous just to hear it.

Eben fetched his flint-and-steel from the split-log mantel on the fireplace, and soon had a lamp burning. With the room lighted, Abner looked around with constantly moving eyes, which, being crossed, gave him a memorable but disconcerting aspect indeed.

"Why are you here, brother?" Eben asked.

"She's gone, Eben. Gone away and left me. And took every penny I had to my name."

"Who are we talking of?"

"My woman, Eben. Who do you think?" Abner's voice was shaking suddenly, as if he might weep.

"Your woman . . . You're talking of Molly Reese?"

"Eben, you know she isn't really Molly Reese. I don't even know what her true name is. She's just a woman I met who, for her lack of a tongue and lack of any moral scruples about living out a falsehood, was willing to take on the role I needed played."

"So you openly admit you're a fraud now."

"Unlike you, brother. Unlike you, who never admits it. You know me, and there's no point in me putting on false airs with you. What you forget is that I know you, too."

"Yes, but I have nothing to hide."

Abner threw his head back and laughed.

Eben stood and paced back and forth in a small space. "Why are you here, Abner?"

"I told you. She took everything I had."

"So you want me to give you money because your harlot left you empty."

"What else would I want from you, Eben? Your respect?"

It was Eben's turn to laugh. "You will have neither money nor respect from me, Abner. You might as well leave."

Abner closed his eyes and took several deep breaths, forcing himself to calm down. "Eben, why can't we be friends? We're brothers, yet you treat me like an enemy. We're both in the same work, serving the same big purpose."

Eben wouldn't hear more. He shook his head firmly. "We are far from serving the same purpose, Abner. I believe in what I preach and teach. You do what you do for the sake of fame and gain."

"How do you know what I truly believe, and what I'm truly trying to achieve? Have you seen the crowds my preaching draws, Eben? Have you seen the people who see their lives made better and brighter? Have you seen —"

Eben interrupted. "I've seen you put forth a woman professing to be someone she is not, and I've seen you live with that same woman in a state of fornication, all the while pretending to be a man of God. You are false, Abner." He paused, then said, "It is just as well that your Molly Reese pretense can no longer be done. It could not have gone on much longer even had the woman not deserted you. Eventually it would have been noticed that the Reese narrative has been around too long for the 'Molly Reese' of your camp meetings to be the actual woman. The real Molly Reese, if such a woman even exists or ever did, would be older than the woman who has now abandoned you."

"How do you know her age, Eben? Have you attended my meetings?"

"I have observed them, hidden among the crowd. As a teacher of true religion, I find it worthwhile for me to acquaint myself with religion that is false, so that I may know my enemy. And as much as I regret it, you, my brother, are an enemy of the truth, and an enemy of me."

"And what of you, Eben? You and I both know the kind of man you have been for years."

"The past is past, Abner. And what God has forgiven, let no man bring up again. Especially one so false as you, yet unrepentant of it. My sins are past. Yours are ongoing and willingly embraced."

Abner glared at his brother, as best a cross-eyed man can glare. "I should have known there was no point in coming to you. You care about nothing but your own precious college . . . which I have yet to see any true sign of."

"I'm fresh returned from Virginia with a supply of books that will create the finest library west of the Alleghenies," Eben said.

"As well as —" He cut off suddenly.

"Go on, brother. Finish what you were saying. 'As well as . . .' As what? I think we both know. I heard about your journey and what took you to Virginia. Much more than books. You received money. Donations. And yet you look at your own stricken brother and refuse to help him."

"Donations for use of the college, Abner. Not for my personal use. Certainly not for yours."

Abner again forced himself to settle and calm. He said, "Eben, I had hoped to find you in a more charitable and Christian frame of mind. It hasn't proven the case. Clearly you are not going to help me willingly."

"I am not. God forbid I should ever do so."

"If no willing help, then unwilling it will have to be." Abner reached behind himself and pulled out the pistol he had tucked into the waist of his trousers earlier. He clicked the lock to half-cock and leveled it at Eben.

"Has it come to this, Abner?" Eben asked. "Are you now to rob me like a common thief?"

"Yes, Eben," said Abner. "It has come to this. Are you going to be reasonable and give me what I demand?"

"I am your brother," Eben said. "You won't shoot me."

But he did.

It was James White who heard the shot and rushed to the cabin where Eben Bledsoe resided. He found the clergyman sorely wounded but still alive, and fetched a young Cherokee boy, the son of the woman who served as a cook at the fort. The boy was sent on the fastest available horse to Fort Edohi, where he fetched Dr. Houser and brought him as quickly as possible back to White's.

When morning came, Eben Bledsoe still lived, but his condition was precarious. Houser sent the Cherokee messenger boy back to Fort Edohi to tell his wife what had happened, that her husband would remain at White's for a day or two, until he knew that Eben Bledsoe would survive.

When Mary Deveraux saw the Cherokee boy ride into the stockade, she screamed and hid herself, sobbing, and would not be consoled until the boy was gone.

As Eben regained some of his strength, White and Houser questioned him closely regarding who had wounded him, and what the motive had been. Eben declared that he had been robbed by a nocturnal intruder, but said he had not known the man, whom he described in a whole-cloth falsehood as about thirty years of age, stocky, and bearded.

Houser asked, "I provided care for a man matching that description. Was he by chance missing a portion of one leg?"

Eben Bledsoe, seeing a chance to fully divert any suspicion that might be turned toward his brother — for as much as he loathed Abner, for the sake of family blood he did not wish to see him hanged as a thief — lied once more and said that indeed the man had been possessed of only one leg, and it was out of pity for him that Eben had allowed him to enter his quarters.

"You were robbed, then, by a man I am almost sure was the infamous highwayman Jeremiah Littleton," Houser told him.

"Yes," said Bledsoe. "I am quite sure that was the man."

"I am pleased to see that you have found each other," said Dill Talbott to the group of travelers when they reached Crockett Spring. "I had hoped that such a thing would happen when I saw young Titus here off on your trail, Edohi. But it is a big and broad country up beyond the Gap, and I had no real confidence you would meet."

"A big and broad country, yes, but the road through it is narrow," said Fain. "We encountered one another on the trail, and a pleasant surprise it was. Now we are going together to Jonesborough, where we have heard that Deborah Bledsoe, or Deborah Corey, if they are one and the same, may be."

"She is a far-ranging woman, then," said Dill. "Why would she follow so odd a pattern?"

"I suppose we'll find out when we locate her."

"I need you to do something for me," Fain said to Potts when the group departed for Jonesborough. "I promised Bledsoe I would send him word of our progress all along, by messenger, and he provided money to cover that cost. I want to pay you to take a letter to him for me. We don't know much, but what we know, I want him to know."

"You don't need to pay me for it," Potts said. "I'll make the trip for no cost to you."

"You *will* take payment. Bledsoe provided money to cover messenger cost, and we will use it. You are the messenger, so it is you who are paid."

Potts argued no further. The letter was already complete, having been constructed by Fain at spare moments as they traveled. Potts tucked it beneath his hunting shirt, said his farewells, and made promise to rejoin the others as soon as his errand was run and he could reach them.

Then he rode southwest toward White's Fort while the others headed east toward Jonesborough.

Chapter Thirteen

Several days later
Jonesborough, State of Franklin

In all her happy girlhood in North Carolina, Constance Harkin had never had a moment of ambition to become a widowed mother of three, operating a lodging house on a dangerous frontier. Her intent had been merely to grow up and marry a man as fine as her father had been, and live a happy life raising a family in some village or town where life was stable and safe.

Life had taken unplanned turns. She had found the husband she had hoped for, and John Harkin proved as good a man as she'd dreamed: hardworking and able, a lawyer of cleverness and skill, and a fine father. John's only flaw had been poor health. Ailments of the lungs plagued him all his foreshortened days, particularly in winter and the moist days of spring. Despite Constance's rapt attention, insistence on his frequent examination by good physicians, and endless prayers for his healing, the man aged before his time and his lungs became ever weaker and more prone to illness. His refusal to give up his single vice of pipe-smoking did nothing to help him, in Constance's opinion, but she had always held herself back from haranguing him about it. Her mother had advised her that "a man must be left to be a man," and she had tried to follow that guidance.

John had somehow persuaded himself that what his health needed was a move out of the Carolina Piedmont country across the mountains to the backcountry where, as he put it, life was "new and fresh and healthy." It made no sense to Constance, who had heard of the heat and humidity of the backcountry summers, but a man must be left to be a man, and she had faithfully followed him to the new town of Jonesborough. There, John had established a law office, one of the first in town, and built his family a snug home, and beside it, a conjoining sturdy two-story log inn with four bedrooms, each with its own fireplace built by the best mason John Harkin could find. For a time it seemed the sheer exuberance of achievement and change did good things for his health, for he thrived and brightened in a way that cheered his wife to no end, and filled her with hope for their future in this town.

Then came the first frost of autumn and the first snow of winter, and John Harkin had declined with astonishing rapidity. By spring he was dead and Connie Harkin was running the inn alone and using the little law office building as a spinning house from which she sold a bit of fabric to make extra money.

She visited his grave daily for the first two months, then found that activity depressed her with no corresponding benefit coming in compensation. She began to talk to John not by his grave, but in her mind and sometimes in audible whispers when she was alone. Over time she began to feel a sense of his presence. Not that she believed in ghosts, merely in continued survival beyond the grave of the sort she had been taught in church. She believed John heard what she said to him and sometimes was allowed by the hosts of heaven to intervene and help her in mysterious ways. Usually simply in giving her an unaccountable sense of companionship and strength, as he had done in life.

For the children, it was difficult. Yet they managed fairly well. Only the eldest, twelve-year-old daughter Maggie, had passed the age of ten. Youth meant adaptability. It seemed to Constance that the youngest, six-year-old James, had adapted to his father's absence better than his older brother, middle child Michael, ten. Michael carried with him an eternal, brooding restlessness and a propensity for nightmares that sometimes broke his mother's heart and filled her with worry.

Maggie tried to manage such things, having appointed herself her father's replacement in shaping and disciplining her brothers. The only problem, from Constance's motherly point of view, was that Maggie followed some of her father's poorly chosen styles of son-raising, using intimidation and fear to prod the boys in the direction they should go. Constance disavowed such an approach, common as it was in her society, but John, and now Maggie after him, had never shied from it. In particular John had established a pattern of using phantom bogeymen to frighten and thereby control the boys. Maggie did the same, and while it appeared to have little effect upon her brother James, Michael was much affected, to the point that Constance secretly blamed some of his nightmares and frequent bed-wetting on the influence of his late father and storytelling older sister.

And there was the further complication in the form of old Benjamin Crawley, a charmingly British silversmith who had moved to the town after the end of the war, joining his son in the former Colonies. That son had worn a British military red coat during the conflict, but had deserted his army, drawn by the notion of life in a new country with seemingly unlimited prospects and room for growth. The son had lived only a year after his father joined him in America, then had been killed by a highwayman.

Though the senior Crawley was old and these days merely tinkered at his silversmithing, he was a popular and entertaining figure in Jonesborough, particularly for children. Gentle and protective toward the young, the old man delighted in sharing with them tales from his native England. Legends of kings and knights and dragons and mysterious dark forests where lived strange people, some of whom perhaps were not people at all. Crawley had the mind of a scholar and of what would one day be called a folklorist. He loved the old tales, and to him, a tale was not a tale unless it was often told.

There was one oft-told tale of Crawley's that impacted nighttime life in the household of Constance Harkin: the tale of Skellenwood Forest lurker Loafhead. Loafhead, a misshapen figure with a great lump of bone and flesh on his forehead. Loafhead, the frightening figure who emerged from England's Skellenwood whenever children were disobedient, or defiant, or ill-behaved, or, most of all, when they wetted their beds at night. Loafhead the punisher, invoked by parents and grandparents — or in the case of Jonesborough's Harkin household, by a sister seeking to control and dominate her little brother. Loafhead the bane of bed-wetting children such as Michael Harkin.

Constance Harkin had firmly commanded her daughter to say nothing more of Loafhead to her brother, and Maggie had promised more than once to obey. But she had not, and Constance knew better than to expect it. The story was simply too compelling, and gave Maggie such a strong hold over her brother's mind, that she was not strong enough to resist. And besides, Michael continually asked to be told of Loafhead, drawn to the story as children often are drawn to that which terrifies them.

"You wet yourself in your bed tonight, and Loafhead will come through that window, that one right there, and tear off your head for a bread loaf," Maggie told Michael night after night. "You feel like you need to make water, you'd best get up and go out to the outhouse, unless you want your head to be Loafhead's bread and your brains his butter."

"But if I go outside — that's where he is," Michael would protest.

"He don't hurt boys who use the outhouse . . . usually," Maggie said, customizing the folklore to fit her own manipulative purposes. "He takes the heads only of boys who wet their beds. Like you do. What's wrong with you, Michael? Will you wet your bed until you're a grown man?"

Michael went to sleep almost every night with his sister's chiding in his ears, tears in his eyes, and Loafhead in his mind. He went to sleep waiting for the seemingly inevitable awakening with the chill of dampness on his body, and his heart full of dreadful anticipation of the shutter rattling open to give entrance to Loafhead, he who ate the heads of bed-wetting boys like loaves of bread.

Loafhead never came, and frequently Maggie received morning scoldings from her mother for keeping alive old Mr. Crawley's terrifying folk story, but for Michael the fear remained very real. Loafhead was to him as solid and alive as the old gum tree in the backyard of the inn, or the feral cats that prowled the night outside his shuttered window, and whose sounds made him certain that it was Loafhead he was hearing. Loafhead, who was moving around in the dark out there, solid and alive and hungry.

Also alive was Michael's shame over his nocturnal inability to control a basic function of his own body. It was a secret humiliation, one he struggled hard to keep from the handful of other children of the town. But he knew that it wasn't really a secret. They knew.

Maggie had told them.

Sometimes he wondered why Loafhead was so concerned about punishing bedwetting boys. Would it not be better if he turned his wrath on cruel and humiliating sisters?

That would be fine by Michael Harkin.

The outlaw Gilly had no idea where he was or any memory of how he came to be there. Only when his murky vision began to clear did he see anything familiar, that being the three faces gazing down at him: Harlow Jones, Bart Clemons, Nathan Sikes. Three longtime associates in crime. Fellow members of the gang that had until recently operated under the leadership of Jeremiah Littleton, until the need for flight and hiding had fragmented the group.

"Boys, have I been out?" Gilly asked, mumbling. His head hurt and he was very disconcerted. He sat up but felt too dizzy to come to his feet.

"You have been, Gilly. Bart had to clout you on the skull bone to calm you down. You was ready to kill us all, and I think you'd have tried."

Gilly frowned, utterly confused. He was seated on the ground, back leaned against a tree. He didn't remember any argument or altercation, didn't remember even being with these men. Hard as speaking was, he said as much.

"Gilly, we run into you by chance," said Jones. "It was plumb providential. We was riding in toward Watauga from over near White's Fort, wondering what had become of you and of Jeremiah, and lo and behold, we got over past Greene County and there you was, camping. You didn't act glad to see us, Gilly. You cussed and fought us and we had to knock you in the head, knock you cold. We need to talk to you about all that, and a few other things."

"Before we hang you," threw in Sikes.

"Hang me? By jingo, boys, what the hell you talking about?"

"Gilly, where is Littleton?"

"How would I know? Hell!"

Jones knelt before Gilly. "Gilly, there's a lot of rumors flying around about Jeremiah, and about you. All of us here know he was mighty angry with you over the murder you done during that robbery, and truth is we're all just as mad about that as he was. When you killed that man you made it all the more likely for all of us that we'll come to our ends on a gallows."

"No more so than you would anyway, with all the robberies we've done. Hell, a man can get hanged for stealing a horse or robbing a coach!"

"But that horse thief will get hanged a lot quicker if he's also a murderer, or part of a gang of outlaws that has a murderer amongst them."

"I killed that man because he killed my father a long time ago. I told Littleton that, too."

"That don't help us none, not now nor when they haul us out to the hanging beam."

"Wait," said Sikes. "When did you tell that to Littleton?"

"What month is it now?"

"September. What? You don't know what month it is?"

"You clouted me on the head. You knocked

the memory of it out of me."

"When did you see Littleton?" Sikes asked again.

"Last month. Over by Fort Edohi."

"Where is he now?"

Gilly hesitated, unsure what he should say. As someone who had vied with Littleton for leadership of this gang, he didn't mind these men learning that Littleton was dead in the bottom of a cliff-side pit, as Gilly believed he was. At the same time, Sikes and Clemons had both been quite loyal to Littleton, and he wasn't sure what might happen if they ascertained that Gilly had killed him.

"Where is he?" Sikes asked again, more forcefully.

"He's dead," Gilly said. "He took a fall off that bluff near the big meadow at Fort Edohi and broke his neck. Fell into a big pit there, quite a drop. I tried to get him out, but he died before I could."

"So Littleton is dead. Mighty handy accident to happen, and mighty big co . . . co . . ."

"Coincidence?" Clemons suggested for his companion.

"Mighty big coincidence, you just happening to be nearby when he fell."

"I didn't just happen to be there. Littleton had called me to meet him on that hill, wanting to talk to me about the same thing we just talked about here. He wanted to know why I shot that man."

"Littleton falling over that bluff didn't happen with any kind of help from you, did it?" Clemons asked.

"Not a bit of it. He just fell."

"Know what, Gilly?" Jones said. "You saying that ain't a surprise to me. Fact is, we already knew about Jeremiah falling into that pit."

"But nobody else was there but me and him. By jingo, boys, I swear it's the truth!"

"That's the same thing he told us. Just you and him there. Nobody else."

Gilly went pale. Then his eyes narrowed and brows lowered. "You're lying. He couldn't have told you nothing. He's dead."

"Somebody helped him out of that pit, Gilly, and it wasn't his neck that was broke; it was his leg. He lost that leg, Gilly. Had to cut it off to free himself. But he's still alive. Clemons talked to him nine, ten days ago. Remember Jimmie Clute? Old horse thief out of Virginia? He's living in the woods near Cumberland Gap now, and Littleton was staying with him awhile. Teaching himself to walk on a wooden peg leg one of Clute's neighbors had carved out for him.

Clute said he was getting right able on that leg."

Gilly was paler yet. "You're a liar. If he came out of that pit, he didn't come out alive!"

"Oh, but he did," Clemons said. "And he said it wasn't no accident that he fell into that pit. You *pushed* him. And he ain't forgot it, nor forgave it. He's going to find you, he says. And he's going to kill you when he does."

"Hell!" Gilly spat, beginning to feel like a man riding a runaway horse of a situation. "He ain't going to do nothing to me! Even if he found me, I reckon I'm able enough to outrun a peg legger. He won't have a chance to do me no harm. I can deal with him as easy as I did the first time."

"Aha! So you admit you caused him to fall!" Jones said.

Gilly, realizing he'd just made an error of judgment, turned a burning eye on Jones. "I didn't say — ah, damn it all, what does it matter now? Hell yes, I pushed him into that hole. And if it didn't kill him, next thing I do to him will. I'll make sure of it!"

Jones shook his head and said, "You'll never have another chance." He stood and stepped back from Gilly. "Gentlemen, we have a confession there from Gilly's own lips that he tried to murder the leader of our sworn gang, and in fact believed he *had* murdered him. So as far as I'm concerned, he's guilty of the crime, same as if he'd succeeded at it, and the proper penalty is his own life. Gentlemen, I say we hang him, for the attempted murder of Jeremiah Littleton, and for endangering all of us without necessity through the murder of that man in the house we robbed."

Gilly looked as if the very soul had just drained from him as the others gave a very ragged "Hurrah!" at Jones's words.

Gilly came to his feet, wobbling, head throbbing terribly now from the blow he had received earlier. "You men ain't going to hang me," he said. "We're friends. Have been a long time."

"I got a rope over on my saddle," said Clemons. "I'll fetch it . . . *friend!*" The word was heavy with sarcasm.

"Boys, boys, listen to me. I ain't done nothing any worse than any of you — 'specially you, Sikes. You know the kind of man you are. I shot that man we were robbing, sure. And I pushed Littleton into that pit. I admit it all. But what you did, Sikes, was a lot worse than that. That poor little girl over in Virginia, just a child, and you treated her worse than if she was a common whore! She was a *child,* Sikes! Anything I done don't compare to such a crime and sin as that! And what's wrong with you, anyway, that would make you have that kind of a lust in you? It ain't normal, a man wanting a child in that kind of way!"

Sikes glared silently and hatefully at Gilly. The others said nothing at all, but proceeded with their preparations.

They performed the deed in the simplest manner, pulling Gilly up off the ground by the neck rather than dropping him. He was in tears when they did it, and unsettled his executioners rather badly by managing to stare at them accusingly even as he swung, eyes bulging and red, tongue emerging between lips.

Clemons said, "He's dying slow. Maybe I should pull down on his legs, make him choke faster. That's what kinfolk of hanged people used to do over in England, I heard once. Made them die quicker."

Harlow Jones shook his head. "Let him alone," he said. "Let him choke. He don't deserve no kindnesses."

"But he's so light of weight, it might take him so long. . . ." Clemons looked up at Gilly's face, the eyes now nearly absent of light. He shuddered and turned away. He was not a man of strong stomach.

"Let's go. I don't want to see this no more." Jones wrinkled his nose. "Good God, I think he lost his bowels."

"It happens sometimes, I hear."

They simply left Gilly dangling there, bug-eyed and swinging and self-soiled, and departed. The weak-stomached Clemons could not resist looking back, as hideous as the sight was to him. With embarrassment he turned again and retched.

Two minutes after they were gone, something stirred in the forest, and a big, strange figure emerged and stood a moment before the dangling Gilly. After moments of silent staring, the figure moved forward, reaching toward the hanged man with powerful arms.

Part Three: Backcountry

Chapter Fourteen

Crawford Fain had expected to be in Jonesborough several days sooner than he actually got there. What slowed him down was illness, a rarity for a man of usual robust health. It arose quickly and knocked him off his feet. Pain in every muscle and joint, a head that would not quit aching, bone-shaking chills that alternated with bursts of furnacelike internal heat that drenched him with sweat. He could hold down no food for three days, and only a little water.

Titus built a half-faced camp in the woods beside the trail and put his father there to recover his health and strength — and neither he nor Micah was willing to mention to each other how similar the arrangement felt to the time they had spent with the doomed Sisalee lying in that hunter's shelter. The difference was that Fain's illness was transitory and not life-threatening, nothing like the apoplexy that had laid the old "white Indian" low. Nor was there an unstable little girl with a hidden pistol and a grudge ready to find lethal expression.

After a couple of days of rest, Fain had begun to improve, slowly. Micah brought in a deer, and from the meat cooked up a thin broth that he swore Fain would be able to tolerate, and which would give him strength.

It did. Fain remained unbalanced, aching, and weak, but his stomach settled and the nourishment did much good. He sat up on his bedroll in the half-faced shelter and, though he would never admit it, found he was enjoying the opportunity for rest and the chance to be tended to. In particular, he valued the time he could spend with his son, who seemed now to actually want to be at his father's side and hear what he had to say. A few years ago Titus had displayed almost no interest in his sire.

"I've come to realize there's a lot about you I don't know," Titus said. "And a lot less I know about your parents. This might be a good chance for you to tell me a few things."

Fain nodded, staring out the open front of the shelter and enjoying the feel of the light breeze on his face. "Son, you're right. And there's some things I didn't tell you when you were a boy because I didn't know you needed to hear them then. Like the fact that your grandfather was in some ways not a good man."

"How so?"

Fain looked over at his son. "He was a thief and bandit, Titus. He broke houses and operated as a highwayman back in his homeland, in England. Might have wound up on the gallows had certain things never happened. And if he'd ended up doing the Tyburn dance, I would never have landed in the Colonies, and you and me wouldn't be sitting here talking right now."

"Tell me more." Titus was surprised and troubled, his father having never given a hint of this kind of thing before.

"Your grandfather was a man of poverty, and of a poor raising. It sent him down the wrong path early on, and he turned to theft as the surest way to make a living." Fain paused for several seconds. "I'm not sure I should be telling you this part even now, but as a boy I was involved with some of his crimes, too. The housebreaking in particular. I was small of frame, you see, and a good climber, and your grandfather would find ways to sneak me into houses, where I would hide myself through the day and then let him in under cover of night. Then Father, with me helping, would take whatever was valuable that we could get out with without waking anyone up. Your grandfather knew places he could sell it. It was a simple system, but it worked. We kept operating like that till I was twelve, thirteen years old. I'm sorry to admit it to you, but you're a man now and you can deal with knowing your father ain't lived a perfect life."

"Pap, you were just a boy, doing what your father told you. Even so, I'm . . . to borrow your word, I'm 'smote.' I had no notion of anything like this."

"I've kept it from you. Best to raise a boy to believe the blood in his veins comes from generations of righteous-living folk, not sinners. But you're no boy any longer, Titus, and you should know the truth about those who came before you."

"What about the highway robbery? Were you involved in that as well?"

"Never. Father kept me from that because it was the most dangerous side of what he did." Fain paused again, then gave a dark little chuckle. "Funny thing, Titus. There were things that happened on both sides of my father's criminal life that didn't just kind of vanish once they happened. Things that had longer-lasting aspects."

"I'm not following you."

"Let me just tell you the stories. The first

one involved me, and happened during one of our typical housebreaks. The last break-in we ever did, in fact. I was thirteen years old and up to my full man's height by that point, though I'm not a tall man. I'd sneaked in through a cellar door into a house my father had picked out to rob . . . and I hid in a room in the upstairs. Well, that night somebody entered that room, a man and a girl, and the man commenced to doing things I've never been able to close out of my mind since. I saw it all out of the darkness where I was hiding, fearing all the while that I'd make a noise or otherwise show myself, and wind up getting caught. But I wished before long that I'd not been so cautious, for it just got worse and worse. Finally that man knelt over that poor girl he'd misused so sore, and, I swear to you, cut the tongue out of her mouth. It was dark, for the most part, so I couldn't see it clear, and I'm glad I couldn't. But I saw enough to bring me out of my hiding place. I lit into that devil and wouldn't let up. He'd hit the girl with a candlestick, and I put my hand on another just like it and struck him with it, hard. I killed that man, Titus. Your father has the blood of that man on his hands and his soul."

Titus was astonished. "Pap, what you did

was help a helpless girl. You did the work of the angels, Pap."

Fain shook his head. "It was too late to help her as much as I should have. She'd already been hurt by him, and mutilated. Her tongue was gone from her head, son. And I'd let it happen, when if only I'd moved a little sooner . . ."

"Pap, I got to say, this tale sounds mighty familiar. It matches that story that's heard so often about . . . What was her name?"

"Molly Reese. Molly Reese who had her tongue cut out by her own father and whose life was saved by an 'angel' from the shadows in a dark room. If it sounds like the same tale, son, it's because it is. I was that 'angel' that came out of the dark and killed her attacker. And the girl was Molly herself, the *real* one. Not the false Molly Reese that Camp Meeting Bledsoe has foisted on the world for a good while now. I've known for a long time that Bledsoe's 'Molly' wasn't the real one, because I'd known the real one when I was young."

"I'm astonished, Pap."

"There's yet more to the tale. After I struck down her pap and got Molly out of that house, I took her home with me. My father and mother, they took her in. For three years she was sheltered by your own grandparents and lived as my sister. She adored me for having saved her that night. It was me who taught her to read and write. And it was my mother — she had a talent with words — who helped Molly write out her narrative that became so famous, and gave old Bledsoe the grist for the mill of fraud he's had grinding away at his camp meetings with that woman pretending to be Molly."

"It surely must be hard for you to know Bledsoe's been out making a false presentment about somebody you knew well."

"It is. I had to listen to him going through all that bilge when he was preaching there at my fort a while back. And that woman was out there holding her mouth open like her wits were gone so folks could come by and see that 'Molly Reese' really had got her tongue cut out. By the way, Titus, Houser the physician came nigh to prompting me that evening into telling him what I've just told you. But I didn't. You are the first I've ever told this to."

"What happened with Houser?"

"At the close of the meeting, Houser looked into the mouth of Bledsoe's Molly and was able to see that her tongue had never been cut out, but just had never grown in, and from that he'd determined that this woman couldn't be the true Molly Reese. Since he figured that much out on his own, it was hard not to just tell him the full tale. But I've made such a habit of keeping all that part of life private that I just held my own tongue and didn't speak. When you get into the habit of silence about a certain thing, it's hard to change your practice."

"Where is the real Molly Reese now?"

"Still in England, far as I know. I lost her trail long ago. She'd be nigh my age now, just a couple of years younger. My father moved your grandmother and me to the Colonies and by that time Molly had already left us and gone back to London. I don't know for sure how she lived, and maybe it's best I don't. I've heard that part of her living came through selling copies of her narrative. But once that became so commonly printed and familiar, I doubt she could find buyers for long, and after that there's no telling what she might have been forced to." Fain shook his head. "You know, it's been so long now I'm not sure I'd know Molly if she walked up to this shelter right now and said hello."

Titus smiled. "Not that she'd be able to say it."

"She'd do better than you'd think. She

learned to make sounds in such a way, even with no tongue, that you could tell what she was trying to say, just about every time."

"Pap, why did your father bring the family to America? And how did you go from being a city boy in England to a woodsman on a whole different continent?"

"That, son, is a whole different tale, and I think I may hold on to it awhile longer. I'll get around to telling you, promise you. It ties in with what I've told you already."

"Tell me now."

"I'm talked out, son. Voice is weak. I think I may sleep for a spell. I'm not accustomed to sickness like this. I hope you don't catch it."

"Me, too. Me, too. Thank you for talking to me, Pap."

"I'm glad I've got you to talk to."

When he had completed his mission and was traveling again, anticipating joining his prior companions at Jonesborough, Potts was glad to leave White's Fort and Eben Bledsoe behind. Bledsoe, in recovery from the brother-inflicted gunshot wound he was blaming on the outlaw Littleton, had been quite displeased with Fain's progress, believing him to be moving too slowly. He was, however, intrigued by the meager information Fain had uncovered, particularly that Deborah now went by the last name of Corey.

"Please let Fain know that I will expect much more from him the next time I see a messenger come riding in," Bledsoe said. "In fact, I expect next time to see Fain himself, and Deborah with him."

"I'll tell him that," Potts said neutrally. "Hope you're all healed up soon, Reverend." He rode away. Next time, he hoped Fain would ask Micah or Titus to play messenger. There was something about the overbearing Eben Bledsoe he instinctively didn't like.

Now that September had come, the heat of summer had given way at last. The days still could grow hot, but the heat faded earlier and evenings were sometimes actually cool. Humidity, the worst aspect of summer in the backcountry, was much diminished and the atmosphere had a clear, crystalline quality.

Jeremiah Littleton had always favored this time of year except for the fact that it led into the fall, when trees shed their leaves and it was harder for a highwayman to hide himself along the sides of trails and roads. It was much easier in the summer, when leaves were lush, to find the proper spot for an ambush.

Littleton, riding along slowly and going east for no particular reason other than random choice, had to smile to himself as he remembered a time he and his gang had gone to a particular spot to intercept and rob a band of immigrants coming to the Cumberland from the Watauga and had gotten themselves into position when they realized they were not alone. Across the trail, in the woods on the other side, was another gang of would-be highwaymen, already hidden, awaiting the same party of travelers. Littleton had come out and confronted the rivals, and then the others of both gangs had joined the gathering, the result being that the immigrants and would-be robbery victims had come up to find two bands of fist-fighting men pummeling one another for no obvious reason in the midst of the forest trail. The travelers, all on foot and with no animals other than packhorses and three milk cattle, simply withdrew into the woods and managed to hide as the bandits finished their fight. The bandits actually had a laugh at their own expense over the absurdity of the situation, and sat down together and drank themselves into a stupor like the oldest of friends. The immigrants, meanwhile, made a new route through the woods, behind a nearby ridge, and simply bypassed the men who would have robbed them had all gone according to plan.

"Don't matter no-how," one of the rival gang had said. "They looked like a mighty poor band of people, anyway."

Littleton chuckled at the memory, but a throb of pain from his foot made the chuckle die fast. The odd thing about it was that the pain came from a foot no longer there, a foot that was even yet wedged in a tight rock crevice in the base of a pit near Fort Edohi miles away, being eaten by insects and worms. He'd heard about such pains afflicting those with lost limbs, but he had never believed it. He believed it now, and it seemed the most unjust thing possible. A man is forced to cut off nearly half his own leg with his own belt knife, and even so is left to hurt in places where there is really nothing there to be hurting? Where was the sense and justice in that?

It had gotten worse since he'd started wearing the wooden leg. At first it had been fine, the stump of his limb fitting perfectly into the cup the wood-carver had hollowed out at the top of the peg leg. Over subsequent days, though, something had changed in the fit, causing pain that was making

Littleton a miserable man.

Determined to tough it out at the moment, Littleton rode on, but eventually each jolt of the horse's motion made his pain unbearable. Littleton found himself actually crying from the pain. Like a child. It made him feel humiliated and angry and glad to be alone. Even when he'd been trapped in that pit with hellish pain radiating up through his body, he hadn't wept. But this was a continuous lower-grade suffering that wore him down physically, mentally, emotionally.

He determined to get control of himself, though, when he heard the sound of voices coming toward him through the woods. Though he was posing now as the fictional Lyle Kirk, he had spent too many years as Jeremiah Littleton, highwayman, to hide very effectively behind a mere false identity. Any group of people he met might include someone who would recognize him.

Littleton rode a little farther, the voices coming clearer. He stopped as a fiercer burst of pain shot up through his thigh and all but paralyzed him. He climbed down from his horse. Odd as it seemed, he had found he could sometimes gain some minor ease from his phantom pains by standing on his false leg. Something about the angle of the pressure on the remnant of his leg, he supposed . . . he really couldn't account for it. But in any case, he dismounted and led his horse on up the trail and around the edge of the stand of woods beside him.

A cluster of people stood gathered around an open hole, tears staining several faces, even as they stained Littleton's. Tears of physical pain in his case, emotional ones for these strangers. A woman was being buried, having died in the process of giving birth to a tiny boy, an infant now held in the trembling arms of the baby's weeping father. The bereaved man looked from the face of the sleeping child, down to the wooden box that held all that physically remained of the woman he loved, then around at the faces of the other mourners. He gazed then at Littleton, seeking to recognize this limping newcomer but failing to do so. But he did see the tears on Littleton's face and assumed them to be the marks of shared grief.

"You knew her, stranger. That much I can see, just from your tears. Come say your farewells."

Littleton hadn't progressed in his criminal career as far as he had without having learned to roll with life's blows, to recognize and take opportunity. This group obviously assumed him to be someone who had known the deceased woman, even if they did not themselves know him in turn. As Littleton tied off his horse to a low-hanging branch, a woman came around the grave and extended her arms toward him, tears streaming and lip aquiver. Littleton stepped forward, held still, and let her embrace him.

"Poor thing! I can see you loved her, too."

"I can't . . . believe she's gone . . . ," Littleton croaked out in his best grieving voice.

"How did you know her, sir?" asked an older man in the group.

"I can't talk . . . about it right now."

Nods of understanding all around, and more tears. It hit Littleton that later on, this bit of playacting would all seem quite funny.

CHAPTER FIFTEEN

Littleton realized that his leg hardly hurt at all now since he had gotten out of the saddle. The leather straps that attached to the wooden leg and, along with the cup that fit over the stump of remaining, held the prosthetic in attachment to his body, felt a little pinched and uncomfortable, however.

The burial service was completed with a prayer and the advance of two grubby men who were obviously ready to fill the grave. Littleton drifted back toward his horse. One of the men in the group, a fellow with a piercing, knowing look that made Littleton nervous, came to him. "Paul Hasker," he said. "Sarah was my cousin, but close enough she was more like a sister."

Littleton smiled through his whiskers and put out a hand. "Good to meet you, Paul. I'm Lyle Kirk. I heard Sarah speak of you."

"How did you know her?"

Littleton was put on the spot by the question but didn't show a trace of panic. He was a practiced liar.

"From church," he said. Churchgoing Lyle Kirk. That was him!

"Is that right? Which church?"

Still he wasn't thrown askew. "The old one," the liar said with a quick flash of a smile, hoping his words happened to fit some scenario of the dead woman's life that would make sense.

"From her Baptist days, then," the other said.

"Uh, yes."

"Was that before or after . . . Well, you know what I'm thinking of."

"Uh . . . after." Littleton hoped desperately that this would lead to no further questions.

Hasker put out his hand again. "Well, it's good to meet you, Mr. Kirk, even though the circumstances are sad. I'm glad you could get here in time to see her laid to rest."

"I just wish there was something I could say to make everyone feel better."

"We all grieve together. But life goes on." Hasker's eyes flicked down to Littleton's false leg. "Might I ask how you came to lose . . . ?"

"Accident with a wagon," Littleton said. He'd decided two days before to use that vaguery as his standard lie about the leg. One repeated lie would be easier to keep track of than different tales told to different people.

"Recent or old?"

"Recent."

Another man, poorly dressed and ugly and bald, joined the conversation. "You carve that peg yourself, that you're standing on, friend?"

"No. A carpenter made it."

The man bent over and looked at it closely. "Going to break right out from under you, it is."

Littleton put his hand out against a sapling and shifted his weight to his real leg, lifting the wooden leg off the ground and tilting it up so he could see it better. "Nah, nah. Nothing wrong with that leg," he said. "No cracks or nothing. Ain't going to break."

"Pshaw!" said the other. "I've did a lot of work with wood in my day, and I know that wood there has a flaw in it. Going to break with your weight going down on it all the time."

"I think this peg will hold up fine," Littleton countered, growing annoyed with this fellow. To demonstrate his confidence, he put his weight back down on the wooden limb and shifted to stress the wood from various angles. "See there?" he said. "Holds up just —" Then, with an abrupt splintering noise, the wood cracked and the peg split almost completely apart, the separated portion bending to one side, leaving the remaining part of the leg with a splintered point that stabbed into the ground under Littleton's weight.

"I told you," said the ugly man. "I could tell it."

Littleton gave a heave and managed to pull the splintered point out of the earth. The other, split remnant, not broken completely off, swung back down against the other portion.

"I can repair that for you," Hasker said. "I'm a blacksmith, and what that peg needs is a good iron band around it, holding it all back together again. A good strap of iron around it would have spared you the break ever happening to start with."

"Could you do that work, Mr. Hasker?"

"I can. This very day. We're not far from my smithy."

"I could see it was going to break," affirmed the ugly man yet again.

"How is it you have such a good eye for wood?" Littleton asked him, figuring friendliness to be his most prudent option.

"Built a lot of cabins, mostly. Or half

cabins. My name's Ott Dixon. I'm a traveling seller of spirits. When I go to a new place, I put up a tavern, usually log on the bottom and tent cloth at the top. I've done it so much I've gotten where I can tell when wood is strong and when it's got weakness in it. That carpenter who made that leg, he would have knowed that was a weak piece of wood, if he'd been worth his vinegar."

"Pleased to know you, Mr. Dixon," Littleton said. "My name's Kirk, and I'd covet the chance to turn up a tankard at your traveling tavern, if it is close by."

"It is, though it's only been where it is for a short time now. I moved it west from where it had been before, up at Greeneville. I got the tent fabric on it just three days back. Follow me and I'll guide you there, Mr. Kirk."

"I am your shadow, sir," Littleton said, already anticipating the taste of rum.

Littleton did not go immediately to Dixon's newest tavern, though. First he took Hasker up on his offer of a repair for the broken wooden leg. Hasker, who unlike Dixon was clearly honestly upset by the death and burial of the woman named Sarah, was just as clearly glad to have a task to distract him from grief. He threw himself into his task, firing and hammering out a strong iron band of perfect proportion to slide up onto the split prosthesis and bind it together again.

"Only one thing I ask of you in how you do that, sir," Littleton said. "Please do not put the band so firmly in place that I can't work it off again with a blade tip."

Hasker frowned. "Very well. But why would you want to do that? The leg can't be walked on if the split-apart pieces are not bound together, so I wouldn't advise that you —"

"I have my reasons, sir, and I hope you will take no offense if I keep them private."

What Gilly remembered the most keenly was the strange, intensely prickling pain that had filled his entire skull after he was taken down from the rope and blood flow resumed. The feeling had been worse even than the pinching of his throat and straining of his neck while he was still hanging.

He remembered also that first gasp of air, rushing through a raw throat, refilling lungs painfully yet giving him an immediate feeling of resuming life. He had a sense of being drawn back from the brink of a great darkness he had seen looming before him, ready to pull him in, irreversibly.

Beyond those things, memory and understanding were murky.

Only this much Gilly knew for a certainty: He had been hanged by his old companions, pulled up by the neck from the earth, his light weight becoming suddenly heavy and throat-crushing. The forest before him, and the faces of the former partners who were doing this to him, first had gone glaringly white, then faded swiftly to gray and finally darkness. His head, robbed of the nourishment of air and blood, had swum and spun. It seemed to him that a long time had passed this way.

Then, when his executioners were gone, and just as the embrace of the blackness had been on the verge of becoming absolute, something very powerful had grasped him about the thighs and shoved him upward, relieving the worst of the pinched feeling in his neck and allowing those terrible, tingling prickles of renewed blood flow to begin their tormenting play. His eyes had opened and he had caught a flickering glimpse of his rescuer. That glimpse had persuaded him that what he was seeing was not real, just some imagined figment that comes to the mind at the moment of death.

He had felt the loosened noose removed from his neck, and at that moment a spasm caused by the resurgence of blood through his brain caused him to break the grip of whoever held him, and he fell. A sharp, breaking pain went through his left ankle, and he had groaned as he passed out.

Next thing he had known, he was bobbing along aboveground, head swinging downward and eyes staring at the back of whoever had rescued him. His left ankle throbbed miserably with every jolt as he was carried like a rolled-up bearskin over the shoulder of a very large man.

He passed out again and knew nothing more for a long time.

Ten-year-old Michael Harkin awakened from sleep to an awareness that it had happened again. Another night with drenched legs, a soaked bed, and a mother who would be angry but try not to show it. Then his sister would be wakened by the activity in the house, and he would face her contempt and mocking once again. And her whispered hints, spoken out of earshot of their mother, that the dreaded ogre Loafhead would appear and punish him for once again wetting the bed.

Michael sat up, the straw tick rustling beneath him. He reached down to verify what he already knew, and to his shock found he was wrong. The bedding was completely dry. He had not wet the bed after all. Astonishing!

Rising, he smiled into the darkness, relieved and pleased with himself. Maybe at last he was past his old problem. Maybe from now on his body would let him know when he needed to go relieve himself, and he could handle the situation like a normal person by getting up and heading out to the privy.

Michael headed toward the door that led out to the dogtrot section between the conjoined log buildings that together composed the Harkin Inn and private family home. The door of his little room opened directly into the dogtrot, which was simply an open passageway, like an alley, between the house and the inn. Roofed timbers extended over the dogtrot so that the two log structures could be considered, superficially, as a single building.

Michael put his hand to the wooden lift latch, realizing from the mounting feeling of desperation in his bladder just how narrowly he had missed another bed-wetting. But he was nearly sure he could make it to the nearer of the two outhouses in the back before nature's call became self-answering. The smaller of the two privies served the

Harkin family; the larger was intended for use of those in the inn. But the larger one was closer to Michael's room, and it was there he intended to go. Closeness mattered.

He looked forward to morning, when he could tell Maggie of his success. Let her mock him *then!* Let her barrage him with her silly tales of Loafhead, the Punisher of bed-wetting boys, and try to make him afraid.

Michael's hand froze on the half-lifted latch. *Loafhead.* The mere thought of the name chilled him into paralysis. The darkness outside his door became heavy and threatening, filled with danger . . . filled with Loafhead.

Pressing a hand to his crotch to help himself restrain his need to urinate, Michael tried not to imagine what it would be like to step through that door into the dogtrot and feel the heavy hand of the Punisher suddenly descend upon his shoulder, grasping him, lifting him to carry him off over his back and find some private spot to eat his head like a loaf of bread. And of course, in trying not to imagine it, Michael forced himself to do exactly that. He remained frozen where he stood, wildly needing to relieve his bladder but too terrified to move.

"There is no such thing as Loafhead," he whispered to himself, repeating something his mother had told him time and again. He'd heard her say it to Maggie, too, scolding her for lying to her brother about such a frightening notion. "There is no such thing as Loafhead," he said again, louder.

Looking back into his dark room, he suddenly remembered that beneath his bed was a chamber pot. He disliked using it, normally, for it filled his room with the smell of urine and made him think of bed-wetting. But tonight the chamber pot provided a welcome option. He could use that and avoid the necessity of going out into the world of darkness and Loafhead. When morning came he could quietly go out and secretly empty the chamber pot, and declare to Maggie that, guess what, he'd gotten up in the night and used the outhouse without fear, not wetting his bed at all, not living in fear of her old English bogart story. She'd never know he was lying about the outhouse visit.

So he went to his bed and from beneath it retrieved the crockery pot . . . but he suddenly gritted his teeth and said, aloud, "No." He stared at the log wall, shook his head, and said it again. "No. Because there is no such thing as Loafhead, and I don't need to be afraid."

It was a matter of pride now, his own pride in himself. He had made it through the night without wetting, gotten up as a normal person should when he felt the need to relieve himself, and he'd be hanged if he'd let some old, false folk tale told by a mere girl scare him now!

He *was* going out that door, down that dogtrot, across the little expanse of yard to the outhouse, and then back again to his room and bed. The chamber pot would remain unused. And he, Michael Harkin, would be victorious. A winner in the war he had fought with himself and his own physical failing, and with his eternal fear of the bogeyman his mean sister would not let die. No fearful pissing into a chamber pot for Michael Harkin! No, he was going outside, to the outhouse. As his father would have. Like a man.

Michael lifted his eyes upward in the dark, forced a smile onto his face, and whispered, "See, Papa? I'm not afraid anymore. I'm not afraid."

And while he still had the determination burning in him, he pushed the unused chamber pot back under the bed, marched to the door, opened it, and stepped out into the dark dogtrot.

■ ■ ■ ■

The south end of the dogtrot opened toward the street, and though Michael needed to go the opposite direction to reach the outhouse, something on the street drew his attention and he glanced that way.

What he saw passing from right to left across the rectangle of dirt street visible to him caused him to suck in his breath as a cold fear gripped him. The side of the dogtrot blocked most of the street from his view, so almost immediately what he had seen was hidden by the intervening wall. Forgetting the outhouse for the moment, Michael moved toward the street and at the end of the dogtrot paused to look out down the street to see what had passed by.

He clamped his hand to his mouth to keep himself from yelling, and his straining bladder gave way and streamed urine down his legs beneath his nightshirt. Whimpering and terrified, he backed into the darkness of the dogtrot, went back to his room, and spent the rest of the night cowering in his bed, afraid even to open his eyes.

Loafhead was real. And he was here. Michael knew. He had just seen him, treading down the middle of the street in Jonesborough, carrying a man slung over his shoulder like a sack of dirt.

Chapter Sixteen

It was often easy for Crawford Fain to forget that he was a famous man in his part of the world, and even in parts he had never set foot in. In his own mind he was simply one more frontiersman, one with particularly apt skills for playing out his role in life, perhaps, but in the end, merely another man.

His arrival in Jonesborough had provided a quick reminder that others were not so casual in their assessment of him. He was more than a man; he was a symbol, of his time and his place and his frontier. Like Franklin leader John Sevier, who found himself thrust into leadership both political and military virtually everywhere he went, Fain could not live the life of an ordinary man. It simply wasn't allowed by those around him.

He had not been in Jonesborough a day before word of his arrival spread and visitors began to pay call. Fain had intended to reside in an inn or boardinghouse, but instead he and his entourage were invited, almost compelled, to join the household of Matthew Stuart, a local merchant and active citizen who had already made a moderate fortune for himself on the east Carolina coast before coming west on a quest to see what further fortunes life might bring him in a new country.

Stuart's house, one of the first and best frame houses in the over-mountain backcountry and considered a mansion by frontier standards, was outside town on property bordering an expansive wooded area. It held two distinctions setting it apart from other properties in and around the town: The first was that Stuart, an avid horseman, had built a substantial racetrack on the one portion of his land suitable for such development. The second was that he had also given over a section of land to provide space for a jail, and on that land had built a facility made of heavy, hewn logs, spiked together to make them virtually impossible to separate. A local smithy made a door of heavy, crossed iron bars and devised a clever locking mechanism.

Fain had never previously met his host Stuart, but had heard of him, and Stuart certainly knew of Fain's reputation. Stuart was eager to host a famous man, and show off his land and buildings to the frontiersman, and welcomed Titus and Micah as part of the bargain. When Potts rejoined his old companions after completing his messenger journey to White's Fort, he, too, was enthusiastically hailed.

The jail building Stuart had erected held a single occupant, a man who Stuart said had identified himself as one Caleb Clark. "He's in quite a weakened state," said Stuart to Fain, privately. "As best anyone can tell, he was choked with a cord or rope. In fact, it appears from the marks on his gullet that he was hanged, then taken down again before he had time to expire. He must have fallen some distance after he was taken off the rope, because his ankle is broken."

Fain looked at the man through the barred door, which was closed but not locked, the man not being there as a prisoner. He was sleeping, snoring loudly, and also making a strange, hissing-air noise in his throat, apparently the result of his throat injury. His left ankle was splinted and firmly bound up in cloth. By the light of a lamp Stuart held in his hand and thrust through the bars of the door, the indentation and abrasion of the rope that had hanged him could be seen.

"I never knew a man could be hanged and survive it," said Stuart.

"I've heard of it," Fain said. "Depends on how the hanging is done, to large measure. Let a man drop a sufficient distance and he'll break his neck and be gone right off. Give him a rope with little or no slack, or haul him up slow and let him dangle, and he might strangle for a long time and still make it through if he's took down in time, especially a light bird like that man there looks to be."

"I'll be!"

Fain went on: "Ever hear of Jack Sheppard, the old English robber? He was a skinny, light-bodied fellow, condemned to the gallows about sixty years back, and he had friends who planned to haul him down from the noose at Tyburn before he expired, and revive him. As it turned out, there was interference and them friends couldn't save Sheppard's life after all. The crowd cut him down and hauled him off before his friends could claim him, thinking maybe those friends were really just folks working in league with the dissectionists."

Stuart gestured toward the man on the cot. "Well, Clark here had better luck than that. I can't tell, though, how much damage might have been done to him that isn't going to go away, at least not very fast. The strange breathing like he's doing there, the way he can hardly get his voice out, and the fact that when he does talk, he strains to make any kind of sense."

"A man has the blood cut off to his head for long enough, no telling what it might do to him," said Fain.

"I suppose so."

"Tell me this, Stuart: Since he can't walk, how did he come to be in town here?"

"That's the oddest part of the tale. He was carried in by someone in the middle of the night on Saturday, and placed on the doorstep of a church where he'd be sure to be found the next morning."

"That's a mite strange. Why bear him in and be secret about it?"

"As best I can figure it, Mr. Fain, I think whoever brought him must have had something to do with his hanging. So he wanted to keep his involvement and identity unknown. Hence the secret visit by night."

"But why would somebody hang him, then rescue him?"

"I couldn't tell you. My guess is that there were second thoughts about the hanging. A change of mind, for some reason." Stuart abruptly chuckled. "Whoever it was who brought him in, he wasn't as covert as he thought. He was seen doing it. Little boy here in town up in the night to go to his outhouse — he saw a man carrying Clark on his shoulder, passing down the street in the dead of night."

"Did he recognize the one carrying him?"

Stuart laughed again. "He says he did. But his identification isn't much helpful unless you believe in bogeyman tales."

"What do you mean?"

"Well, this hasn't been told out across the town, but this boy told his mother that the one he saw was . . . well, have you ever heard of the old English bogey called 'Loafhead,' Mr. Fain?"

Fain made a sudden noise in his throat and took a backward step. Stuart lost his smile and held the lamp up to illuminate Fain's face more clearly.

"Are you well, Mr. Fain? Your face just drained of color." Stuart paused. "I'm not to take it, surely, that you *believe* in this 'Loafhead' bogey?"

Fain shook his head. "No, of course not, sir. I beg your pardon for my reacting like this, which I know seems odd. Suffice it to say that there is a reason for it. Your mention of that name strikes close to home for me. In the old legends, you see, Loafhead lived in the deepest part of Skellenwood

Forest. And Skellenwood is the very place I spent many of my young years."

"You are an Englishman?"

"By birth only. By life and choice I am an American and a free man, obliging to no king or royalty. But a man's birth is what it is, and it was in old England I was born."

"I am intrigued that such a great American woodsman as you had his beginnings in an English forest. How did you come to live in such a place?"

"My father was a huntsman and woodsman in the employ of the landowner. I learned to track, to make shelter, to hunt and fish and harvest foods that grow in the wild . . . all in Skellenwood Forest. An unusual home indeed my father made for his brood there. Walls of split logs, but roofless, built inside a hillside cavern that provided good shelter from rain. Thus the lack of need for a roof."

"Fascinating, Mr. Fain. And unexpected. From Skellenwood to the over-mountain backcountry . . . what a journey!"

"Aye."

"There is a man in this town I want you to meet, Mr. Fain. A silversmith and himself an Englishman. I have heard him tell the Loafhead legend to the children here. . . . He will be intrigued indeed to meet someone who grew up in the forest that is at the heart of the legend."

"I'd be pleased to meet him. As will my young friend Micah Tate, who has with him a piece of rock he has been planning to have a silversmith or goldsmith examine. It came from a family he met on the Cumberland."

"Crawley will be able to tell him what it is. The man knows his stones, precious or plain."

"I'll look forward to meeting him."

The sleeping man moaned and moved and his bleary eyes opened slowly. He looked around the log-walled cell until at last his gaze settled on the men looking in at him. His focus centered on Fain.

"I know you," he croaked out. "I know who you are, Edohi."

"I can't say I know you, Mr. Clark, sorry to admit," Fain replied. "I am sorry, though, that you have been hurt."

Clark lifted his hand to touch his damaged and tender neck.

"How do you know Mr. Fain?" Stuart asked Clark.

Fain said, "I've learned over time how familiar a figure I am across this wilderness, Stuart. I'm known by sight to more people than I can account for."

Fain knelt by Clark's bed and squinted at

the creased abrasion around his neck. "Hanged?" he asked.

"Yes," Clark croaked out in his damaged voice.

"Then they took you down."

"Not them. Another."

"The same one who carried you into town?"

"Yes."

"Why did he do it as he did? Why did he just leave you on the church doorstep and vanish?"

"Don't . . . know."

"Who was he?"

Clark shrugged, tried to speak but this time couldn't, and lifted his left hand to his brow. Cupping the hand, he covered his eye and extended his fingertips up to his hairline.

"A lump over his eye and brow?" Fain asked.

Clark nodded.

Stuart asked, "Do you know who it was, Mr. Fain?"

"Can't say I do. But I know of a family that has — No. No. I'll not go linking somebody up to a situation like this when I've got naught but secondhand knowledge of the matter."

Stuart grinned. "Well, it sounds like Mr.

Crawley's Loafhead character to me."

"Loafhead lived in Skellenwood. Not in the American backcountry," Fain replied.

"In the legend, you mean."

Fain paused, then grinned. "Of course. In the legend."

When the pair was gone, Gilly Cobble, now going by the name of Caleb Clark, rolled over and tried to find a posture that would relieve some of the discomfort in his throat and neck. It was difficult, and his ruined ankle was stabbed with jolting pain as he moved.

He lay there wondering why the famous Crawford Fain had come to visit him. He'd never known the man, though he'd seen him several times before in public settings, or from a distance as he had that day with Littleton beside the camp meeting ground at Fort Edohi. Thank God he'd had the foresight to give a false name when he'd been found on that church doorstep. Fain and others would probably have known well who Gilly Cobble was, if he'd let his real name slip. And then that cell door standing open nearby would have been locked, and Gilly would have been soon facing a noose from which there would be no last-moment rescue.

He pondered the strange figure who had removed him from the rope, and wondered who the man was. If man he had been at all. . . . What Gilly had glimpsed in that moment just after he'd been taken down had looked only somewhat human. The head had been horribly misshapen, a great mass of flesh growing out of the brow and covering one of the eyes. Horrible to see.

But the man or creature or woodland ogre or Cherokee skinwalker or whatever it had been, had certainly been strong. He'd managed to carry Gilly for miles, on foot.

Most of what had happened between the time Gilly came out of the noose and awakened on the doorstep of that church with Jonesborough townsfolk gaping down at him, he was unaware of. But he did recall occasional moments of consciousness when he was being hauled along over the big man's shoulder in the middle of the night. He'd tried to look around but found it too painful to move his neck enough to see much.

He knew why he had been hanged. What he didn't know was why he had been rescued, or just who had done it.

Chapter Seventeen

"There ain't no such thing, you know," said Maggie Harkin to her brother. "You sound like a fool, saying you saw Loafhead carrying a man into town in the night."

Michael glared at his sister. No such thing as Loafhead? That certainly didn't match what she had told him time and again as she mocked him for his bed-wetting.

"You'd best not say anything like that to anybody besides me and Mother," said Maggie. "The whole town will laugh at you."

"I *ain't* saying it to nobody else. Even though it's the truth. I know what I saw."

"I know what *I* see right now. A fool. A fool who believes bogeyman tales are real."

"I got you figured out, Maggie," Michael said. "You change your story to be whatever suits you, as long as it makes me feel bad or look bad or whatever it may be you want. Next time you're trying to scare me into not pissing my bed, I bet you'll tell me Loafhead is real *then!*"

"It's just an old legend, Michael. You're old enough you should be able to tell a legend from a true story, even if I tease you with it. You're a little fool."

"Bible says if you call somebody a fool, you're in danger of hellfire!"

"Bible also says you ought to tell the truth. And it's the truth that you're a fool, and I'm telling it."

"I ain't a fool. Old Mr. Crawley tells me I'm one of the smartest young men he's known."

"Yes, and then he tells you another Loafhead tale and you run off believing it, and he laughs at you behind your back."

"No, he don't."

"Yes, he does!"

"You're lying. You're a no-good liar!"

"Well, you're a bed-pisser, and that's *sure* no lie. And everybody in town knows it and laughs at you for that, too."

Michael's rage, hot inside his chest, threatened to erupt in tears and shouts. He determined not to let that happen, not to let Maggie get the best of him.

"I ain't talking to you no more," he said. "I'm going to go down and talk to Mr. Crawley, and just ask him straight out if

Loafhead is real. Because I can tell you, sister, that whether there's a Loafhead or not, I did see somebody who sure looked like him carrying that hurt fellow into town. Big old ugly knot on his head, all bulging out . . . You'd have said it was Loafhead, too, if you'd seen him."

"Well, I didn't see him because I wasn't up roaming around because I'd peed on myself in my sleep. I don't do that. I'm not a pissy baby like you are."

"I had got up so I could go to the outhouse. That's when I saw him going down the street."

"Loafhead, you mean."

"Whoever it was. A big man with a lump on his brow."

"Then you peed on yourself from being scared."

"Well . . . yes."

Maggie shook her head and sighed loudly. "That's no better than peeing your bed," she said. "Maybe it's worse. Pissy baby! Pissy baby!"

"Don't you say that!" he shouted in her face.

She backed away. "Your breath smells bad, *pissy baby.*"

"I'm going to knock your teeth out one of these days, Maggie. I swear I will! And if there really is a Loafhead, I'll send him to get *you!* I will! I'll really do it, Maggie!"

"And after that what will you do? Piss your pants again, pissy baby?" She laughed scornfully and marched away from him.

The breeze was up and pleasantly cool as Michael strode down the street toward the silversmithy of Ben Crawley. Walking hard and fast helped Michael burn out some of the fury he felt toward his sister. He wished she wasn't able to make him so mad. That anger gave her control over him.

The little shop housing Crawley's smithy stood on the right side of the street near the base of a hill on the edge of town. Michael turned down a little alley and circled around to the rear doorway, knowing it would be open because Crawley loved a good breeze. That back door was Michael's usual portal into the smithy, where he enjoyed studying the fifty or more hammers of various sizes and shapes that hung on Crawley's rear wall, above the smithy bench where he did his work.

Not that Crawley did much of that anymore. When he had lived in Virginia, on the edge of Williamsburg, he had been a busy man, some of his work making its way to the cabinets and tables of the governor's palace. Wealthy buyers frequented his premises. He'd done well for himself there, but worn himself out, too. When he'd come west over the mountains, he'd been happy to leave hard work behind and to content himself with sitting in his mostly idle shop and talking with the citizens who came by to enjoy the music of his accent. On rare occasions he would work, if he felt like it, or if there was a job to be done. In an area where most people had little money and modest possessions, a silversmith's services were not much in demand.

Michael slipped through the rear door at just the right moment. Crawley was talking with someone in the front area, which was separated from the work area by a tall, solid-backed shelf displaying some of Crawley's best work. Michael sneaked to the corner of the shelf and peeked around into the front of the shop. There was Crawley in his usual chair, side toward Michael, and before him a stranger who had been pointed out to Michael, by his mother, as the famous hunter-explorer people sometimes called Edohi, but whose true name was Crawford Fain.

He had caught the men in midconversation. Crawley was saying, "I am astonished to learn that so famous an American as you, Mr. Fain, come not merely from a different land, but also the same land of my own origin, and the same region of that land. Skellenwood Forest is the soil where my roots first planted themselves."

Fain nodded. "As did mine. And not merely the region, but within the forest itself. My father was the huntsman of Skellenwood, and our home was built within Skellendale Cavern."

"Blast me! Within the same cave that was the legendary home of the fearsome Loafhead?"

On the other side of the shelf wall, Michael stifled a gasp. Keen-eared Fain glanced back that way, but persuaded himself he had heard nothing.

"The very cave," he said.

Crawley laughed. "And did you ever encounter that ogre?"

"Knew him personally."

Crawley laughed again. Michael bit his knuckle, trying to absorb what he was hearing.

"Whatever do you mean, Mr. Fain?" Crawley asked.

At that moment, Michael shifted position and his foot slid beneath his weight and bumped the base of the shelf. Fain came around the shelf.

"Hello, young man," he said.

"Hello, sir." Michael reddened at having been caught as an eavesdropper.

Crawley came around as well with slow and stiff old-man movements. "Michael? I didn't know you were there, lad. Do you know Mr. Fain?"

"I know who he is. Everybody in town's been talking about Edohi being here."

"Why are you hiding like this?"

"I came in the back door and heard you speaking, and didn't want to interrupt."

Crawley looked at Fain. "Well raised, this lad is. And his sister Maggie as well. I delight in their visits here to my smithy."

"A pleasure to meet you, Michael," Fain said.

Crawley brought his visitors back around to the front of the shop. Michael took his usual place in a corner, seated on a log section substituting for a stool. Crawley said, "Speaking of what you saw, it so happens that Mr. Fain and I were talking about something I have told you stories about before, Michael."

Michael said, "Loafhead. I heard you talking."

Crawley said to Fain, "The question of Loafhead's reality has been a concern to this young man. Am I right, Michael?"

The boy nodded abashedly.

"Michael," Crawley said, "I have told you of being born in the climes of Loafhead's district . . . but I have learned that Mr. Fain here has done me one better. He lived within the very forest of Loafhead, Skellenwood. In a house built within that very huge cavern where the ogre was born and lived."

Michael saw in his memory the figure with the distorted brow, moving down the dark Jonesborough street bearing the body of a senseless man. Overwhelmed, he had to ask: "Sir, Mr. Fain, is he real? Is he real? Loafhead?"

"There is more than one kind of 'real,' young man. The kind of 'real' that makes you afraid of Loafhead, the walking, living, breathing kind of real . . . he isn't that kind of real. Not anymore."

"He is dead?"

"He died years ago."

"How do you know?"

"I do know. Know it absolutely. You can trust me on that, son. I promise."

"But he was alive once . . . He was real?"

"There was once one who some people called Loafhead. He was no ogre, just a man. A man who knew misfortune in his time and was forced to live mostly apart from other people."

"Was there . . ." Michael cupped his hand

over his eye and brow, imitating the deformity he had seen on the man on the midnight street. "Was there this?"

"There was. There from his birth. He covered it almost always beneath a cloth mask worn over his head."

Crawley listened intently. These were things he had not heard before about the legend from his homeland.

"Loafhead died in his cave?"

"Not in his cave. He died here, in America. He came here aboard a ship. He lived in America for several years, and took to the woods just like he had done in his homeland."

Crawley was silent, absorbing lore that to him was as new as it was to the boy. Crawley had known the tales of Loafhead for years, but none of them had spoken of his death or of a journey to America. Was Fain spinning tales of his own creation, or were there parts of this legend Crawley simply had missed?

"Mr. Fain, could there have been more than one Loafhead? Maybe another one living in America? Maybe still alive today?"

"To my knowledge, son, there was only one who was ever called by that name. He lived; he died. He was a human. Then he was a legend. The human passed; the legend went on. Loafhead is not real, not anymore. I can tell you that, son, with great assurance."

■ ■ ■ ■

Part Four: Crale

■ ■ ■ ■

Chapter Eighteen

Littleton leaned back on the bench and rested his shoulders against the wall of the newest incarnation of Ott Dixon's traveling makeshift tavern. With a grimace of effort and some pain, he hefted his peg leg up across his knee so the drunken woman near him could see it better.

"I never saw a real peg leg before," she said. "I've seen men with crutches and walking sticks and such, but never a wooden leg. She reached out toward it, hesitated, then touched it and drew her hand back as if fearful she had violated some limit of acceptability. "Is it hard to walk on it, Mr. Kirk?"

"Easier all the time," Littleton said, his own voice slurred by the effects of rum. "The longer I wear it, the easier it gets. Pinches sometimes, though."

"How did you lose that part of your leg?"

Littleton drew in a deep breath and put a

cocky expression on his face. "Cut it off. Pulled out my knife and just sawed it right off."

The woman gasped and put her hand to the base of her throat. "Oh my . . . oh . . . oh my!"

"Didn't have much choice about it," Littleton went on. "I was trapped down in a hole in the ground. A sorry scoundrel had pushed me into it, and my foot and the bottom part of that leg were stuck in a crack in the rock, and already shattered up and ruined. Even if I'd been able to pull free, which I couldn't, I'd have lost the leg anyway. Somebody would have had to cut it off, or it would have mortified and rotted off. . . . Only thing I could do was cut myself free."

"How could you endure such pain, Mr. Kirk?"

Littleton smiled at her. "You can call me Lyle. I can endure a lot. I'm a strong man."

She smiled weakly. "You must be! You must be so very, very strong!" Then a long sigh, hidden poorly.

She asked, "Who pushed you into the hole in the ground?"

"Man name of Gilly. Worthless piece of rubbish . . . scrawny rat of a man. Outlaw and murderer. His intention was to murder me."

"Men like that come to bad ends. That's what my papa used to tell me. Bad ends."

Littleton wondered if her papa had ever warned her about the ends that could came to women who drank too much liquor and talked too freely to strangers. He hoped not. At the moment, he was looking for a woman without scruples, without inhibition, without morals or fear of consequences.

Littleton said, "Gilly will find his bad end, and bad it truly will be. I already have something in mind for him, me and old peg leg here." He rapped the wooden leg with his knuckle.

"What are you going to do?"

"Something Gilly would never forget the rest of his life . . . though he won't have a 'rest of his life' ahead of him at that point."

"You've got to tell me!"

Littleton shrugged. "If I tell you, maybe there's a thing or two you could do in return for me. Kind of a thank-you." It was as subtle as Littleton was capable of being.

Her expression rapidly transformed into one of smiling comprehension.

"My cabin is just up the hill from here," she said.

Littleton chuckled, taking another swig of

rum. "I don't even know your name," he said.

"It's Rachel. But it don't matter what my name is."

"I think I'm going to like you, Rachel."

"Oh, Mr. Kirk, Lyle, I *know* you're going to like me! I'm going to make sure of it!"

"Then let me show you Gilly's 'bad end,' " Littleton said. He drew out his knife and pressed the tip of it beneath the metal band the smith had made him after the leg cracked and split at the roadside burial. The band held the split wooden leg in one piece. Littleton worked the band loose and slipped it off. Then, with the splintered section of the leg swinging off to the side almost as if on a hinge, he showed Rachel what he had in mind for Gilly, whenever he got his hands on him.

Littleton had never had much attention from women, except those willing to exchange feminine affections for money. Thus he was surprised when it began to appear that Rachel's willingness to be with him bore no financial motivation. She simply accepted his advances. He hardly knew what to think of it.

Once the iron band was back on the peg leg so that the prosthetic would function again as a single piece, Littleton left Dixon's with his female companion and followed her as fast as his handicap would allow as she took them up a trail through thick woods behind Dixon's tavern. Watching her move along in front of him, he noticed an oddity in her gait, a limp that revealed that she, too, was somewhat lame. Her right leg was slightly shorter than her left, giving her a decided stutter in her stride. Suddenly, Littleton's pride in himself for having attracted the affection of this woman lessened. Might she simply be paying attention to him because he and she were both cripples?

The trail narrowed as it climbed and they passed through a laurel thicket that crowded in on both sides. Beyond the laurel was a clearing and in it a small cabin. Smoke poured from the chimney and Rachel came to a halt, Littleton coming panting up beside her.

"Oh, I'd forgotten," she said, watching the smoke curl up.

"What is it?" he asked.

"There's someone still here. I thought he'd be gone by now. I'd forgotten he was here at all."

Littleton wondered if maybe Rachel was merely a sporting woman after all. Not many women would take a man into their home overnight and then simply forget about him.

"I reckon I should go," Littleton said, annoyed that he'd been forced into an uphill trek, a difficult task for a man on a wooden leg, only to have it lead to nothing but having to turn around and retreat the way he'd come.

Rachel started to speak, but stopped when the cabin door opened and a sandy-haired man stepped out. He was average in every way, from height to size to appearance. On his nondescript face was a beaming smile.

"Good day to you, Rachel, and to you as well, sir!" He advanced at a fast clip, hand out.

Littleton, accustomed to a life of dodging almost everyone and of mistrusting strangers, reflexively wanted to draw back from this oncoming incarnation of friendliness and good humor. He wished for half a moment that he had kept his rifle with him, as he usually did, rather than having accepted Dixon's invitation to store the weapon with Dixon's own guns inside the tavern. But as the man reached him, grin intact and with nothing threatening visible in his demeanor, Dixon decided there was nothing to be concerned about. He put out his own broad hand and engulfed that of the stranger, who said, "James Corey, sir. I'm pleased to make your acquaintance."

"Lyle Kirk," said Littleton. "Pleased as well."

Corey pumped vigorously at Littleton's hand. Littleton looked over at Rachel, thinking of what surely would have happened with her had this stranger not appeared, and wondering why all his luck seemed to inevitably turn bad.

When Corey learned that his new companion, "Kirk," had been traveling through the region, his interest in him intensified, and questions began.

"I've been on the move myself," Corey said. "Trying to find my wife, who has gone missing. Her name is Deborah and her hair is yellow. Her real identifying mark, though, is her left eye, which has a streak of gray — here." Corey pulled down his lower eyelid and pointed at the bottom portion of his iris.

Littleton stared past Corey, his mind pushed back to the day he had lost his leg and the night he spent on a pallet in the home of Crawford Fain at Fort Edohi. Corey's words brought to mind things he had overheard Fain talking about in the darkness to the other, younger man who had been there that night.

"There's somebody else besides you looking for your wife," he said. "Crawford Fain. The one they call Edohi."

"Edohi?" Corey frowned. "How do you know that?"

"I heard Edohi himself talking about it to another man when I was at his fort. He's been hired by someone to find her. I don't know who hired him. If he said, I didn't hear it."

Corey's expression darkened. "Who would hire the famous Edohi to find *my* woman? And why?"

"I don't know, sir. I heard what I heard, and no more. But I saw a yellow-haired woman with a marked eye myself, once. At Crockett Spring on the Holston."

"She was well?"

"Seemed to be, as I recall."

Corey was different after that, the light friendliness replaced by an intense, brooding manner. He paced incessantly and quizzed Littleton nearly to the point of rudeness in hope of figuring out more regarding why the famed woodsman Edohi would be seeking his woman.

When Corey left Rachel's cabin to resume his journeying, Littleton went with him. This partnering up was not planned or thoroughly talked out; it was just a natural progression of events and conversation. Littleton had lost interest in Rachel, who seemed more plain every time he glanced at her, and who was out of reach, anyway, with another man hovering about. Having a traveling companion actually become more appealing than the idea of a dalliance with a plain-faced, lame slattern.

They retrieved their horses from Dixon's horse pen, and Littleton's rifle from the tavern, and took an eastward route. They went east because Corey had heard a rumor of late that Deborah might have been seen in the vicinity of the town of Jonesborough.

They had traveled no more than two miles from Dixon's tavern when they met a man on the trail, walking back toward them. The man carried a small jug and had it tilted up to his lips when first they saw him.

"Thirsty gent," said Corey as he and Littleton reined to a stop.

Littleton was looking intently at the man on the road. The uplifted jug partially blocked his view of the face, but when at last the man lowered the jug, Littleton made a little noise of surprise.

"What is it, Lyle?" asked Corey.

"Do you know who that is?" Littleton asked.

"Never seen him before that I know of."

"I have. Last time I saw him was at Fort Edohi. He was outside it, up on a platform, preaching to the crowd."

"That man's a preacher?"

"That man is *the* preacher! That's old Camp Meeting Abner! Abner Bledsoe himself! You know of him, don't you?"

"Course! Everybody knows about him. Your religious folk will travel miles just to hear him jabber. But that can't be him, not drinking like that. That wouldn't be his way. He preaches hard against drunkenness."

"It's him. No doubt about it at all. That's Bledsoe."

The man on the road hadn't noticed the two riders until he'd finished his long draw on the jug. Now he looked at them with an expression of worry and the manner of one who might turn and run at any moment. But he didn't run, and Littleton put his horse into motion and rode slowly up to the man.

"Good day, preacher," he said.

The man gave a very nervous chuckle. "Preacher? Why do you call me that, sir? I am no preacher!"

"I know who you are, Bledsoe. I can tell it from your crossed eyes, and I've heard your voice before, too. Heard it while you was preaching."

The man's lips moved without sound, a look of distress came onto his face, and he stepped back. The jug slipped from his fingers and struck a stone embedded in the ground at his feet. Shattering, the jug spilled its last dwindling contents into the dirt.

"Confound and blast!" the drunken man said. "I've lost the rest of my . . . water."

Littleton wrinkled his nose. "Might be for the best, sir. From the smell of it, I think your water has had some corn get in it and go to whiskey."

"Whiskey! No, sir, I think not. Why would a man such as myself, a man of God, partake in whiskey?"

"Oh, so despite what you said, you *are* a preacher!"

"I am . . . I . . . I mean to say . . ." He let the thought die. Then, to Littleton's surprise, the man's eyes grew livid and moist. He was beginning to quietly weep.

"Sir, it was just one small jug," Littleton said, feeling uncharacteristically empathetic toward another person.

Corey drew nearer, "I'll go back and fetch you another from Dixon's, if you want me to."

The older man shook his head and stared at the ground. "No. Best I just do without.

A man in my position has no business drinking himself drunken, anyway. It'll ruin me if word of such got out."

"You're Bledsoe, ain't you," said Littleton, not as a question but a statement.

Bledsoe surrendered, and dodged no more. "I am. And I've backslidden bad, my friends. Turned away from the right to embrace the wrong. The very kind of thing I've condemned in others I've done myself." He paused, frowning in thought. "And for the first time, I think I understand a little better those who fall prey to such things. I have maybe been too harsh a judge in my time."

"Well, sir, one thing I can tell you: You'll face no judgment from the likes of me. Nor, I suspect, from my friend Mr. Corey there. Neither of us is a stranger to sin, nor prone to wag a finger at others."

Bledsoe swabbed his face with the heel of his right hand. "I am grateful for such lack of condemnation, sir. You are a man of kind heart."

Littleton chuckled. "That's me: one kind heart, ten good fingers, and five toes."

Bledsoe, noting the wooden leg, laughed at Littleton's joke. "You are a big man, sir, to laugh so at yourself. I'm afraid I, for one, have lost much of the ability to laugh at all in the past several days."

"May I ask you what's happened, Reverend?"

Bledsoe seemed to wilt. His voice was weak and trembling as he replied, "A woman, sir. A woman."

"Somebody you met?"

Bledsoe shook his head. "If you mean recently, no. She traveled with me, helped me with a portion of my meeting presentations. . . ."

"The Reese woman."

"You know of her?"

"I know she was generally part of your camp meetings. You'd tell her story and she'd sit there and loll her mouth open for folks to see where her old daddy carved out her tongue. Right?"

"Right indeed. But she's departed from me. Took my money and abandoned me. Just a common harlot and thief she turned out to be. Treated me easy indeed."

"Well, at least she couldn't jabber at you like a lot of women do, talking your ear off."

"You might have been surprised, sir. She was more capable of talk than most might have guessed."

"Well, sir, I'm sorry you were ill used by her. Such is the way of too many women. It's a damned shame."

"It is, sir. And ill used I was, and that after I had shared so much, so freely, with that woman. I had truly come to love her, and I thought she loved me. But she proved a common jilt."

"Hell with her, Reverend. Go ahead and say it. Hell with her!"

Bledsoe set his jaw and stared up at a treetop. "Hell with her," he slurred drunkenly. Then louder, "Hell with her!"

"That's the spirit, sir! You keep that spirit and you'll forget about her before you know it." Littleton grinned. "And you keep on drinking of the kind of spirits you dropped on the ground there, you'll forget her faster yet."

"I must say, I wish I hadn't spilled it," Bledsoe said.

"There'll be more. We're traveling to Jonesborough. If you wish to join us, you are welcome. Have you got a horse, a wagon?"

"What she didn't take, I sold. I am afoot. Like the very Son of Man, I have no place even to lay my head."

"Well, we'll find you a horse along the way somewhere. You see this horse of mine?" Littleton looked around as if the woods had ears. "Stole it. From Fort Edohi."

"There was a time I might have railed at

you for such a sin," Bledsoe said. "But I find now the sermons have mostly gone out of me."

"Let me ask you something, preacher. Was that woman really Molly Reese?"

"What do you think?"

"I think no."

"You think correctly. She was a jilt in more ways than one." They traveled, Bledsoe walking along in silence beside Littleton's horse. Finally he sighed loudly and said, "I was a duplicitous and fraudulent man in so many ways, Mr., uh . . ."

"Kirk. Lyle Kirk."

"Mr. Kirk. Quite the bearer of false witness, to speak bluntly about myself. Yet I had persuaded myself I was doing the true work of God . . . most of the time, in any case. I suppose I was a deceiver of myself as well as of the congregation of believers."

"You're just a sinner like all of us," said Littleton.

"The chief of sinners, as Paul called himself. Do you know, sir, that I actually shot my own brother? Another man of the cloth?"

"No! Did you kill him?"

"He was alive when I left him. I don't know if he survived after."

"You hear that, Corey? Camp Meeting

Abner here shot his own brother!"

"I heard him say it."

Littleton reached down and gave the preacher a slap on the shoulder. "Drinking, shooting folks, telling false tales to the righteous — hell, you're *my* kind of preacher, Abner! God bless you, sir! God bless you!"

"How did you lose your leg, Mr. Kirk?"

"Call me Lyle. I cut it off, preacher. Stuck down in a pit on a hillside while you were preaching over at Fort Edohi. The leg was wedged and ruined, so I cut it off just to be able to get out."

"Well, brand my backside! What a story, Lyle! What a story!"

"I'm full of them, preacher. Every now and then I even tell a true one."

"Like the one you just told?"

"Yes, sir. That one was as true as gospel."

Bledsoe was staring at the wooden peg leg. "You cut off that leg even as I was preaching, you say?"

"Yes, sir."

"Tell me how you managed to get out of that pit with one leg gone."

"Well, sir, I had help. A young fellow appeared at the top of that pit and reached in to help me out. If he hadn't come when he did, I might be in that hole yet, rotting like a throwed-out tater. It was nigh as if he was an . . ."

"What were you going to say?"

"That it was nigh as if he was an angel sent to rescue me." Littleton laughed. "So in some ways my story ain't too far removed from the tale of Molly Reese."

Bledsoe stopped in his tracks and began rubbing his chin. "You are right, Lyle. Right indeed."

"Change a few things around and I could just about do the same thing she was doing at your meetings . . . except all I'd have to do is just show my cut-off leg, not hang my mouth open like she did."

"Lyle, it may be that *you* are my angel, sent to my rescue. There may be some possibilities left for this old preacher yet! The Molly Reese business was growing stale, anyway."

"Preacher, I don't know about doing such a *public* deception." Littleton was thinking about the possibility of being recognized as he stood before one of Bledsoe's big camp meeting crowds.

"If I may say so, you don't seem the kind of man to suffer greatly from moral qualms, Lyle. And if you are, let me assure you from my own experience that those qualms, like wind on the belly, pass in their time. Ha!"

"Truth is . . ." Littleton looked over and summoned Corey to draw closer so he could hear as well, and looked around to make sure there were no unnoticed listeners about. He had just decided to make a sensitive revelation: "Truth is, my name ain't Lyle Kirk. Keep it under your hats, men, but my name is Jeremiah Littleton. And a lot of folks know that name, and would like to see the neck of Jeremiah Littleton wearing a rope cravat, if you take my meaning. I've done a lot of crimes, men. Stealing, highway robbery, fighting, stabbing, shooting . . . and one of my gang did a murder not long back. I'm a man who has to hide himself, not one who can stand out in front of a crowd of hundreds of people where I could be recognized. I have no ambition to dance with my feet not scraping dirt."

Bledsoe was crestfallen. "What a shame it is. If only there were a way to make you difficult to recognize, to make you not look like the man people know, Lyle . . . er, Jeremiah."

"Keep on calling me Lyle. I don't need to have my true name being called. The wrong ears might hear."

"It would be easy to change his appearance," said Corey. "How long you worn them whiskers, Lyle?"

"Years now. Ever since I was old enough to grow them."

"Shave them off and you'd be a different man then. Starve yourself awhile and you'd be half the size you are. Not a soul would know you."

The spark was returning to Bledsoe's countenance as he took that in. "Mr. Kirk, you who were rescued by an angel who appeared at your moment of need, summoned to the scene through the power of my preaching in the meadow nearby, you and I, sir, could do some lucrative work together. What say thee?"

Littleton rubbed his hand through his whiskers, trying to imagine how it would feel to be beardless. "These whiskers do sweat me fierce in the heat of summer." He grinned at Bledsoe. "Let us see what we can do as a team, me and you, Reverend Bledsoe."

The preacher laughed joyfully for the first time in days.

Chapter Nineteen

Micah Tate had the attention of Benjamin Crawley the moment he walked in the silversmithy carrying the stone he had been presented at the Colyer house where he and Titus had taken young Mary Deveraux after the massacre at her home in the Cumberland Settlements.

Crawley rose from his chair with his eyes locked on the stone. "Hello, sir," Micah said. "My name is Micah Tate and I came to town with Crawford Fain. I have here —"

"Yes, I can see," Crawley interrupted, reaching out and taking the stone from Micah's hands. He hefted it, held it in a shaft of sunlight from the window, and put his eye so close to it that eyeball nearly touched stone.

"That stone belongs to a family named Colyer over in the Cumberland country, but the stone itself came from a man out of

North Carolina, or so the Colyers told me. They don't know what it is, nor do I, but I'm wondering if it might be an ore of some sort."

"I believe, Mr. Tate, that there is gold in this stone."

"Gold?"

"It will take more time and work to know, but that is what it appears to be to me."

"If there is gold there, can you get it out?"

"I can. If there is sufficient quantity, I can create an ingot. I have only one question. If this stone is not yours, will there be objection from those who own it to me melting out the metal?"

"It was given to me for the purpose of finding what it is and what the value might be," Micah replied. "The only way to do that, I am sure, is to give you freedom to do what you must."

"That is sufficient for me, then."

"How long do you need?"

"Come back in two, three days. Or if I finish sooner, I'll look you up at Stuart's. That is where Edohi's band is lodging, is it not?"

"Indeed. Very good, sir. Gold . . . I'm blasted!"

Two days later, the silversmith would be holding in his hand a gleaming, four-inch ingot of gold, marveling at its beauty and trying his best to calculate its worth.

Micah said his good day to Crawley and left by the front door. Distracted by the thought of gold, he paid insufficient heed to his movement and plowed straight into a young woman walking past the smithy. She staggered under the impact out into the dirt street and went down hard, tripping over her own feet. Micah landed in the dirt beside her.

He was up again in a moment, bursting with apologies, and put out his hand to help the woman up. She ignored the hand and bounded to her feet on her own, spryly, and glared at him.

"What's wrong with you, boy? Don't you know how to watch where you're going?"

Boy. He felt the sting of the word, especially coming from a young woman. "I'm mighty sorry, miss. It was my fault. Please pardon me."

"Ma'am, is this man bothering you?"

The voice came from elsewhere on the street and caused both Micah and the young woman to turn. Titus Fain was striding in their direction, a reproving look on his face as he eyed Micah.

"Titus, I caused a problem here without

meaning to. I came out of the smithy there and didn't give sufficient heed to where I was going. Knocked this young woman down, and myself, too."

Titus looked intently into the face of the woman, who was well featured and maybe twenty years old. "Are you hurt?" Titus asked.

She smiled. "I am well enough. Startled and a bit jolted is all. But your gentlemanly behavior restores my cheerful frame of mind."

"I said I was sorry," Micah protested feebly from the side. "*I'm* a gentleman!"

"A gentleman watches where his big canoe-sized feet carry him to begin with," Titus said. "Miss, my name is Titus Fain, and I am a visitor to town. I'm forced to admit that this stumble-foot here is my friend, Micah Tate. I assure you that, despite all appearances, he isn't as bad as he seems. Just not particularly smart, that's all."

"I see." She smiled more broadly. "Fain, did you say? Are you the son of Crawford Fain, or Edohi?"

"I am."

She put out her hand. "My name is Amy DeVault. I am pleased to know you, Mr. Fain. I had heard your father was in town with a band of travelers."

"Pleased to know you, too, miss," said Titus.

"And I'm also pleased to know you," Micah threw in. "And I *am* sorry about what I done."

She glanced at him without interest and gave a curt nod. Finished with him.

"It's a notable event when my father arrives in any town or settlement," said Titus. "When I arrive it's not a matter worth much notice."

"You have been noticed, I assure you," Amy said boldly. "I have several friends here in Jonesborough, all of them young unmarried women as I am, and when you rode into our street here for the first time, you perhaps did not realize you possessed an audience watching from behind cabin window shutters."

Titus, never much aware of his own looks and qualities, actually blushed. Micah grunted with annoyance and strode swiftly away, as unheeding as before, and nearly ran into another woman, this one a large matron of about sixty. He dodged her at the last moment, drawing from her a startled little cry. There was no collision, though Micah did trip on a mounting block and fell clumsily on his face. He rose looking like a man who knew full well he'd made a fool of himself, and continued down the street a little slower and more watchfully.

"How did you end up with a man like *that* as a friend?" Amy DeVault asked.

"Despite what you've seen, he's a good man. Clearheaded and capable. I'd as soon have Micah Tate with me on a hunt or on the trail as any man I know. You mustn't judge him from one accidental run-in on the street."

"I'll take your word for it, sir."

"Let me ask you something, miss. Might you have a relative by the name of Andrew DeVault? Over on the Cumberland?"

"My brother, sir. Coming here to visit me with his new bride any day now. I am keeping a watch for his arrival."

"I met him, with his Cumberland Scouts. Good man."

"He is indeed."

Abner Bledsoe was in a rage. "No printer in this town? Well, I'm confounded. How is a man to obtain what I need if there is no printer to do the work?"

Constance Harkin gave the complainer as sympathetic a look as she could muster, but her thought was that she wished he would follow the pattern of his peg-legged traveling companion and remain calm and quiet.

It was certainly not her fault that Jonesborough had yet to attract a printer, not her fault that this new-arrival preacher could not have broadsides printed to advertise his upcoming camp meeting.

What did a preacher want with broadsides, anyway? It seemed to Constance that a preaching event shouldn't be promoted in the same way as a traveling piece of playacting or music. Shouldn't it be, well, *above* that sort of triviality? Especially given that this particular preacher had already made a name for himself and surely could draw a crowd merely by word of mouth.

Constance drew upon her own natural propensity for diplomacy and found a way to express those thoughts to Abner Bledsoe without sounding offensive or insulting.

Bledsoe sat down wearily on a nearby stool in the common room of the Harkin Inn. "You are a wise woman, ma'am," he said. "But you misunderstand my needs. My desire to find a printer is not to print announcements, but to provide myself a text printed large for my aging eyes to read."

"You read your sermons?"

"Only one portion of my presentation is read. In the past that portion — which I finally mostly learned by heart through sheer repetition — was the famous story of

Molly Reese of London. Are you familiar with that oft-told tale?"

"I am, sir. A remarkable story, though I admit to a certain degree of doubt as to whether her rescue was the result of an actual angelic act, or something with a more earthly explanation."

Bledsoe waved his hand dismissively. "It doesn't matter now. Though for quite a long time I provided Molly Reese with a marvelous platform to share her story, she has chosen to abandon my holy work. But thanks to my new friend Mr. Kirk and his equally remarkable story, Miss Reese can safely be replaced and forgotten. Mr. Kirk also has seen the rescuing hand of God as administered through angelic visitation. In the very tragedy of being forced to lose a portion of his own leg, he attained the rescue of his life through the intervention of an angel drawn to his aid by the sound of my own nearby preaching."

"That is . . . extraordinary."

Littleton, who was nearby, cleared his throat and spoke, though the act drew a look of remonstrance from Bledsoe, who clearly was enjoying monopolizing the attention of the young widow innkeeper. Littleton, who had shaved off his whiskers, was beginning to lose weight, and looked very little like his former, infamous self, said, "I fell victim to a ruffian who caused me to fall bodily into a pit that was surely the mouth of hell, trapping and ruining my left leg and forcing me to take a knife to my own flesh to free myself. But even after that I remained trapped in the pit and certainly unable to climb. And though there was one of Reverend Bledsoe's camp meetings taking place nearby, no one could hear my call for help." Littleton paused and glanced at the preacher. "No one but God, who hears even the silent cry of a worm. And he sent to me a helper, an angel in the form of a young man, who drew me from that pit and carried me on his own back to where help could be found. My life was saved, just as Molly Reese's was saved so many years before, by the power of one of God's servant spirits."

Bledsoe took advantage of the pause to jump in and take over again. "And it is *that* story, Mrs. Harkin, that I am most anxious to have printed in large letters, so that I may read it with ease in the pulpit. My eyes are not what they once were, you see, and like St. Paul, I need the benefit of large letters that can be clearly seen and read by dim eyes in the even dimmer light of torches."

"Sir, if it is merely a legible and large text

you require, we can provide that to you here, without need of a printer. My young daughter has a most excellent hand and can produce for you a piece of text to equal or exceed the quality and usefulness of anything you would obtain from the operator of a printing press."

Bledsoe pondered it a moment, and nodded. "Ma'am, you yourself are surely an angel sent to help God's servant in his time of need! I would be most happy to accept such assistance from your lass. Can she write it from my spoken dictation, or need I write it for her to copy?"

"You may speak it, if you can do so at a slow enough pace to allow her to keep up."

"God's blessings on you, ma'am. You will see rewards eternal for this aid you are giving an old servant of the Most High."

"I am pleased to be such a help, sir, as I know my Maggie will be, too."

The process started that night. Bledsoe paced back and forth in the front room, young Maggie seated at the table with quill, ink, and paper, scribing away steadily but at a pace not quite satisfactory to Bledsoe, who continually swept in and leaned over to examine the girl's meticulous work. "Your letters are becoming progressively smaller," he said more than once, inaccurately. "They must be a thumb-width tall if I am to see them, and you cannot use narrow lines. The aim is to produce a text I can read from some distance, in imperfect and flickering light."

Maggie struggled with her patience, and with a vague sense of discomfort that the preacher roused in her, a feeling that something was just not right about the man.

At length she realized what it was, and asked her mother about it that night before retiring. "Mother, should a preacher have the smell of whiskey on his breath? Because the Reverend Abner Bledsoe does. He would leave the room from time to time, saying he was going off to pray, then come back in and his breath would smell stronger of it. Is that a bad thing?"

"I can only hope you were mistaken, dear, because yes, it is a bad thing. A man of God should not be given to much liquor. But preachers, I suppose, are nothing but men, just like other men. And men are often weak and prone to sin."

"I think Reverend Bledsoe might be like that."

"Perhaps so."

Of the three outlaws who had hanged Gilly,

Bart Clemons had been the most unsettled and repelled by the process. Yet he was drawn back to the scene days later, wondering whether Gilly might still be hanging there as a bird-pecked corpse. It was the strongest of unwanted compulsions. He simply had to *know.*

He had no reason to expect the body would not be there. The hanging had taken place in a remote area, away from common trails and roads, hidden by forest and undergrowth. Most likely Gilly was still dangling, weathered and decaying, a sight Clemons dreaded seeing and was sure he would never forget after he did. Still he was driven to go there, because however horrible Gilly's remains might be up on that rope, they were there because of what Clemons and his partners had done, and he, for one, could not shy away from it. Clemons knew he would never rest as well again until he had faced the full, sickening results of their act.

As he clambered up a timbered hillside and began to recognize that he was indeed at the right spot and growing very near to where Gilly had to be, Clemons began to brace himself for the stench of death. By now Gilly would surely be growing quickly ripe, baked in the sun, infiltrated by maggots, and damaged by the carrion birds of the forest. As bad as the sight promised to be, the smell would probably be worse.

Yet as he neared the place, Clemons smelled nothing. The breeze was quite fresh and clean, though it blew from the direction of the place where Gilly had died. Clemons paused repeatedly, sniffing the air and wondering whether his sense of smell was failing him. Surely there would have to be a stench!

There was none, though, and when at last he reached the location and, after bracing himself, strode boldly into the clearing to face the results of what he and the others had done, there was nothing to be seen. Nothing but an empty noose, moving slightly in the wind. No corpse swinging, no corpse on the ground, and judging from the lack of smell, no corpse dragged into the woods nearby, either.

Gilly was gone. It was as simple as that. They'd left him hanging dead — for surely he'd been dead, with his eyes bulging and unblinking and his tongue thrust out between his swelling lips, an image Clemons could not shake from his mind — and yet he was gone. As if his body had simply turned to smoke and blown away.

Or been carried away by something or

someone.

Fear overcame Clemons. If someone had found the hanging body, there might be interest out there in finding the responsible parties. He glanced around as if suddenly the forest around him might belch forth an entire posse of vengeful regulators, coming to get him and punish him for what he, Sikes, and Jones had done to their old partner in crime.

He fully grasped for the first time the fact that it didn't really matter that Gilly had deserved the hanging they gave him. The hanging party had not been constables or sheriffs or officers of the court, carrying out a prescribed sentence of law. The hangmen had been common criminals themselves, acting on their own.

Clemons pondered this, froze where he was a few moments, then turned and ran into the woods as if hounds were upon him. In his mind was an image not of Gilly, but himself, hanging from a noose with his eyes bulging and tongue protruding.

He ran a long way before exhaustion brought him to the ground. As he had done before when they had hanged Gilly, he retched violently.

Chapter Twenty

"I have somewhere I want to go, and I'd like you to go with me," said Crawford Fain to his son.

"Where is that, Pap?" Titus replied. The pair were walking in the vicinity of the cabin of Christopher Taylor on the outskirts of town. The Taylor house had stood nearly a decade, one of the oldest residences in the backcountry. The late lawyer John Harkin had used it for a partial template in designing his own house and inn.

"Well, it just came to me yesterday that it's been a long time since I've been this far to the east, and there's a reasonable good chance I'll never be this far over again. And I've got an old friend I ain't seen for the longest time, living in the Doe River country. You ever heard me mention McCoy Atley? Old trader amongst the Cherokee, and one of the best dang hunters I've ever shared powder with?"

"I have heard you talk of him, yes."

"I got to take my chance to go see him. If he's still there to be seen."

"What do you mean?"

"McCoy is an older man than me. Good ten or twelve years older. I've heard a rumor he had died. I don't know that it's true, but I need to know. I'm going to take myself a little hunt-and-hike trip down to the Doe and look him up. If he's there we'll have us a good visit. If he's gone I'll give my respects to his widow. Half-Cherokee white woman name of Polly. Good gal."

"You want me to go with you?"

"I do. It'll give me some good time with my son with nobody else about, and I can tell you more of that family history I got started telling you before we got to town here. Without other ears around to hear it and other heads and hearts to pass judgment on it all."

"Pass judgment . . . What the deuce are you going to tell me, Pap?"

"You got to wait to find out. And you got to agree to go on this hunt with me."

"No Langdon Potts or Micah Tate to go with us this time?"

"Not this time. Just me and you."

Titus scratched his temple. "Sounds good to me, Pap. Right good at that. I never been to the Doe River country."

Fain slapped his son on the shoulder, grinning widely. "It'll be a good journey, son."

"What about Eben Bledsoe's daughter? We were sent out to find her, and so far we ain't. Story we heard was she'd been seen here around Jonesborough, yet here we are getting ready to traipse off somewhere else."

"Well, I ain't found her in Jonesborough since we got here. Have you? And I've been asking around just about everybody I meet. Nobody's seen a yellow-haired woman with a marked eye. Maybe we'll find her along the Doe somewhere. Meantime, Potts and Micah can keep on prodding around here for her and maybe they'll turn her up, if she's really hereabouts."

"Sounds like you're determined to do this, Pap."

"A man's got to do certain things sometimes. And what I've got to do is call on my old friend McCoy Atley."

Jeremiah Littleton had never been much of a tobacco smoker, but with him seated comfortably in the common room of Jonesborough's Harkin Inn, his false leg propped on a stool that was just the right height to maximize his comfort, the clay pipe he puffed on was providing a good deal of pleasure. Adding to that was conversation with a man who had dropped in to have a gander at his wooden leg. Since becoming a "hopper," as he sometimes called himself since his leg loss, he'd been surprised at the level of unabashed interest people took in the novelty of a wooden limb. It had actually worried him some before he shaved off his beard. Now that he was whiskerless, and starting to lose some of his corpulence, he did not believe it probable that any casual interaction with strangers would be likely to prompt recognition. He was actually beginning to think of himself as Lyle Kirk every now and then.

The man with whom Littleton was chatting had come over from Limestone Creek on some matter of personal business, and had seen Littleton thumping down the street on his peg leg. He'd followed him a short distance, unnoticed, then watched Littleton enter the Harkin Inn. Needing a bed for the night himself, he'd rented a room from the Harkins and buttonholed Littleton into conversation by the cold hearth.

"You do good on that leg, Mr. Kirk," the man said to Littleton. "I saw your skill at it while you was tromping down the street earlier. I knowed a fellow who lost his leg at the King's Mountain fight, and he never did learn to use a false leg. And all he'd lost was his foot and ankle on the right leg. So he had more left to work with than you did, seems to me. But he never did learn that peg leg and wound up on crutches. That's how he gets by today, just crutching along, swinging that leg with the missing foot."

"I reckon I was lucky, getting a peg that fit me well," Littleton said. "That carpenter knew what he was doing, and he got the inside part, where the end of my leg slips in, so smooth that it fit like a glove. I had some trouble for a while, with it pinching and my leg hurting and all, but now it seems the best it's been. I can walk at a right smart pace, as you saw."

"Surely so," the man said. Just as he spoke, the door opened and Langdon Potts walked in. Potts nodded a friendly greeting at Littleton. He didn't recognize Littleton, despite having seen him in Fort Edohi, because of Littleton's missing beard.

But when Potts looked over at the man who had been conversing with Littleton, he stared in surprise. The man gave a similar look back to him.

"John? John Crockett? Am I remembering right?"

"Hello, Potts! Fancy seeing you here! I

thought you was going on over to Fort Edohi."

"Been there and a few other places since I saw you last, John," Potts said.

"You two know each other?" Littleton asked.

"We met back in August," Potts said.

"Eighteenth of August," Crockett said. "I remember because it was the day after my latest child was born."

"How is little David?" asked Potts.

"Growing like a weed, sir. Like a weed."

"Congratulations to you, sir, on the child," said Littleton to Crockett. He stuck a hand out toward Potts. "Name's Lyle Kirk."

"Langdon Potts. Just call me Potts. Good to meet you, Lyle."

"Small world we live in, I reckon," Littleton observed.

"I reckon so," Crockett said. "Seems it happens quite often you'll run into a stranger and find he's not really a stranger at all."

"I've been traveling with Crawford Fain," Potts said. "And it seems there ain't no strangers with him. He knows most everybody, and everybody surely does know him."

"Famous man," Littleton said. He was eager for the subject to change. He feared the talk about Fain might cause Potts's mind to drift back to that night of the camp meeting at Fort Edohi and the one-legged, bearded man who had slept on a pallet in the corner. Recognition would not be welcome, especially considering that Littleton had stolen a horse when he fled Fort Edohi that night, and it could have been Potts's horse, for all he knew.

For Littleton, the world grew even smaller with Crockett's next question to Potts. "Did you stop by Dixon's and get yourself a drink as I told you to that evening?"

"I stopped. Didn't drink, though. He nigh threw me out because of it."

Crockett laughed, nodding. "That's Dixon for you!"

Littleton asked, "Are you talking of the Dixon who moves from here to there setting up taverns? Ugly fellow, no hair?"

"That's the one. You know him?"

"Drank at his place recently. He ain't in Greene no more. Farther west now."

"He moves a lot," John Crockett said. "Made me mad as spitfire when he left Greene County, though. I turned up many a cup at Dixon's, and I miss that place."

"It truly is a small world," observed Potts. "I heard in town, Mr. Kirk, that you are now a partner with the famous preacher Bledsoe, and will be presenting, at his camp meetings, the story of a rescue by an angel that you experienced?"

"That's true. The reverend is a fellow lodger in this very inn and is paying my own lodging because I'm working for him now."

"I saw Abner Bledsoe the night I visited Dixon's near Greeneville. He came in to announce his camp meeting soon to be held at Fort Edohi."

"That was the very meeting that was taking place when I lost my leg, but was given angelic rescue."

"As we've been saying, small world it is."

"Destiny is at work, gentlemen, bringing us all together in one place," said John Crockett, a far more philosophical comment than he was typically prone to give.

"I'm not sure I believe in destiny," Littleton noted. "It's not truly so strange that folks would meet up more than once, considering how new this country is and how few still the towns and settlements are. Men move about, their paths will cross."

At that moment, Michael Harkin walked into the common room, tossing and catching a coin. As he'd been taught to do, he smiled politely at the visitors and nodded his head. "Always be cordial to our patrons," his mother had directed him.

"You've come into some money, son!"

Crockett said.

"Yes, sir," replied Michael, holding the coin between thumb and forefinger and showing it to the men. "It's pay I earned from Mr. Stuart for carrying supper to old 'Jingo' down in the log jail. Mr. Stuart didn't want to do it himself this time, and had had no one else handy for the task, so he hired me. Paid me good, too."

"Who is this 'Jingo'?" asked Littleton.

"Oh, that ain't his real name," said Michael. "It's just what I called him because he says it all the time. 'By jingo' this and 'by jingo' that."

Littleton scooted quickly to the edge of his seat. "What's this fellow's real name? For I used to know a man who turned that phrase every few minutes when he spoke."

"This fellow's name is Clark, I think," said the boy.

"Is this the fellow who was seemingly hanged, yet lived?" asked Crockett.

"That's the one, sir. The mark on his neck is clear to see."

"I heard talk of him on the street today," Crockett said.

"Hanged?" Littleton queried. "What story is this?"

Michael waited to see if Crockett would

answer, but he did not. All eyes turned to him.

"Well, sir, Clark is a man who was carried into town by night and left on the church doorstep. He'd been injured about the neck, the marks showing that he'd been hanged alive, but taken down before he had time to die. The one who took him down, not the same as who had hanged him to begin with, carried him into town on his shoulders and left him. Mr. Stuart, who owns the finest house in town, took him in to let him recover. Clark is being kept down in the log jail building, and Mr. Stuart is keeping him fed from his own larder."

"What's this fellow Clark look like?"

"Very thin, small-framed fellow. That's how he was able to live for a time while hanging, Mr. Stuart thinks. If he'd been heavier he'd have choked faster."

Littleton nodded. "And this Clark says 'by jingo' frequently?"

"He said it three times just during the time I was bringing in his supper tonight," said Michael.

"Why is he locked in the jail?"

"He ain't locked in, sir. He's just there because there ain't no prisoners there just now, and it's a safe place for him to heal up. He could leave anytime he wanted, if he wasn't lame."

"Lame?"

"Broken ankle. It seems likely that it happened when he was took out of the noose. He dropped and broke it. Then the one who'd taken him down heaved him up on his shoulder and marched him all the way here into Jonesborough, dead of night."

"Sounds like another 'angel rescue,' " Crockett observed, his eye on Littleton.

Littleton spoke: "So this hurt fellow now is laid up in an unlocked cell room in the big log jail building. And if he was able to walk, he could get up and leave whenever he wanted."

"That's right, sir. He's free to come and go as soon as he's able, and other folks can just as easy get to him."

"That's what I wanted to know. I may have to pay a visit to Mr. Jingo before long."

"I can take you there if you want me to," the boy offered.

Littleton shook his head. "I can find him. I'd rather go see him alone."

Shortly after one o'clock the next morning, Gilly Cobble woke up to find a stranger standing by his cot and looking down at him by the light of a candle in his hand. Gilly looked up at the face in the flickering light and noted the smile, but also a familiarity in the looks that he couldn't quite pin down.

"Confusing, ain't it, Gilly, seeing me without my whiskers?"

Gilly sucked in a hard breath. Oh God. Oh no. Not *him!* But he knew the voice. And now that the whiskers had been mentioned, he recognized the face. Particularly the eyes. He'd always be able to know Jeremiah Littleton by his eyes if nothing else.

"Jeremiah . . ."

"Yep, it's me. And you thought I was dead, didn't you!"

"I — I'd heard you got out alive. I'm glad you did, Jeremiah. I never wanted no harm to come to you!"

"That right? Is that why you shoved me over the edge of a bluff and just ran off and left me there in that hole? 'Cause you didn't want no harm to come to me? You figured I'd be safe and sound down there?"

"I'm mighty sorry, Jeremiah. Mighty sorry."

"You ain't even started being sorry yet, Gilly. But don't fret. You'll get your chance. But it won't last long. You'll not be feeling anything at all when I'm done with you. Except maybe fire and brimstone in a place you and me are both bound to go."

Gilly sat up, wincing with pain as his ankle

scooted on the cot. “Dear God!” he said tightly.

“Why, what’s the matter, Gilly?” Littleton asked with deep sarcasm. “Are you feeling some pain? Let me tell you about pain, partner. Pain is having your leg shattered and crushed up until there ain’t much left but a kind of meat pudding or bloody mush, and having it stuck down in a pinching rock hole with your own weight pushing down on it. But you can’t pull out because if you tried it would hurt even worse. That’s pain.”

“I’m mighty sorry that happened to you, Jeremiah. I am.”

“I bet you are. ’Cause you know how a man like me is prone to deal with such things. I’m an eye-for-an-eye kind of fellow. Hurt me and I hurt you.”

Gilly began to cry, and instinctively pulled away on the cot to increase the distance between him and Littleton.

Littleton glared at him bitterly. “You know what also hurts, Gilly? Taking your own knife and carving your own flesh away, cutting off the pulp that used to be your leg, just so you can maybe get free if somebody helps you. But all the time you’re figuring that there ain’t nobody going to come, and you’re going to just be where you are until you die. That’s pain. That’s more than one kind of pain, all put together."

"I heard you were walking on a peg now. I hope it works good for you."

"You're just full of kind wishes, ain't you, Gilly! Just as kindhearted a soul as a man could hope to meet. Yeah, my peg works good. I hobble along as well as anybody could, I reckon. But it ain't a real leg, and I know that every time I bear down on it and feel the squeeze and pinch on the stump where a leg is supposed to be. And that makes me think of you, every time it happens. Ain't it nice, knowing there's somebody been thinking of you every time he takes a step, Gilly?"

"Jeremiah, please . . . please . . ." Gilly looked longingly at the open cell door.

Littleton laughed. "You want to leave, Gilly? Then leave! Get up and walk out. Oh, wait. I forgot. You got a busted ankle, right? Can't walk at all."

Gilly wailed childishly.

"Get out of that bed, Gilly. Get out and lie down on this good puncheon floor. On your back, please."

"I — I can't get out of bed. My ankle. It would hurt too bad."

"I'll help you." Littleton grabbed Gilly's arm and dragged him off the cot. He hit the floor hard, and screamed terribly in pain as his ankle struck the puncheons. The sound was intense in the little room, but the thick log walls guaranteed that no one who might be outside at this late hour of the night could hear anything.

Gilly's screams faded to moans, and his lip quivered like a dead-of-winter shiver.

"Time for settling up, Gilly. And I know just how I'm going to do it. Had it planned for a little while now. My wooden peg leg broke on me, see. Fractured right in two, though the two parts didn't come full apart. That's why I have that iron band around it. Holds them back in place just like it ain't even broke. But that band can be slipped off." Littleton bent and worked at the band, which soon loosened and slid down to the floor. He stepped out of it, letting part of the broken peg leg tilt away to reveal the sharpened splinter tip of the other portion.

"Littleton, what are you thinking of doing?" Gilly asked pleadingly. "Jeremiah, please . . . please . . ." Littleton grinned at him again, cruel-eyed.

"Just going to show you how I can walk on my peg leg," he said.

"Please, Littleton. Have some mercy!"

"Let me stand for a minute and think on that," Littleton said matter-of-factly. Then, unhesitating, he lifted the peg leg, aimed the point of the broken piece at the center of Gilly's chest, and stepped forward.

Gilly did not scream this time. There was not time. His life ended too quickly.

Littleton stood there a full minute, the sharp point of the peg leg piercing all the way through Gilly's chest to touch the floor below. At last Littleton pulled it free of the corpse, pushed the halves of the peg together, and set about to working the iron band back into place around the splintered pieces.

"No, Gilly," he said to the man who was beyond all hearing now. "No mercy."

With the peg leg put together again, he studied by candlelight the copious amount of blood staining it. Someone would be sure to notice if it remained that way. But it was dark and the street would be empty at this hour. He could make it back to the inn without anyone detecting the bloodstains. Then, in his room, he could whittle away the stained wood and burn the shavings in his fireplace.

He didn't do it, however. As he considered the inevitability of the discovery of Gilly's death come morning, and the fact that it would immediately be detected that Gilly had been murdered, he realized he needed to be gone. He went to the stable where his stolen horse was, saddled it, and sneaked it out. Within minutes he was riding out of Jonesborough, heading in the direction of the Doe River country, where the surrounding terrain was rugged and mountainous and a man could find a hundred places to hide.

He pondered the fact that he was abandoning the preacher Bledsoe, who would be furious that yet another "angel-rescued" human display had left him in the lurch. The hell with him, Littleton thought. Bledsoe was nothing but a fraud and deserved any hard times he found.

Littleton was a murderer now. And murderers had to flee. It went with the status.

Chapter Twenty-One

James Corey awakened from a deep and very restful slumber, and had no immediate notion where he was. He lifted his head from the feather pillow, then sat up and looked around the cabin. Only when he looked out the window to his right, a window built into the rear wall of the one-room cabin, did he see the woman and feel the murk of alcohol-enhanced sleep lift sufficiently to let him remember.

He'd met her on the road while he was traveling with the preacher and the one-legged man. They had not seen her, hidden as she was in roadside brush, but he had, and had caught her signal to leave her presence unrevealed. He had subtly signaled back, hoping she could rightly interpret his silent instruction to stay where she was; then he'd ridden on nearly a mile with his companions until they had drawn near enough to their destination of Jonesborough to see the first cabins on the far outskirts of the settlement. Then, making the excuse of having dropped his knife somewhere along the last mile or two, he'd parted from his traveling companions and gone back.

She was still there, as he had hoped. And also as he had hoped, he soon learned that she was exactly what he'd thought she would be: a "woman of easy virtue." He'd known so many women like this one that he could usually tell the breed with little more than a glance. This one he found more appealing than most he'd encountered through life: She was raven-haired and well proportioned and possessed a starkly beautiful pale-skinned face that contrasted intriguingly with the black of her hair. He learned from her that she had been sleeping in the brush along the trail when he spotted her. The noise of the first two travelers passing had awakened her and she had sat up in time to see Corey, and for him, alone of the three, to see her in turn.

Her name was Sadie Cleaver, and she was a woman of road and trail. Much like Ott Dixon plying his liquor trade from settlement to settlement, she moved through the countryside selling the only thing she had to offer: her "favors," as people tended to so delicately put it. And though she was often lonely and felt of little worth in the world, she was happy at least to be unencumbered and to make her home wherever she happened to be. She was sure she knew the backcountry as well as any scout or hunter, or even Indian. She doubted there was a single hunter's shed or unused cabin or dry cave she did not know the location of, and had not occupied at one time or another, sometimes alone, sometimes with paying male company.

Sadie had led Corey to the cabin in which he had just awakened and had entered the place so casually he was sure it must be her own. There were signs the place had been occupied and used recently.

She had left Corey sleeping in the cabin and gone to a nearby creek for a wash, but when she returned he was awake and waiting for her. "I'm going to go on to Jonesborough this morning," he announced. "The ones I was traveling with are probably wondering what became of me. When I left them I told them I was going back to look for a dropped knife."

"I hope what you found was better than just a knife." She smiled coyly at him. She secretly loathed the men she consorted with, and despised their very looks and touch, but she was a woman of business.

Teasing and flirting with good-paying customers such as James Corey were simply part of what had to be done.

Corey laughed. "Oh, much better, much! And if I didn't feel the press of time on me, I might be ready for another round of 'knife hunting.' "

"I'm going nowhere. If you can put off leaving for a little while, and if you've got another coin or two tucked away somewhere, we can . . ."

Corey didn't reply directly. He waved a hand at the cabin. "Is this yours?"

"Oh no, no. Just one of the places I'm allowed to stay when I need to. This is a Crale cabin."

"Crale cabin?"

"One of Tom Crale's lodgings, in fact."

"Am I supposed to know Tom Crale?"

"No. Few folks know the Crales, or even know *of* them. The Crales keep it that way. Most of them don't even use the Crale name, just to keep themselves that much more hidden. They ain't a usual kind of family. Tom's the most different of all of them, the most secret. He uses the Crale name, but it don't matter in his case because he's almost never met or seen by anyone."

"Is he one of your paying customers?"

"Oh no. No!" She paused and shuddered

like a cold wind had hit her. "The very thought of — No! I wouldn't be able to bear touching him, much as I 'preciate him."

"What's wrong with him?"

"The Crale lump."

"The what?"

"The Crale lump. There's been several Crale men to have that over the years. At least one or two Crales with such a lump are alive at any given time, as a general rule. It grows out of the forehead and goes down over one eye, usually. Tom's is that way. His grandfather had the Crale lump, too, but it didn't cover his eye."

"What a family! How did they come to be like they are?"

"I think they kept too much amongst themselves. In ways they shouldn't have, if you follow me. That's one of the reasons they use other family names besides Crale. It helps them disguise that they're marrying among their own kin."

"Oh." He looked at the cabin again. "Why does this Tom Crale let you stay here, if you give him no favors?"

She looked Corey square in the eye. "Because Tom Crale may be the single kindest, tenderest man I've ever known. You know how I met him?"

"How could I know?"

"I ran into him way over by the Nolichucky River. He was returning baby birds to a nest. They'd fallen out in a storm, and he found them, and took time to use the one working eye he has to find their nest. How many men do you know who would do that? Tom Crale is a good man. A truly good man."

Corey had known a few truly good men in his day. He didn't like them because they were so different than he.

"Why isn't Tom Crale here now?"

"He has places he stays all over the overmountain country. Mostly with other Crales, but he's also got cabins like this one, and old hunter stations, even a couple of big hollow trees he's been known to curl up inside of to sleep. Little secret refuges. He goes wherever he can be that people ain't likely to see him. That's why so few know of him. He lives in secret, and listens, and watches. Everything. He watches cabins being built, settlements going up, fields being broken. He watches the Indians along with the whites. Some of them know him; they respect him as having a special place on the land. They believe his face, the way it is, comes from being touched by God and made special. They don't hurt him and he doesn't hurt them. But whatever he does, wherever he is, he hides. He might as well be a spirit, the way he can hide himself."

Corey thought about that. "He hides because of his . . ."

"Because of his ugliness. The Crale lump. He spends his life mostly apart so folks won't make sport of him or be afraid of him. Children cry to see him, and it torments him. He loves children, loves birds, animals, hates even to hunt, though like anybody he does hunt to stay alive. He's like the Indians in thanking the prey he kills for having given up their lives to help him keep his."

"How do you know so much about him?"

"I've spent hours talking to him on those rare times I'm able to find him. He's one of the few men I've known who is happy just to talk to me. He doesn't judge, or condemn; he's just kind. And he listens. He's one of my few real friends."

"But even somebody like you, who thinks the world of him, can't even consider touching him."

"It's true. And sad."

"All I can say is better him than me. I'm too fond of the female touch to even think what it would be like if every woman ran from me. Hey, all the Crales don't have that same kind of growth on them, I take it?"

"Most look just like anybody else. Though

there's been a lot of them sickly in various kinds of ways because of kin marrying kin."

"Kind of a sorrowful tale," Corey said. Though in fact he cared not at all. Empathy was not part of his nature.

Sadie paused. "Come here," she said. "I want to show you something."

"Well!" Corey declared with a nasty smile. "I like the sound of *that!*"

"That's not what I'm talking about. Nothing like that at all. This has to do with Tom."

"Well . . . ain't *that* wonderful!"

She led Corey across a small meadow to the base of a hillside pockmarked with great limestone outcroppings. The entrances to narrow caverns and tunnels, most of them mere cracks in the rock big enough to accommodate a small animal but certainly not a human, covered the face of the rumpled stone bluff. But when Sadie led Corey around a large, slablike boulder embedded in scree at the base of the escarpment, he saw a larger cavern entrance, wider than a cabin door and big enough for a man to enter without having to stoop very deeply to do it. Sadie led Corey to that entrance, then paused to look at the angle of the morning sun. She nodded happily. "Good," she said. "We've come at the right time. For a little while in the morning, there is enough sunlight spilling onto this cave door to maybe let you see what I want to show you. I hope so, anyway." She ducked inside.

"You've got me puzzled, woman."

"Come on in."

At first Corey thought what he was seeing was the product of some earlier people who had roamed this land, some native tribe who had left their marks in colored images on stone. He'd seen a painted cliff like that once in one of the more rugged mountain areas of North Carolina.

A closer look at this particular bit of artwork on the stone, though, showed it to be the product of a much more recent hand. For one thing, the art, apparently produced mostly in the media of colored clays, coal, crushed berries, and chalky stones, depicted cabins and wagons and men bearing long rifles.

"Tom Crale drew these?" he asked Sadie.

"He did. He's quite an artist."

"I reckon so."

There was more farther back in the cave, where the wall was smoother, but the light was mostly lost and Corey could not clearly see what Sadie pointed out to him. All he could tell was that it was seemingly the image of a face. Farther back yet, there was something else painted, but Corey could not make out at all what it depicted.

"We need light," he said. "I've got my fire makings."

He exited the cave, gathered what he needed, and with his flint and steel and punk got a small fire blazing. Lighting a little bundle of sticks and shielding the flame with his cupped hand, he reentered the cave and illuminated the image of the first face on the wall.

"So that's him?" he asked Sadie. He was looking at a quite well-rendered image of a deformed face, one side of the brow expanded and drooping like melted wax, lolling out and over, completely hiding one eye. Though it was merely an image, Corey found himself reflexively pulling back from it, moving his little torch away so darkness could mask the unpleasant visage again.

"Good God! Is it really that bad for him? Is he really that . . . ill made?"

She nodded sadly. "He is."

"Why would a man take time to paint a picture of his own face on the wall of a cave? Especially if he is so ashamed of it that he hides it from the world?"

"Bring your light down a little farther."

The fire played on the next image, the one that could not be made out at all before.

Corey studied it by the flickering little torch flame, and when he glanced around at Sadie, he saw that her face was tearstained.

The image on the wall was another face, yet also the same one. It was Tom Crale as he would have been with no deformity. The man had drawn an image of himself, from his imagination, as he would have liked to be.

"I'll be," Corey muttered.

"He showed it to me himself," Sadie said. "It made me cry to see it, and he couldn't understand. He asked me why I was crying to see his face when it was beautiful." She tried to say something further to Corey, but her voice choked and she could speak no more.

He studied the face on the wall. "I'll be," he said again.

Sadie spoke. "Tom has drawn pictures in hidden places like this all over the mountain country. This is the only place I have seen him draw his own face, though."

"What does he draw other places?"

"Mostly the kinds of things he drew at the front of this cave. Things he has seen while watching people. Farmers digging, hunters bringing in game, Indians building their homes or traveling . . . things like that." She paused and looked again at the rendering of

Crale's undistorted face, drawn to it. "Most people don't know of Tom by name, or that he is the one who makes these images. Most just attribute them to the 'cavern man.' But I know it's Tom, bless him. I've seen him doing his work."

Chapter Twenty-Two

It was Stuart who found the body of Gilly Cobble, alias Caleb Clark, lying dead on the floor of the little cell room. The blood pooled beneath him was substantial, having drained by pull of gravity out of the ugly chest wound that pierced clean through him, and was needled in and out with splinters of wood.

"Great God above," Stuart muttered when he got a close look at the injury. "How in the name of heaven . . . and *who* . . ."

The sheriff was summoned and questions both official and informal were fired all around. The story spread fast through town and it did not take long for suspicion to be cast on the peg-legged man who had come to Jonesborough with the Reverend Abner Bledsoe, Lyle Kirk. And Kirk, intriguingly, had apparently vanished in the night. His rented bed in the Harkin Inn was unused, and the horse he had stabled earlier was gone.

It was none other than John Crockett who suggested that the murder might actually have been committed with the wooden leg as the weapon. He had taken a close enough look at the prosthesis to see that it had a split in it held together by an iron band, and that one of the separated portions had possessed a sharp point the size of the wound in Clark's pale chest.

"So he killed this poor sod by stepping on him with a sharp-pointed piece of wood," the sheriff said after Crockett pronounced his theory. "Little different than having a stake drove through the heart. Makes you feel like we ought to be burying this gent in a crossroads with a stake through him, like you bury a suicide."

The sheriff's band of manhunters were duly gathered and sworn in under authority of the state of Franklin, and then, for good measure, one of the number had the others thrust their hands up and swear under authority of North Carolina as well. "Must make sure we're legal all around," he said when questioned about it.

"Maybe we should swear to act in accordance with the laws of the emperor of China, too, just in case," a wag commented.

"Gentlemen, we're missing an opportunity

here," said another of the group when they were ready to set out. "We have in town one of the great trackers and hunters of the west, Edohi himself. Should we not include him in this group?"

Micah Tate, who had volunteered his services to the manhunt, spoke. "Edohi is not here at the moment. He and his son left for the Doe River early this morning."

"We can surely track down a peg legger without Edohi, gentlemen," the sheriff commented.

"Has his horse got a peg leg, too?" someone asked. "Because a peg-leg man can ride as fast as anybody else."

"Then all the more reason to move on without delay," replied the sheriff. "Gentlemen, you are all duly sworn. Pay heed to my orders should confrontation arise, and good fortune to all of us."

The band rode out on what seemed the most likely route, though they had no clear indicator what direction Lyle Kirk had taken. Outside town, though, they found a good and fresh set of horse tracks, and a mile on, a spot where the horse had been stopped and someone had dismounted, apparently to urinate beside the trail. The tracks showed one footprint and a round depression of the sort a peg leg would make in the ground.

Confident now they were tracking in the right direction, the sheriff's party moved on, the best tracker among the group taking the lead and riding bent forward so he could keep in view the tracks that led them.

Kirk's horse was strong and sure, and it soon became obvious they would not quickly overtake it. "But even the best horses tire," pointed out the sheriff. "He will stop eventually, and we will catch up to him."

Bart Clemons awakened slowly, which wasn't typical for a man who often slept on the ground, as Clemons had done throughout the prior night. Hard ground had a way of making a man want to rise, even if a part of him ached for more sleep.

He'd managed to make himself a particularly comfortable bed, lying in layers of moss and soft ferns until he had a surface more restful than many a straw tick he'd occupied in his life. So when morning had come he had barely noted it, rolled over, and snored again.

Now, though, it was time to rise. The sun was edging up steadily, the air was warming, and dew was almost completely dried off the vegetation. Clemons stretched and yawned and looked around the woodland clearing in which he'd passed the night. It struck him that a further reason he had slept better was that he had not dreamed of Gilly's bulging face as it had been when he was hanging in that noose. He'd managed to bury that image deeply enough in his mind that it simply hadn't emerged in sleep. Clemons was grateful.

"Sluggard, arise!" came a voice from behind him, playfully Falstaffian in tone.

Clemons sucked in his breath and bounded to his feet, turning at the same time. The effort tangled his feet and he sat down hard on his rump, facing the man who had entered the clearing unnoticed just as Clemons had been waking up.

"Did that hurt, whomping down on your arse like that?" Littleton asked Clemons, who was staring up in surprise combined with the stupor of lingering sleepiness.

"Littleton, where did you come from?"

Littleton was in a remarkably light mood for a man who had just driven a piece of broken wood through the heart of another. "Well, Clemons, that kind of thing begins when a man and a woman fall in love with each other. The two of them stand up before a preacher and say some vows, and then they commence to living in the same house and sleeping in the same bed. And then —"

"Littleton, shut up! Everything's got to be a big jest to you, don't it! Well, haw-haw-haw! Damn!"

"Ill-humored this morning, I see!" Littleton said. "I guess I better straighten up and fly right so as not to make you mad, reckon?"

"You better."

Littleton knelt beside Clemons's cold campfire, his one knee popping loudly as he did.

Clemons said, "If there's any embers glowing in that, stir them up and feed some twigs and such to them. I need to get a fire going to cook some breakfast. Got a couple of squirrels skinned in my hunting bag yonder. You et yet?"

"I ain't hungry, but thank you for asking. But the fact is, I can't build up your fire, Bart. I probably got hunters on my trail right now. I'm talking manhunters. Law. Smoke of a fire would draw them here."

"What did you do?"

"I killed Gilly. Over in Jonesborough."

"Gilly? I'll be! They know it was you who done it?"

"They're bound to know. Though they believe my name is Lyle Kirk, which is the false name I've been using lately."

"When did you shave off your whiskers, Jeremiah? Or Lyle, or whatever you want me to call you now?"

"Go with Lyle. I cut the whiskers off so I'd be harder for folks to recognize. See, there was this plan for me to become a defrauder for a traveling preacher, who was going to tell a big tale about me being rescued by angels from that pit Gilly pushed me into. To get folks riled up in their spirits and ready to give gifts and money and such, you know."

"Haw! *You* were going to become a religion seller?"

"Yes, sir, it was the plan. Working with old Camp Meeting Abner hisself! Might have been some good money in it, too, though I got a feeling old Abner would have found a way to keep most of that for hisself."

"Yeah, never trust nobody who lives declaring themselves righteous. Hey, you said you killed Gilly?"

"I did. Funny thing with Gilly — he'd been hanged alive. But he survived it. Somebody took him down from the noose before he had a chance to choke all the way to death, and hauled him in to Jonesborough in the dead of night, dumped him in front of a church house."

"I — I found the empty noose. But I

didn't know what had become of him. It was us who hanged him, Jeremiah. The other boys and me. We hanged him because of what he had did to you. But it wasn't us who took him down. Wasn't me, anyway. I can't speak for the others. We split up after the hanging and went our different ways."

"Them boys was bad company for an upright citizen such as you, Clemons."

"You ain't never serious, are you, Littleton?"

"I try not to be."

"How did you come to kill Gilly?"

Littleton told the story in some detail, finishing by taking the iron band off his peg leg and showing Clemons the splintered point he had driven into Gilly's midriff. Clemons, weak-stomached as he was, grew pale hearing the description of the blood gushing up around the peg leg and spreading in a pool beneath Gilly's back.

"He didn't live but a moment or two," Littleton said. "I'm right sure I drove that wood right through his heart."

"Good God, Littleton. Good God!"

"That's what they say. Don't know he's ever done much for me, though. Unless that boy that pulled me out of the hole really *was* an angel."

Clemons shook his head. "Ain't no angels,

Littleton. Ain't no goodness or heaven or hell or nothing like that. There's nothing but us, and this dirt and rock and trees and the sky, and I reckon it just goes on forever with nobody living up there or looking down to bless us or curse us. Ah, Lord. I reckon that's surely the way it is."

"I don't know, Clemons. Maybe you're right. Or maybe you ain't. All I know is, if there's blessings to be had, I sure ain't earned them. I ain't been nothing but a bad man all my days."

Littleton immediately wished he hadn't said it, because Clemons's lip quivered and tears bolted from his eyes. He tilted his head upward, eyes closed, and wept.

Littleton had seen Clemons like this before. Odd fellow, Clemons, Littleton pondered. He'd seen the man so full of life and excitement that he could hardly sit still, full of plans and hope and brightness . . . then, virtually in an instant, he would become as he was now: gloomy, tearful, depressed, and empty. Utterly hopeless. How could a man transform that way, so completely, and so suddenly? Littleton had seen this phenomenon enough times with Clemons to know that there was a good chance the man would the next morning be as hopeful as he was hopeless now, as full of cheer and life as he was of sorrow and hollowness at the moment.

"Cheer up, Clemons," Littleton said, though he knew from experience that such banalities did nothing to change Clemons when he was in this state of mind.

"I can't cheer up. Know why, Littleton? Know why?"

"I don't know."

"Because of the kind of folk we are, that's why! Look at us, Littleton! What kind of men are we?"

"Bad ones, according to most. The way I see it, we're men who do what they have to do to survive. We're survivors."

Clemons firmly shook his head. "No, no. Not us. It's good people who survive in the end. For the bad, wickedness turns around on them and bites them. It's going to bite us. It's time for it to bite us. Ain't no justice if it don't."

"Well, maybe when it bites, it'll catch me on my wooden leg and I'll not even feel it!" Littleton laughed at his own wit, but Clemons was in no mood for humor.

"Don't laugh, Littleton. Think for a minute about what we've done. We've robbed, we've hurt people, we've even murdered. Gilly killed that man who was doing nothing more than keeping quiet and hoping we'd finally leave his home and let him be. Gilly shot him dead. And then there's Will Sikes, worst of us all. Hurting, raping little gals, just children. It's evil. We're evil. The lot of us. And it can't go on. *We* can't go on."

"But we will go on. That's the way life is, Clemons. It goes on. If we need to change our ways, well, we can work on that."

"Too late. Too late for us, Jeremiah. Hell's waiting."

Clemons stood and walked over to where his pack lay up against a log. With his back toward Littleton and his body blocking view of what he was doing, he produced two small flintlock pistols and quietly checked them. He put the muzzle of one in his mouth and bit down on it, holding it in place, still hidden from Littleton. Then he turned, aimed the other pistol at a startled Littleton, and shot him in the chest.

Littleton rose, staggered weakly, and tilted on his wooden leg. He fell down hard, writhed, tried in vain to speak, then flopped facedown in the dirt.

Without hesitation, and filled with a sorrow that flowed through him with the liquidity of blood, Clemons took hold of the other pistol gripped by his mouth, tilted the muzzle up to the roof of his mouth, and fired. He collapsed, dead before he struck ground.

"I want to hear more about the family, Pap," Titus Fain said to his father. They were riding slowly along the trail that would take them ultimately to the rugged country of the Doe River. Jonesborough was behind them now, the sun climbing.

"I don't remember all I got told to you before," Fain said. "I told you my father was a criminal, a housebreaker and a highwayman."

"You did. And you told me you took part in the housebreaking, but not the highway work."

"That's right. I was protected from that by your grandfather, who feared I'd be more likely fodder for the noose if I was ever caught in highway robbery. So I never was permitted to do that."

"I'm glad of it. Tell me how your father became a woodsman in Skellenwood."

"In that tale, son, lies the key to our family being in this country today, and me being the man of the wilderness that I am.

"Your father wore a mask in all his highway robberies, just a kind of sack pulled down over his face and head. So his face went unseen. He never harmed a soul in all his robberies, beyond stealing from them. He brandished a pistol, but never used it, and I don't think ever would have used it. And because most of his robberies occurred on the Skellenwood Road, he was known as the Masked Bandit of Skellenwood. Quite a dramatic name, eh? And he was known for his cordiality to those he robbed, and the fact that he'd never harmed any one of them."

"Bandit of Skellenwood. Worthy of poetry."

Fain cleared his throat and continued. "There came a day when something went wrong — but which turned out to be the best thing that could have happened for my father. A new coachman was on the road, driving his team carelessly, far too fast, some rich passenger urging him on because he was late to a business appointment, and a little boy stepped from the edge of the road at the wrong moment and was hit. Your grandfather was preparing to stop and rob that very coach, his eye on the purse of that same man of business who was in such a hurry. But when he saw the boy being struck, the robbery was forgotten.

"The coachman drove on, abandoning the lad, but Father went to him and saw he needed the help of a physician. He carried that poor injured boy in his arms all the way to the nearest house, a great estate mansion. The boy, it turned out, had come from that very place. The estate was that of his uncle, and the boy was recently orphaned and had been taken in by that uncle, who was Lord Skellen, the landowner of most of Skellenwood Forest."

"Let me take a guess," Titus threw in. "The landholder was grateful for the rescue of his nephew, and gave your father the job of woodsman in Skellenwood."

"You are exactly right, son. And not only was he given the task of woodsman, but he was allowed to do it in a secret manner. That was how the house of the Fain family came to be built within the very entrance chamber of Skellenwood Cavern. It allowed for secrecy. And Father was given safety from the consequences of his highway robberies. Influence and power . . . Lord Skellen possessed them, and used them to Father's benefit and protection."

"But you told me that the housebreaking went on into your youthful years."

"That is true. Lord Skellen knew only that my father was a highwayman, but nothing of the housebreaking. It was a failing of Father's that he could never put aside housebreaking. He started it as a means of survival in his most impoverished days, but eventually it became a kind of vengeance."

"Against whom? Or what?"

"Against an injustice done his mother, my grandmother, by a Scotsman of wealth, rank, and power. That Scotsman's own home fell victim to my father's housebreaking, with my aid. A tremendous take of gold and silver, most of it in coin. The most successful effort of the sort we ever engaged. I still carry a silver piece taken in that robbery. It is my intent to have Houser place it as a decoration in the stock of this fine rifle he made for me. That way I can keep my two most prized physical possessions together."

"That's an excellent notion, Pap."

"I think so."

"It was after all these things happened that Molly Reese came to be part of your family for a time."

"That is correct. She lived within the cave house with the rest of us. And she was sensible and foresighted enough, when she and your grandmother were putting into words her famous narrative, to make no record of that portion of her life, her time in Skellenwood. She understood the need for secrecy, you see. For the sake of Father."

"Pap, are you hungry? I could stand to

stew up a bit of hardtack and jerky meat, myself."

"As could I, son. And that provides us a good point for me to close my mouth and rest my voice a spell."

"I am the son of Edohi and the grandson of the Bandit of Skellenwood. Quite a heritage I have, eh, Pap?"

"You do indeed, son."

"There's more you can tell me?"

"The main part of it all you've now heard. Any lesser details I'll present to you as they come to mind, and as circumstances allow."

They made camp, built a fire, and prepared a hunter's stew of hardened bread simmered with jerked beef in a small travel kettle that Fain never journeyed far without. They ate and Fain told a few more tales, mostly of boyhood adventures in the wilds of England's Skellenwood Forest.

Chapter Twenty-Three

The inner fire had him again. It was like that . . . like a flame inside him.

When it struck, Nathan Sikes felt he had no control over what would happen after. The decision seemingly already had been made for him.

He had come to the town of Jonesborough to get out of the wilderness, where he had been spending most of his time for weeks now, and also to find a way to quench the inner fire.

When he was a boy, he'd perceived the life of a criminal as something likely to be fun and thrilling and full of romance of the most classic kind. Instead it was mostly a life of worry and hiding and wondering which of his last steps had been a misstep he just hadn't recognized yet.

Even so, criminality had its compensations. Oh yes, sometimes very good compensations indeed, the kind Sikes loved above all else life had to offer. Specifically, the compensation that came from giving in when the inner fire gripped him. It was so much easier to say yes than to resist. And much more gratifying.

He would be saying yes very soon. This very night, if he proved lucky. All it would take would be finding the right kind of target, then watching and following and looking for opportunity that he would seize the moment it came.

He looked up and down the street, walking lithely and without worries, grateful that he, unlike Littleton, was almost entirely unknown, not a criminal with a name or a face much anyone would be familiar with.

He saw his target. He identified her the moment she crossed his field of vision. Familiar thoughts, anticipations, and vile plans fell into place, and he began to follow her. Sikes knew how to do it in a way that would never catch her attention. And he knew how to look for the opportunity to get her alone, where she would become his possession.

He'd done it so many times before. It was dangerous, deviant, and — Sikes knew full well — deplorable, but he had trained himself not to care. He couldn't imagine living without the inner fire, or the fulfillment of it.

He wondered what her name was. Her age he could easily guess: twelve, probably, or maybe thirteen. Just what he was looking for.

He was glad he'd gotten away from Clemons and Jones. His partners, though criminals themselves, despised his practice of taking his pleasure with young girls. They considered him depraved and purely evil for it, and their glares and comments and palpable disgust interfered with his enjoyment of the process.

He was alone now. Following his latest target in a town where he was sure no one knew his face or name.

The girl would never know what was happening until it happened. She would not escape him. Nor would she identify him. He would make sure of that by letting her know what would happen to her family if she dared to speak of it to anyone. If it came to it, he would have his way with her and leave her corpse to the carrion.

The girl walked fast, and Sikes pushed hard to keep up without getting too close. He made sure to maintain the appearance of looking past her or nearby her, not directly at her. He'd grown adept at watching his targets from the corners of his vision. Should someone call to this girl, or some other distraction cause her to turn in his direction, she would see only a man looking elsewhere, minding his own affairs and merely chancing to be walking some distance behind her.

She'd never figure it out until it was too late to run, too late to stop him. He knew how to make it work.

He'd done it so many times before.

Maggie Harkin was not as unaware of the man following her as the man supposed her to be. A precocious girl who had been trained by a sensible mother to be aware of those around her at all times, Maggie also knew she was old enough, and physically mature enough, to draw the attention of men. Some of them, anyway. And she lived in a society in which many girls no more than three years older than she were married, and no one thought it odd or hurried.

She had managed to catch three quick glimpses of the man without alerting him that she had caught onto him. A part of her, the mature-beyond-her-years part, wanted to step into an alley or recessed door or dogtrot, then come out and confront him and demand to know why he was following her. The other part of her, the scared-little-girl part, and also the sensibly cautious part, knew such a move would not be prudent.

As the daughter of an innkeeping woman, Maggie had been trained to be cautious not to offend newcomers and visitors to town, because such were those from whom the ranks of inn guests were drawn. One was expected to avoid creating situations that could potentially insult or embarrass a guest.

Maggie took advantage of a barking dog behind her and down the street, and turned abruptly to pretend to look for whatever the dog was barking at. The man was much closer, which startled her, and this time she caught him looking straight at her. He averted his eyes quickly, but there was no question he had been watching her.

Her decision was made. She was nearly sure that her mother was at the moment in her spinning house, where the Harkin law office was located when her father was still alive. Maggie drifted across the street in the direction of the little shop, planning to duck in quickly.

The door was closed tight, and bolted on the inside. Maggie froze. Her mother was not here after all . . . and when she turned, the man was gone. For a moment there was relief, but then his absence made it seem that he might be around any corner or behind any wall.

Maggie suddenly wanted to be nowhere but in her own room at home, locked safely inside, away from strangers and followers and the kinds of fear that lived on the street, even in small, friendly frontier towns.

She ducked through the alley beside the spinning house and went to the back of the little cabin. Preparing to make an off-street run around to the Harkin Inn and her home, she trotted past the end of the next alley.

His arm seemed to materialize from nowhere, wrapping firmly around her neck and pulling her back. His face was at her ear, his breath hot and foul. She felt the sharp sting of a knife tip against her neck as he pulled her into a cluster of bushes growing at the rear of the near building.

"Not a sound from you, not a scream, not anything at all to cause me a problem. Do you understand me, girl?"

She nodded, terrified.

"Don't make me mad, girl. Whatever you do, don't make me mad. If you do, you and your family die. Do you understand *that?* Don't think I'm lying. I've done it before."

She nodded again, tears starting now. She realized she had not breathed since he grabbed her, and gasped loudly for air. Apparently thinking she was about to scream, he held her tighter and pressed the knife hard enough to break the outer layer of her skin.

She did not scream. She would not dare anger or disobey him. There was no question in her mind that he would do exactly what he had threatened and end the lives of the entire Harkin family.

"Now, we're all going to be good, ain't we?" he said. "You and me are going to walk out of town together, off the street, and we ain't going to make a sound or raise a single peep. Are we friends now? Sure we are, girl. Me and you, we're friends, and we're going to be even better friends before long. You hear me? Good, good friends."

She walked with him somehow, but her legs were numb and lifeless and moved as if they belonged to someone else.

If only her father were alive! He would stop this man and rescue her. If only . . . if only.

An old hunter named Braxton Card was the manhunter who first spotted the two unmoving forms lying in the camp clearing. It was Micah Tate who discovered that one of them was Lyle Kirk, weak and wounded but still breathing.

The other man was a stranger to them all, and not alive. The pistol that had fired a ball through the roof of his mouth into his brain lay at his side.

The sheriff knelt beside Littleton, who was declining fast, his face taking on that unique gray hue that signals approaching death. "Who did this to you, son?"

"Over . . . there. Him."

"He's dead, you know. Seems he shot himself in the head. Through his mouth."

"I never even heard . . . the shot. Too busy . . . dying myself."

"You ain't dead. Not yet. You're Kirk, ain't you?"

"I am."

"What's the dead man's name over there?"

"Bart Clemons."

"Why did he shoot you? And himself?"

"Because we're . . . bad men. He was . . . bothered him that we were . . . what we are."

The sheriff didn't know what to say to that, so he simply rose to his feet and walked away a few moments, staring down at the corpse of Clemons. The others of his party stood unmoving, watching.

The sheriff returned to Littleton's side. Littleton was struggling hard to breathe, and the effort was draining him. His eyes were closed until the sheriff leaned close and spoke to him.

"Was it you who killed the man in Stuart's jail in Jonesborough?"

Littleton nodded weakly. "It was. I . . . owed him."

"Money? So you killed him not to have to pay it?"

"Not money . . . death. Owed him death."

The sheriff looked Littleton over. "From the looks of you, it appears that same debt might be coming due to you very soon. Got any people who'll need telling after you've gone on to the other side?"

"My . . . mother. She's still living . . . Carter's Valley. Maude Littleton. Widow woman."

"Littleton? I thought your name was Kirk."

Littleton managed one weak shaking of his head. "Jeremiah . . . . Littleton. Tell her . . . tell her her boy was fixing to go to work for a preacher, soul-saving . . . before he died. She'll be glad to hear . . . that. It will give her hope . . . for me."

"We'll find her, son. We'll tell her. But tell me this: Are you the same Jeremiah Littleton who led a gang of thieves and bandits in these parts?"

Littleton was beyond answering. He had

spoken his final words and drawn his last breath.

Maggie was numb. So far the man who had abducted her in town had done nothing to harm her beyond the superficial pinprick cut he had inflicted on her while threatening her family, but the girl knew far worse was intended for her. And because she could see him clearly and he'd made no effort to hide his face from her, a suspicion was arising that he had no intention for her to be around to identify him later.

He would hurt her, misuse her, and kill her. Maggie was sure of it.

As a well-raised, sheltered girl, Maggie had only a minimal grasp of this variety of evil. She knew only enough to comprehend that there were those in the world whose interests and passions were distorted, people who would hurt others for reasons Maggie could not wrap her mind around. People to be avoided, fled from, feared.

Too late to flee this man. She had tried, but he had her.

She remembered hearing something her father had said once, when she was much younger. The frontier country, he had said, drew two types of people: good ones fleeing to find a better situation and a better life for themselves, and bad ones fleeing from trouble in the East.

He'd said as well that the backcountry would never be fully settled until it had a strong and stable system of law, but Maggie had been too young to comprehend or retain much of that. What she was left with out of it all was simple: People, especially children, must be very, very careful of strangers in a place where there were not many sheriffs and constables and prosecutors and such around to make sure bad people behaved themselves.

"Bad people run from good ones," she remembered her father saying to her. "They run away from law. That is why there are so many bad ones who go to the border country, the places where the law is weak or not there at all."

Maggie suspected that this man who had taken her must be the kind who felt the need to run, because he was leading her far away from town, and pushing hard as if they had to hurry as quickly as they could. And he kept stopping and looking behind him, then around him, and telling her he had heard something or someone nearby, and she must be very quiet if she didn't want bad things to happen to her and her loved ones. He had repeated such threats over and over again, each repetition making her will become weaker and her fear greater. And Maggie was smart enough to know that was exactly what he was trying to do . . . to break her resistance, to make her so afraid she would not fight him when he did things to her she could not bear to think about.

"Where are we going?" she dared to ask.

"To visit an old friend," he replied. "A friend who enjoys some of the same things I do."

She lost track of time and distance, and soon was lost in hills, mountains, and hollows. They followed narrow, seldom-used trails and streams she did not recognize, and came at last to a place where a rotting cabin sat on a rocky ledge thrusting out from the side of a wooded hill like the lower lip of a pouting child.

The man held her firmly by the wrist and all but dragged her to the door of the cabin. It stood ajar and he pushed it in without hesitation, as if confident the place was empty.

It wasn't. Inside was a fat, very dirt-encrusted old man, his massive bulk spread like a blob of melting grease on a buffalo-skin pallet spread out across the floor in a corner. He looked up with weak-looking eyes as they entered, and grunted in some sort of apparent greeting at Maggie's captor.

"Hello, Sam," said the captor.

"Sikes," said the blob on the pallet, his voice as slimy as his appearance. And now Maggie knew at least part of the name of her abductor.

Sam, who didn't seem to see well, noticed her for the first time and thrust his fleshy face in her direction. "What you got there, Nate?"

"Something you'll like a lot. Something we'll both like. Going to have us a good time this evening, Sam. I can promise you that." Then Sikes laughed in a way that would have made Maggie toss up her gorge if there was anything in her stomach. There was not. She had already heaved up her breakfast during their hurried travel as she pondered what was likely to become of her.

Sam squinted hard as Sikes pushed her near, and the smell of the amazingly obese man, a smell like that of one who had literally never washed in his life, was revolting beyond description to the little girl. And from the words Sikes had just said, she knew there was an intent that this man would misuse her right along with her captor. That thought was so indescribably horrific that Maggie's throat closed up tight and for long moments she could not breathe at all. Then came the inevitable compensatory gasp, and her head and lungs filled with the loathsome stench of the cabin and its occupant.

Sikes didn't seem to notice the smell. He was grinning happily, but the look turned evil when he turned his face to the girl. "You ain't even told me your name yet, girly. What is it?"

She shook her head and said nothing. His look turned more wicked yet. "You tell me, or I'll grab a handful of that hair and tear it clean out. Then I'll give it to Sam here and he can use it to wipe hisself with." That notion seemed to strike Sikes as hilarious, and he laughed wildly, his breath battering the girl.

"Maggie," she managed to whisper, noticing her voice sounded strange, as if it belonged to someone else.

"Maggie," repeated Sikes. "Hear that, Sam? This here is Maggie, and she's going to be a good little friend to you and me tonight."

"It's pretty. I like it," said Sam. "I like it a lot." He licked his lips with a tongue the size of a child's hand.

"Don't you get your feelings hurt, Sam calling you an 'it,' " said Sikes. "Sam always calls the girlies I bring up here 'it.' That's just his way."

Maggie was beginning to feel faint, but she was afraid to let herself lose consciousness even if only for a few moments. A lot could happen in a few moments, and none of it, in this place, would be good.

"Where's old Wash?" asked Sikes of the other man. "I figured to hear him baying and barking at me when I drew close in."

"Wash is dead," Sam replied. "Lay down and just died one day. I boiled up his meat and et on it for near a week."

"Well, sorry to hear he's gone. I liked that old dog."'

Sam pointed up to his left, and Sikes saw a fresh canine skull, boiled clean of all hide and flesh, stuck on the wall by means of a branch stub extending out from a wall log. Sikes looked closely and nodded.

"Yep, that's old Wash. Fine old hound you were, Wash."

"Tasted good, too," said Sam. "Needed salt, but I got nary of that."

Sikes was looking at something on the floor in the corner opposite to where Sam was sprawled. "How long's Wash been dead?" he asked.

"Two week now. Two week."

"Well, that pile over yonder is way fresher

than two weeks," Sikes said.

Sam grinned and showed gums with only a few teeth. "That ain't Wash's pile."

Sikes laughed and Sam laughed, too, and Maggie, sickened nearly to her stomach, lost her battle not to faint. She went limp and collapsed straight down on the dirt floor, eyes rolling up into her head beneath lids that fluttered closed.

Chapter Twenty-Four

A sharp, flat sting on her face, the ugly sound of fingers slapping flesh, and Maggie came awake. Her eyes opened and she found herself staring at the feet of Sikes, who was kneeling beside her and had just slapped the upturned side of her face to try to bring her out of her faint.

"It fell down," the great blob of flesh slurred in his stinking corner. "It hurt?"

"No, Sam, it ain't hurt," Sikes replied. "She — *it* will be up in a few moments."

"Then we commence," Sam said, and chuckled.

"Oh yes. Oh yes, we commence."

Maggie, coming around quickly, heard it all, and fast as her own thoughts, saw opportunity and seized it. There was no time to plan, only to act, and act she did. Seeing that Sikes was crouched on his heels and delicately balanced, she lunged upward and shoved his chest, knocking him back onto his rear. Shaking off the lingering dizziness of her swoon, she turned and darted to the open door and out.

Behind her, curses and shouts, Sikes's voice high-pitched and nearly wailing, Sam's a molten slurring of sound. She ran toward the path they had followed to get there, knowing that, at least, that route was open and passable. She did not want to attempt a run through untrodden forest and risk hanging herself up on laurel or rhododendron.

As she entered the head of the trail, she glanced over her shoulder and saw Sikes bearing down upon her, much more fleet than she would have expected. Beyond and behind him, the cabin door was filled with the bulk of Sam, who had managed to push himself to his feet and stagger after her, but who had literally wedged himself in the doorway, too big to get out of his own dwelling. He was red-faced, sweating, and shirtless . . . and had lost his trousers, too, in the process of rising. All in all, an uglier vision young Maggie had never seen.

Hastening, she pounded along the pathway, hearing Sikes keeping pace behind her and sometimes gaining. Surely, she thought, she could outrun a grown man. She was young and light and fleet, and surely far more motivated to escape than he was to catch her.

He would *not* catch her! The thought couldn't be tolerated. She would outrun him if she had to wear her feet off doing it. She pushed harder, her heart hammering as fast as her feet.

Her foot struck a root and she went forward, hard, her chest hitting a humped area of ground and driving every bit of air from her lungs. Her vision swam and blackened a few moments and she thought she would faint again. Stunned, she forgot for a moment that she was being pursued, but when she remembered, she rolled onto her back and prepared to kick her feet upward and pound him heel-to-crotch.

He was not there, not where she had expected him to be, anyway. She sat up and gaped.

He was back down the trail, having been stopped in midpursuit, apparently about the same moment she had fallen. The one who had stopped him was fighting him hard at the moment, big fists pounding and guttural voice grunting with each blow. Sikes was making sounds, too, high and almost girlish wails of pain as he was trounced by the one who had come bursting out of the brush beside the path and knocked him down.

Maggie, with lungs gasping and refilling with air, looked at the one who had stopped her pursuer and now seemed intent on beating him to death. Her eyes bulged. She recognized the stranger who was protecting her.

Loafhead.

For the second time in mere minutes, Maggie Harkin fainted.

Above, the sky was making a fast change, suddenly darkening and going gray, thunder rumbling like an angry deity off to the west. A storm was coming in.

Maggie lay swooned and senseless, unaware of the approaching storm and no longer hearing the sound of fists on flesh coming from a short distance back on the trail. The guttural sounds had stopped now, as had Sikes's reactive squeals.

Finally even the sound of blows came to a halt, and the big man with the misshapen head left the body of Sikes where it lay and walked up the trail toward the spot where Maggie lay unmoving. When raindrops began to fall, driving down through the trees, Maggie stirred beneath the impact of the cold drops as the man knelt beside her.

Back behind them, Sikes's form also was

pounded by the mounting rain, but he did not move at all, and never would again.

Maggie was only partly aware of it when strong arms slid beneath her knees and shoulder blades and lifted her up. She groaned softly and felt herself carried along through the rain.

The storm covered almost the entire overmountain region, whipping the waters of the Holston, causing surges in the Nolichucky, hammering the Watauga, turning Lick Creek from a mere stream to a temporary wide river.

Riding along on increasingly skittish horses in the Doe River area, a region of gorges and bluffs and wooded ridges, Crawford Fain was beginning to reassess a statement he had made to Titus earlier, that the storm would pass over quickly. At present it looked likely to linger for an hour or more.

Lightning fired down suddenly, striking a tree atop the ridge beneath which the two frontiersmen rode. The tree splintered in an eruption of fire and noise, and smoking wood dropped toward the riders, a large piece barely missing Edohi. The crack of thunder was simultaneous with the strike, as close as it was, and as loud as a cannon fired mere yards away.

"Pap, we have to find shelter," said Titus. "This ain't one we can ride out here in the open."

Crawford Fain nodded. "Let's go over yonder way . . . might be some shelter amongst the rocks."

They rode toward the base of the escarpment and into a maze of boulders and slabs that had collected there over a century or more as the bluff eroded and broke apart above. Hoping for an overhang to keep the worst of the rain off them and the horses, they did better than that, finding a large natural tunnel opening into the hillside, a cave that instantly put Fain in mind of the cave in which he had lived far away in England's Skellenwood in the days of his boyhood. They were able to enter the cavern without having even to dismount.

"Have you known this place before, Pap?" asked Titus.

Fain shook his head. "Never seen it, although I've traveled the Doe country many a time. But never in this exact part of it." He looked around. "Quite a place."

With the storm darkening the region, combined with the natural shadowing of the cavern, it was difficult to see much except when lightning flashed outside. With each flare the cavern flooded for a second with penetrating light, revealing dank stone, fingers of rock reaching from cavern floor to ceiling, and places where water trickled down the stone to stream out in a rivulet that ran in a gully along the base of the wall.

The light also revealed evidence of previous human use of the cave, mostly in the form of places where fires had been built for light and heat, fire locations perhaps generations old and used by both native and later-settlement inhabitants of the region.

"Son, I say let's scrounge up some wood and get us a fire burning," said Fain. "You look about and see what firewood might have been left in this place by folks before us, and I'll pull in some from the outside."

"Anything from the outside will be soaked, Pap."

"Lord, son, you shame your name! Wet bark pulled off uncovers dry wood."

"So it does."

They began their separate quests for fuel. Fain didn't much mind the rain — his attitude had always been that it was only water, after all — and he gathered up several armloads of wood quickly and deposited them inside the cave. When lightning flashed, he could see Titus moving about, gathering wood scraps carried in by past users of this cavern. At length Titus used some hickory wood he'd found to create a torch and explored farther back into the cave, where the cave ceiling was lower and the open, broad space of the entrance diminished to tight, small passages that appeared to simply vanish into the rock of the mountainside.

Fain watched Titus's light go dark as the young man entered one of the passageways, the torchlight suddenly hidden. Fain returned to the outside and fetched one last armload of sodden wood, and when he came back into the cave, Titus was waiting for him, a strange, intense expression on his face.

"Come here, Pap. There's something you have to see."

"What?"

"Just come and I'll show you."

Fain followed his son back into the cave, following the light of Titus's torch.

Rain on her face as she was carried along is what awakened Maggie Harkin from her faint. She had no idea where she was or what was happening to her at the beginning, and her body stiffened in fear as she thought for a moment that she was being held by the man who had captured her and taken her to the foul cabin with the horrible fat man in the corner. The memory of that swept back, and then she wondered if maybe the wicked men had already misused her, and she simply didn't remember. With a great feeling of dread, she sent her mind roaming through all the parts of herself, examining every feeling, every nerve . . . until at last she decided she had not yet suffered any intimate physical abuse. Relief overwhelmed her, but tempered by fear.

Who was carrying her? The memory rushed back of what she had seen that had caused her to swoon: a figure that appeared to be the legendary Loafhead himself, beating her captor. Drawing in a shuddering, deep breath, Maggie forced herself to move her head until she could see the face of the one carrying her now, and when she did, she thought she might faint again.

A broad, ruddy face, an ugly bulge extending down from forehead and across one eye . . . How could she ever have told her brother that Loafhead was not real? She had to face the fact that he had been right in his fearful belief in the ogre, and she had been wrong.

But was he an ogre? So far he had defended and rescued her. And was this misshapen man really Loafhead at all? Might he be someone else with a similar deformity?

Maggie dared not speak to him. The very idea was too daunting. So she merely held on, and let him hold on to her, and was carried along the woodland trails in the driving rain, lightning glaring every few moments, sometimes far, sometimes close.

At length the man's trot slowed as he became fatigued, and Maggie suspected he was looking for a place to stop. Soon they reached a little clearing with a half-faced camp, and he ducked into the slant-roofed shelter and deposited her on the ground. Then he sat down beside her, panting for breath. His form was so tall and muscle-bulked that he nearly filled the little shelter alone. She drew her legs up close to herself, wrapped her arms around her bent knees, and scooted as far away from him as the shelter would allow.

Finally he turned to look at her, and by the glare of lightning she got her first fully clear look at his face. Her shock must have been visible, because when he realized she was looking at him, wide-eyed, he put his hand over the misshapen lump marring his face and turned away. "Don't look," he said in a voice she could only later describe to herself as *muddy.*

"Sir?" she heard herself ask, curiosity overcoming caution. "Are you Loafhead?"

He turned back to her, his only visible eye squinting in a frown. "I know nothing of 'Loafhead,' " he said. "I am Tom. I am Tom Crale." He looked away again. "I am ugly."

"Are you going to hurt me, sir?"

"No. I will not hurt you. I took you away from the bad men. Did they hurt you?"

She felt bashful suddenly, and now it was her turn to break away her gaze. "No. No . . . but they would have hurt me if I hadn't run, and if you hadn't stopped me from being caught again."

"They were bad. Very bad men. They do bad things to young ones."

Maggie began to realize how great a horror she had escaped. However disconcerting and, indeed, ugly Tom Crale was, he did not horrify her like the memory of the two men in the stinking cabin she had fled.

"Who is Loafhead?" Crale asked.

It was awkward, hearing that question. How to answer?

"There is an old story, from across the ocean, about a . . . a dweller in a forest who eats the heads of children who do bad things. He has a face that is . . ." She looked at him and pointed briefly at his deformity. He winced.

"No. I am not Loafhead," he reaffirmed, forcefully. "I am a *man,* Tom Crale. I don't do . . . what you said, eating the heads of children."

"I don't think there really is a Loafhead," Maggie said. "It's that you made me think of him, and I was already afraid, and my little brother believes that one time he saw —"

Crale rose and stepped out of the shelter, seemingly unwilling to hear more. The rain had stopped, though it looked likely to be merely a lull, not a full cessation.

Maggie felt a wave of guilt. She had insulted and hurt the man who had rescued her, and it seemed the worst thing she could ever have done.

He never left her view. For long minutes Tom Crale wandered in the woods before the half-faced shelter, but never did he let himself go out of sight.

Maggie had the impression he was watching her, but despite his horrific appearance and endless vigilance, she did not feel his attention was threatening, as had been the attentions of the other two men. Rather, she was sure that Tom Crale was guarding her rather than attempting to possess and control her. There was nothing amiss in his interest in her.

At length he returned to the shelter, his

sensitivity over her indelicate "Loafhead" question seemingly abated. "What is your name, little girl?" he asked her.

"Maggie Harkin. But I'm not a little girl. I'm nigh grown up now. I live in Jonesborough. Do you know Jonesborough?" She realized she was speaking to him in the same tone she might use with a smaller child, and asked herself why she was doing that. Crale seemed odd, sensitive, injured . . . but he had given no evidence of mental slowness. The slight slur she heard in his words seemed to her to have a physical basis, perhaps a misshaping of the human mechanical instruments of speech, related, maybe, to the same malady that had distorted his head and face.

"I know Jonesborough," he replied. "I have been there. In secret."

"Did you carry a man there in the night recently? A man who had been hanged?"

Crale looked at her with surprise. "Yes. I found him hanging but took him down. He was still living, so I carried him to the town so he could be helped." Crale paused. "Did he live?"

"The last I was aware of, he was still alive," she said. The timing of her abduction had kept her from being aware of the murder of Gilly. "Do you know who hanged

him, Mr. Crale?"
"No."
"Could it have been the same men who tried to hurt me?"
"Don't know."
"Who were the men who tried to hurt me, Mr. Crale? Do you know them?"
"Only Sam. The fat man. He is Sam Crotty. He is like me . . . an alone man. Hidden man."
"But I think he is a bad man . . . and I think you are not a bad man. So he's not like you *that* way."
Crale nodded. "He is a bad man. He has hurt others. Girls, like you. Young. He hurt them with the help of the man I saved you from. I don't know that man's name."
Maggie was pleased that Crale was becoming more talkative and open. There was much about this curious woodland figure she wanted to know. Where had he come from? What was his life? Why was he . . . the way he was?
Perhaps she could learn some of those answers. But instinct told her she needed to be patient and not overinquisitive.

Fain stared silently at the pigmented image on the cavern wall that Titus's torchlight revealed. Titus had discovered it during his hunt for cast-off wood back in the cavern, and it was this that he had fetched his father to see.

The longer Fain looked, the more he was sure the well-rendered face was who he took it to be. The details all matched, from the yellow hair to the clearly visible streak of gray in the lower portion of the iris of the left eye. Someone had painted this image, using pigments derived or compounded from nature, with meticulous precision and detail.

"Is that her, Pap?"

"I suspect so, Titus. Almost has to be."

"That was my thinking, too. You reckon she put this picture up here herself?"

Fain paused, mulling something over. "Son, you ever heard reference made to the 'cavern man'?"

"I ain't sure."

"Well, the story has it that he's somebody who puts pictures like this on rocks and such, mostly in caves, like this. I don't know if it's somebody doing it that made the legend come about, or whether the legend is there and every now and then somebody goes and does something such as this picture here, just to make the legend seem real."

"Why would somebody bother to do that?

Don't make sense to me."

"Who can say what makes people do what they do, son? All I can say for sure about this picture is a couple of things. First off, whoever did this cared a lot about it and took a lot of time to make it look just right, and two, this picture surely does look to be an image of Eben Bedsoe's daughter. Who else could it be? There wouldn't be two women in the same wilderness with such an unusual features as marked eyes, 'specially two marked in just the same way. Has to be her!"

"But we still ain't found the real woman."

"No. But this here picture gives me some hope that there's a real woman to be found. Hold your torch up closer there . . . see? That coloring is right fresh. That ain't an old picture. Somebody done that not all that long back."

"Pap, you said folks talk about a 'cavern man' who does this kind of thing. I ain't never heard of the 'cavern man,' but I have heard somebody talk of a man who maybe does something like this. Somebody I knowed in the Cumberland Settlements who had come from Watauga told me about him. I believe he said his name is Tom Crale. Reckon Tom Crale and the cavern man could be one and the same?" Titus paused and looked intently at his father. "Pap? You all right?"

"Let's don't talk more about this now," Fain said. "We've got our wood now. Let's get us a cook fire going and get dried out, and get us up a bit of supper. And we need to feed the horses."

"Pap? You know this Crale fellow?"

"Later, son. Let's talk about it all sometime later."

Chapter Twenty-Five

Tom Crale had returned to the shelter and now sat as before, staring out from it into the woods. The storm had stopped for a time, then returned in milder form with a steady rain that poured through the crude roof of the half-faced camp shelter in several places. Maggie had managed to find a dry corner in which to shelter herself, but Crale sat unheeding of the two streams of water that poured down on his head and shoulders from the leaky, sloping roof.

"What do you do?" she asked him, because he had begun to show some evidence of willingness to talk about himself. "Are you a hunter? A trapper?"

"I do what I must do to live. I live among the animals. I am more like them than I am like people, I think."

"Are you around people much?"

"Some. Mostly I watch them. That's what I do. I watch."

"What do you mean?"

"I go to the towns sometimes, or to the forts, and even the towns of the Cherokee, and I watch. Without being seen. I see how people live, the things they do, the places they go, the things they try to hide from other people. And I hear the words they say to each other. The songs they sing when they are alone. That is what I do. I watch. And I listen."

"Do you not talk to the people?"

He shook his head. "I cannot be among people."

"Because of . . ."

He waved his hand in front of his face and lumped brow. "Because of this. I scare them. They think I am a devil, I believe, the way they run if they see me."

"That makes me sad, Tom Crale."

"Yes, Maggie Harkin. Me, too."

"Tom, do you think the man who was chasing me is dead? When you hit him, do you think it was enough to —"

"He is dead. He will hurt you no more."

"I should go home. My mother and brother will be worried for me."

"I will take you home."

"Do you have a family, Tom Crale?"

"There are those to whom I am kin. I seldom see them. Some of them fear me just like others do. Even though many Crale men have had . . . this." Another wave toward his face. "It is called the Crale lump. Mine is the worst, I think. The ugliest there has been."

"Have you had it all your life?"

"Since I was a boy. It has grown as I have grown."

"Oh. Do all the Crale men have such . . . lumps?"

"Not all. Some who have had them have been father to boys who grew to be old men and never had the Crale lump. But their sons or grandsons had them. There have been brothers born, one with the lump, the other without."

"So perhaps one day you might have a son without the Crale lump."

He looked at her oddly. "I will never have a son," he said. "Because I will never have a wife. I am too ugly."

"Have you ever tried to find a wife?" Maggie was astonished at her own daring questions, yet noticed that he seemed eager to talk. She doubted he got the opportunity to converse with another person often.

"In all my life, I have known only three women willing to talk to me as if I am a man, not a beast. One is named Sadie, and she roams about, living here and there, like

I do. The other is Deborah. She has lived in different places, and she has a husband, but not really a husband. His name is Corey and she has taken his name like a wife. But they are not truly married. Deborah has been kinder even than Sadie has to me. Deborah tells me I am" — His voice cracked — "beautiful. Because of what is inside. Because I am kind. That is what she says."

"Where is Deborah?"

"She is rich. She has gold. A mine in the mountains, across on the eastern side, that only she and Polly know the way to. She lives there now, guarding her gold."

"Who is Polly?"

"She is the third kind woman. An old woman whose husband was named McCoy Atley and is dead. She may be dead, too, now. I have wanted to see her, but I have let it go too long without going to her. She is a good woman, kind to me. She lives in a cabin in the Doe River country. I have taken her food many times. My cousin John Crale takes her food as well. I hope he has been able to do so these past weeks, when I have been neglectful of her."

"We will go see her. I will go with you."

"You must go back to your home."

"After we go see Polly. Then I will go back."

Crale's one visible eye glared deeply at the girl. "Are you hoping to get gold from her?"

Maggie was jolted by the question, but had to admit, reluctantly, that such a hope probably was part of what made her willing to extend her absence from home a little longer. Her late father had once told her he believed there was gold to be found in the mountains, and the thought of that had always intrigued Maggie. She did not want to miss a chance to see if it might be true.

"I don't want her gold," Maggie said. "I just want to see what it looks like. And I want you to have a chance to see Polly if it is important."

Crale's rather broad and crooked mouth crumpled into a smile. He bobbed his oversized head at Maggie and said, "You are now my fourth kind woman."

She was touched, but said, "I am not a woman, Tom Crale. I am just a girl."

"You will be a woman someday. A great one. I hope you will think of me as your friend."

"You are my friend indeed, Tom Crale. You are my rescuer and hero."

He smiled a little more broadly and looked back out at the forest, still ragged and glistening from the storm.

Tom had hardtack and parched corn in a little bag slung over his shoulder, and he and Maggie ate before moving on. Maggie wondered about the wisdom of leaving shelter when the day would soon be through, and the threat of a renewed storm still existed . . . but she trusted Crale. He lived as a free-roaming denizen of this mountain country, and he would keep her safe.

They passed the night at another of Crale's many lodgings, this one a vast hollow tree with a large opening at the base, opening into a space just the right size for Maggie to curl up in and sleep.

Tom Crale slept outside the tree, guarding the girl and unheeding of any lingering threat of storm. He told Maggie that he knew the mountains, and that despite the distant thunder, he knew it would not rain again that night.

It did not rain.

As fate would have it, Crawford and Titus Fain approached the clearing where the Atley cabin stood from the angle that brought them directly to the graves nearby it. Fain looked at the grave that bore the name of his old friend McCoy Atley, and touched a tear away from his eye. "I'm too late, then," he said. "He really is dead and gone."

"His wife, too," said Titus. "Her name was Polly, right? That's the name marked on this grave beside McCoy's. It's fresher than his grave. Looks no more than a few days old to me."

"God, I'm sorry she's gone. I've frittered away my time and come too late to see either of them," Fain said. He pulled a rag from his hunting shirt and loudly blew his nose. "I wonder who buried them."

The voice came from behind. "I don't know who buried McCoy, but it was me who buried Polly."

They turned in their saddles and looked over their shoulders to see a yellow-haired woman with a gray mark in her left eye looking coldly at them, a rifle leveled.

"Deborah Bledsoe Corey, I presume," said Fain, hoping the woman did not have a nervous finger, the rifle in her hands being on full-cock. She did not appear nervous. Her gaze was as flinty as that of old Hanging Maw, a Cherokee chief with whom Fain had once had a tense stare-down.

"The Deborah is right, but I know nothing of Bledsoe, and I have decided never to use the name of Corey again. I am free of him now and forever, and I choose my own name. I am Deborah Atley, by my own choice. Who are you, old man?"

Fain calmly replied, "I'll begin by saying that I am not old. Gray, to be sure, but not old. Age is in here, and youth." He tapped his head with his finger.

"Reckon you could lower that rifle?" Titus asked. "Ain't no cause for us to be threatening each other."

"It appears to me that I'm doing most of the threatening here," Deborah said. "As such, I'm the one who decides if or when we change things, not you."

"Understood," Titus said, hands in the air and his eyes flicking back and forth between the woman and the butt of his flintlock rifle, which hung on the side of his saddle.

"Finish telling me who you are, old man," she said to Fain.

He sighed. "My name is Crawford Fain, sometimes called Edohi," he said. "This jumpy young fellow with me is my son, Titus."

The rifle lowered slowly. "I know you, then, Edohi. Who you are, anyway. I beg your pardon for raising my rifle on you."

"I don't blame you at all, ma'am. May we talk? I have things I must tell you."

"We will talk," she said.

■ ■ ■ ■

"So you recall nothing of your youngest days?" Fain asked Deborah. "You truly did not know that your original surname was Bledsoe?"

They were seated in the cabin where both McCoy Atley and his wife, Polly, had died. Deborah had been occupying it for some days now since she had found the freshly deceased body of Polly Atley lying on the bed.

"I was very small when I was taken," she said. "No, I scarcely remember anything of my young childhood. What little I do remember is pain. A man with rough hands, quick to strike blows. I remember him telling me I was his daughter and it was his duty to spare not the rod."

"Eben Bledsoe," said Titus.

"I've heard that name, and I confess that there have been times when I have heard others speak the name 'Bledsoe' and have felt a sense of dread I could not account for," she said. The woman was clear-spoken and articulate, intelligence shining through both her eyes almost as visibly as the gray marking glistening in her left one. "Maybe some part of me did remember my last name, and associated it with cruelty and fright."

"He sent me to find you," Fain told her. "He wants me to bring you back to him."

She shook her head unhesitatingly. "I will not go back to him. The brief time I knew him was enough."

"I don't blame you for that, ma'am. Though I will say I don't believe he has any ill intent in wanting to see you. He is simply an old man wanting to see the daughter he lost."

Deborah thought that over deeply, and finally said, "He is creating a school, I have heard. That is a good thing. I will send him gold, by you, that he can use to help build his academy."

"He'll be grateful, I'm sure. May I ask how a woman living alone in this wilderness comes by gold?"

"There is a mine, the location of which I alone know. McCoy Atley found it, and took some ore and nuggets from it, and showed it to me after I befriended him and Polly once when they were both very ill of an ague. He seemed to view me as a kind of daughter . . . and better it would have been for me, I can imagine, if such a man as McCoy Atley had truly been my father."

"McCoy was a fine man. I regret I didn't

get by here to see him before he passed on. How did Polly fare without him?"

"Not well. She was old and sickly and at the last was mostly in her bed. I was here with her through her very last days, but before that she relied mostly on the help of a family here in the mountains. The Crales. They brought her food and saw to her care, particularly John and Tom."

"There's that name again," said Titus. "Crale."

Crawford Fain was suddenly looking very ill at ease. He quickly shifted the subject. "Deborah, we found a picture of you painted in a cave wall. A very good image, too, for being able now to look in your face I can see that it caught your looks almost exactly. Did you make that image?"

"I did not. That would be Tom Crale's work. Tom makes images of those things that matter to him, the things he thinks on and sees from his hiding places."

Crale again. Fain looked unhappy, and Titus wondered what was behind his father's strange reaction to a mere family name.

"Tell us your story, Deborah, if you would," Fain encouraged.

She drew in a long breath and began to speak.

■ ■ ■ ■

The next day, Tom Crale walked across to the Atley cabin, young Maggie at his heels.

When Fain saw Crale, he went pale as snow and was unable to find his voice for a long time thereafter.

Just short of three weeks later, Fain repeated most of Deborah's story at White's Fort to Eben Bledsoe, who looked as if he'd aged a decade since Fain saw him last. Recovering from the shooting he'd suffered at the hands of his brother had drained much life from the man, and Fain had his doubts that the reverend professor would live to see the full-scale operation of his own college. He might linger to see it begin, but Fain was quite sure the man would be gone before the first graduate passed in review.

The clergyman received his daughter's donation of gold gratefully, and seemed also to accept Fain's explanation that Deborah had been unable to come see her father because she was recovering from a broken limb. Titus had urged his father not to lie about Deborah's reasons for not coming to see her birth father, but Fain was a man of empathy and put himself in Bledsoe's place, imagining how it would be to be told one's own offspring chose to absent herself from her own father's life in his failing days. So he lied to spare the man pain.

Fain accepted Bledsoe's payment for services rendered, but gave half of it back for use of the new college because he had failed to bring Deborah to his bedside.

Bledsoe said, "Tell it to me in brief, one more time, Fain. I want to be sure I heard it rightly."

"Very well. Deborah was never taken by Indians at all," he said. "She was taken instead by a man whose child, a girl of her own age, had died. Deborah became the replacement for that child, but she did not remain long in that family, whose name was Pells. The man of that family sold her to a younger man, named James Corey, who was only a few years older than Deborah herself. She became Corey's companion and servant, though he called her his wife and insisted she use his name as her own.

"Corey was not a good man, and Deborah ultimately escaped him, and found friendship and refuge with an old friend of mine, as chance would have it: McCoy Atley. Had she simply stayed there, she might have avoided much later trouble. Instead she decided to go to Virginia. Corey somehow found her there, and made her more his captive than ever. She never revealed to him where the Atleys lived, in fact did not reveal even their existence, because she wanted to be able to find refuge with them again should she manage to flee Corey another time. And there was also the fact that McCoy Atley had discovered a source of gold along a particular stream in the Carolina hills, and she knew it would not do for Corey to learn of it.

"Escape Corey she did, one more time, and made her way back to the Atleys. Corey did his best to track her, but with little success. The short of it is that the Atleys died and Deborah reclaimed the gold mine, which she worked entirely in private, hoping to put the gold to good purpose. I think you should be proud, Reverend Bledsoe, that her 'good purpose' has ended up being your new academy."

The old clergyman nodded. "Her gift will help generations that come after her," he said.

"Amen, preacher. Amen."

"But how I wish I could have seen her! There are many things I need to say to her. Things I regret from the earliest of her days."

"You write them down and seal them and

I'll take them to her with my own hand," Fain said.

"You would do that for me?"

"I would."

"Bless you, sir. God bless you!"

"He often has."

"Pap, did you do what I asked and keep a bit of gold aside so that I might have a ring made of it in Jonesborough?"

"I did. Felt a bit like I was stealing . . . but stealing's just an old practice of the Fain family, I suppose."

"You'll like her, Pap. Prettiest girl I ever saw."

"DeVault, you say? Sister to Andy of the Cumberland Scouts?"

"That's right."

"Good family, anyway. Good family. But, son, you just barely met this gal. Why you figure she's going to marry you?"

"Some things you just know, Pap. I don't know how you know, but you do."

"I'll trust you on that, son."

There was a long pause as they rode along side by side. "One more question, Pap: I noticed more than once that you reacted kind of odd to mention the Crale family name. And when you saw Tom Crale, I thought you would fall out senseless on the ground. He's a hard sight to look at, I'll grant you, but that just ain't your way, being weak of stomach. What is it about that name and that family that stirs you up?"

Fain sighed and finally answered. "Let me answer you by telling you the one remaining piece of our family history I ain't told you yet.

"I told you, Titus, that my father, your grandfather, wore a mask when he robbed coaches passing by Skellenwood. There was more reason than just a wish to hide who he was. He had a deformity on his visage, one almost exactly like that you saw on the brow of Tom Crale. He wore the mask partly out of shame at his disfigurement. It was the same kind of disfigurement that had run in the family as far back as anyone could remember, though sometimes generations would go by before it would show itself in another male child."

"I'll be hanged!"

"Your grandfather wearing that mask and living in Skellenwood caused a legend to come about, one made up by nurses and mothers and fathers and grandfathers to keep their children behaving right."

Titus said, "Loafhead?"

"That's right."

Titus pulled his horse to a stop. "My

grandfather was Loafhead?"

"No. There never was no Loafhead, not really. There was just your grandfather in his mask, a mask that didn't do a particularly good job of fully hiding the lump. You could still see the bulge of it from his brow. So some clever soul decided to put the fear of God into her children one night and used your grandfather as inspiration for a new bogeyman tale. Loafhead was born. Your grandfather gave rise to a legend."

"I don't know what to say."

"Just say a prayer of thanks that you didn't inherit the deformity yourself. I'm grateful for you and me both that we didn't."

"But if I have a male child, he could have such a disfigurement?"

"It appears to be the case. Always the men, never the women, and usually two or three generations between the appearance of it."

"That gives a man a lot to think about, Pap."

"It does. Oh, and there's one further thing you should know. We're Fains. I'm a Fain, you're a Fain, and your children will be Fains. But that ain't always been the family name. It was changed from the original name to Fain a few generations back, 'cording to my father. Exactly why, nobody remembers. Probably somebody trying to hide who they were because of crime, or debt, or some other trouble."

"So what was the family name before they changed it?"

"It was Crale, son. Crale."

The wedding took place in the spring, at the foot of a high, round hill outside Jonesborough. The ring that Titus Fain slipped onto the finger of Amy DeVault was made by Benjamin Crawley from gold that came from the Atley mine.

When Titus kissed his new bride, even Micah Tate clapped and cheered, though a part of him still wished it was his lips pressed to those of the prettiest young woman in the state of Franklin, which was doomed to be gone as a legal entity within a few short months.

Langdon Potts did not attend. About a week prior to the wedding, he had been introduced to a young Scottish beauty named Katherine McClure, a recent arrival in America on her way to visit relatives at and around White's Fort, whose population was burgeoning and would soon be part of a city to be named Knoxville. Potts and Katherine spent the hour of the Fain-DeVault wedding taking a long walk together in a meadow just outside town, talking intently and so enthralled with each other that they didn't even notice when they trod directly across the fresh grave of the troubled preacher Abner Bledsoe, who had been found in the privy behind the Harkin Inn, slumped back against the wall with a bullet hole in the roof of his mouth and a pistol still gripped loosely in his hand.

Nearly the whole town of Jonesborough, and many of the residents of the surrounding countryside, turned out to see the son of the famed Crawford Fain take his new bride. Conducting the ceremony was a clergyman Fain fetched in from White's Fort for the occasion, the academy builder Eben Bledsoe, who had grieved only briefly beside the grave of his unhappy brother.

There was one wedding observer, though, who watched from the woods at the top of the hill, out of view of the crowd, seeing it all through only one functioning eye.

The wedding image that would soon appear on a flat stone inside one of the region's many caves would linger for more than a century, until at last it weathered and faded away and was forgotten.

AFTERWORD

In the case of novels such as *The Long Hunt,* which present a fictional central story played out against a historical backdrop, it is useful for authors to clarify what is real and what is made up.

In the case of *The Long Hunt,* the central story line is almost entirely a work of imagination. There were real-life long hunters, some of whom became well-known, but no actual Crawford Fain; there were, and are, individuals and families with propensities toward physical deformity, but no Crale family (at least no Crale family identical with the one presented in this novel), and there was in fact early-day gold mining in portions of North Carolina and what is now Tennessee, but most of that came a little later than the time period of this novel, 1786–87. There was no historical Atley mine.

There were, as well, preachers and educators, and combinations thereof, on the Carolina-Tennessee frontier, but the Bledsoe brothers are entirely fictional. Also fictional are Littleton, Gilly, and their outlaw companions, as well as the traveling liquor seller Ott Dixon.

The towns of Greeneville and Jonesborough, Tennessee, which provide part of the setting for this story, certainly were and are real, and existed in the time period depicted. For storytelling purposes, however, some liberties have been taken regarding those towns and the individuals living in and around them. The Harkin family and inn, the silversmith Benjamin Crawley, and Jonesborough leading citizen Matthew Stuart are all fictional creations, for example. Stuart's character, along with that of Dr. Peter Houser, draws some inspiration from the historical figure of Dr. William P. Chester, a native of York County, Pennsylvania, and an excellent Jonesborough physician, who opened an inn in Jonesborough in 1797. The Chester Inn remains a beloved Jonesborough landmark to this day.

Also still present at Jonesborough is the rounded hill from which Tom Crale watches the wedding of Titus Fain and Amy DeVault in the closing portion of the novel. It stands beside Highway 11 East, a short distance beyond the Dillow-Taylor Funeral Home, on the left side of the highway when traveling from Jonesborough toward Greeneville, and is a noticeably steep and beautiful hill quite familiar to Northeast Tennesseans.

John Crockett was, of course, entirely real, and lived at the time and place depicted. His son, David, became one of the nation's most famous frontiersmen, achieving legendary status as "Davy" Crockett.

There is no real-life legend of a British "bogeyman" figure called Loafhead, though folklore does abound with many similar legendary figures of fright. Nor does England possess, to my knowledge, an actual forest named Skellenwood.

The character of Tom Crale was inspired by an unknown individual with a similar facial deformity I saw once as a boy. He was seated in the passenger seat of a car in a grocery store parking lot, apparently awaiting the return of the driver, and I have never forgotten him, though I never knew his name or actually met him.

White's Fort, where Fain first meets with Eben Bledsoe, is real, and a replica of it still stands in the heart of downtown Knoxville,

Tennessee. James White, who founded the fort and is generally seen as the father of Knoxville, is buried in a cemetery not very far from his fort.

There was no Edohi Station in actual history. Nor did the Cumberland Scouts, who respond to the raid that killed most of the Deveraux family, exist. The fictional group is loosely based on an actual organization, however: the Cumberland Guard, which provided armed escorts for travelers going from the settlements around what is now Knoxville to the Cumberland Settlements in and around what is now Nashville. It was a dangerous road to travel, particularly in the days when the Lower Cherokee, or Chickamauga, were defending their frontier against white advancement.

The state of Franklin was entirely real, though it never found permanence and is not much remembered outside the areas it once encompassed. Established by over-mountain settlers who were isolated from both the North Carolinian and the federal governments, it made a valiant but contested effort to achieve full statehood, but instead slowly died away. It did launch or bolster the careers of various early leaders of the region, however, including that of John Sevier, who went on to be Tennessee's first governor after serving in the same role for Franklin.

Cameron Judd
Greene County, Tennessee
April 2011

The employees of Thorndike Press hope you have enjoyed this Large Print book. All our Thorndike, Wheeler, and Kennebec Large Print titles are designed for easy reading, and all our books are made to last. Other Thorndike Press Large Print books are available at your library, through selected bookstores, or directly from us.

For information about titles, please call:
(800) 223-1244

or visit our Web site at:
http://gale.cengage.com/thorndike

To share your comments, please write:

Publisher
Thorndike Press
10 Water St., Suite 310
Waterville, ME 04901